Doctor Attraction

Doctor Attraction

The Mackenney Family Saga Book Two

by Caz May

First Published 2020

ISBN 9780648499862

Published by Caz May

To anyone who has found it hard to let go of a first love.

Also by Caz May
11

(Prologue) Addison
13

(1) Zane
15

(2) Addison
18

(3) Zane
21

(4) Addison
27

(5) Zane
31

(6) Hunter
34

(7) Zane
37

(8) Hunter
40

(9) Addison
44

(10) Zane
46

(11) Addison
50

(12) Zane
52

(13) Addison
55

(14) Zane
58

(15) Addison
61

(16) Zane
63

(17) Addison
66

(18) Addison
72

(19) Addison
77

(20) Zane
82

(21) Addison
85

(22) Zane
87

(23) Addison
94

(24) Zane
97

(25) Quentin
103

(26) Addison
107

(27) Zane
109

(28) Quentin
112

(29) Addison
115

(30) Hunter
120

(31) Addison
127

(32) Zane
131

(33) Addison
134

(34) Samantha
137

(35) Quentin
141

(36) Savannah
147

(37) Samantha
152

(38) Quentin
156

(39) Zane
160

(40) Addison
163

(41) Zane
165

(42) Addison
167

(43) Zane
171

(44) Amy
174

(45) Addison
177

(46) Hunter
179

(47) Addison
182

(48) Hunter
187

(49) Samantha
192

(50) Quentin
195

(51) Savannah
203

(52) Addison
209

(53) Hunter
212

(54) Savannah
215

(55) Zane
221

(56) Addison
225

(57) Zane
227

(58) Addison
232

(59) Jett
238

(60) Addison
242

(61) Zane
245

(62) Jett
247

(63) Zane
249

(64) Addison
252

(65) Zane
254

(66) Zane
258

(Epilogue) Addison
262

Playlist
265

About the Author
266

Also by Caz May

The Mackenney Family Saga

Bk 1-Country Secrets

Always Only You Series

Bk 1-Roommates Don't Kiss & Tell

Bk 2-Friends Don't Say Goodbye

Bk 3-Feelings Don't Play Fair

Bk 4-Hearts Don't Steer Us Wrong

A Holiday Romance Duet

Bk 1-Take Flight

My Girl Duet

Bk 1-Not my Girl

(Prologue) Addison

Seeing Hunter at the end of the aisle, a stupid grin on his face makes my heart constrict.
I should have been walking towards him, in a big white dress, not the ruby red strapless one I have on.
But I'm not the one marrying him.
I'm the Maid of Honour for his wedding to someone else.
And it's truly painful.
It wasn't as though I could have refused when he'd asked for me to a part of his special day.
Savannah, his soon to be any minute wife doesn't really have any friends in town since leaving her past behind in the city and stumbling into Hunter's farmhouse nearly two years ago.
Plus it isn't that I hate her. I can't. She's just too sweet.
And I'm around them a lot more than I want to be at times, as I'm godmother to their gorgeous son River.
I swear I've never seen a kid that looks so much like his father.
The kid is gorgeous, just like his Dad Hunter is.

Get a grip Addison. Seriously, you're not the one marrying him.

Taking a deep breath I start to tentatively walk down the aisle, scanning the crowd for my older brother Jett. He hadn't really wanted to attend his ex-best friends wedding, but I begged him to come along, desperate for the moral support.
It also doesn't help that I'm also stuck being partnered up for the wedding with Hunter's annoying, but somewhat attractive younger brother Quentin.
We'd slept together a year or so ago, and it was pretty damn hot, but he'd had to make it complicated by confessing he was in love with me.
Part of me knew I should have gone along with his advances and given him a chance.
Or even taken a chance with someone else.

But I can't let go of his older brother, even now as he's about to marry someone else.

I sigh, realising I've reached the front of the aisle.

I step to the side, feeling Hunter's gaze on me.

I plaster a fake smile on my face, mentally telling myself to suck it up.

He is marrying someone else.

I need to move on.

(1) Zane

Getting posted to Ridgehope Hospital, six hours from the city was just what I needed.
There was too much pain everywhere I turned in Adelaide, and always that hope that Amy would walk back in the door, like she'd never left.
It wasn't that I blamed her for leaving me, but still it hurt like a bitch.

It was though our wedding vows meant nothing to her.
In sickness and in health she'd promised, but she apparently only promised health, not sickness.

I couldn't think about her leaving me now though.
I was in Ridgehope for a new start and the country air was welcoming the minute I drove up to the rundown house on the outskirts of the quaint one main street town.
It needed some TLC but it was a roof over my head and I was unlikely to be spending much time there anyway.

That was another reason Amy had left me.
Apparently I was married to my job.
I was hoping that moving to a small town like Ridgehope might make that less likely to happen.
Not that it really mattered now when I was single and heartbroken from her walking out on me three months earlier.
I was after a fresh start, although I was hesitant about getting to know the people of such a small town. No one, except my close family and friends knew me in Adelaide, but here it seemed everyone would know my name.
I wasn't sure if I was ready for that.

Come on Zane, put your big boy pants on.

I have to suck it up, and get out of the car.
My brand new black V8 Ford Mustang seems a little out of place in this town, but I love her and I'm hoping the cops aren't anal about speeding, as I plan to take her out for a speedy drive down the back roads and really run the engine in.

Ok, Zane, big boy pants, get out of the car.

I open the door slowly, stepping out, scanning my surroundings, taking in everything I can.
I press the button for the boot and it springs open, revealing my two suitcases.
I'd not brought much with me, just some basic everyday clothes, underwear and a few black slacks and white shirts. The hospital would have brand new scrubs to wear and I often didn't wear them when not in surgery anyway.

Wheeling my two suitcases towards the house is quite a feat in the soft red dirt.
It's wispy and feels like it's getting everywhere, under my clothes, through my hair and in my fucking eyes.
It stings like pins stabbing me, but I blink hard, desperate to get inside the house.

Thankfully I'd not needed to worry about furniture as the house is fully furnished and quite pleasantly too.
Dropping the suitcases inside the door I race straight to find the bathroom to flush the dirt from my eyes.

Looking at my eyes in the mirror, they are bloodshot, my face sporting a serious five o'clock shadow and bags under my eyes so dark you could mistake them for two lovely black eyes.

I've not slept for days, worried about the move, but also feeling some pains in my legs that have me worried too.
It's only mid afternoon, but I need sleep.

Doctor Attraction

Stumbling down the hallway, only just able to see out of my dirt irritated eyes I search for the bedroom, falling against the bed the minute I see it.

I drift to sleep, thinking about what the hospital might be like when I start there tomorrow.

(2) Addison

I'd heard the car pull up the street from me.
It's engine rumbling deep, almost like a roar.
No one in Ridgehope has a car like that.

Curious I peer out my curtains of the front room but I can't see anything, so step out onto my front porch. I'm only wearing knickers and a t-shirt.
The weather has been seriously hot for autumn.

So what does it matter if anyone sees me?

The car owner appears to have stopped three doors down from me and I can't see through the dark tinted windows. The car is as black as night, the windows almost blending into the paint.
It's a damn hot looking car.

I watch it, for a minute or so, wondering what the owner might look like.
I have a feeling it's a male, and think it might be the new Doctor the chief had mentioned.
He's apparently coming from the city, and is some hot shot surgeon who also dabbles into obstetrics and emergency cases. He sounds like a complete arse who is out to steal my job.
I've only just come back to Ridgehope, in my despair and I can't lose my job, as well as possibly losing hope of ever getting Hunter back.

I'd been stupid to reject his proposal a year ago, but I had my reasons.

I can't think of that now, focus Addison, mysterious stranger incoming.

The car door is opening and a tall, disheveled looking male is stepping out.

Doctor Attraction

He has a clear five o'clock shadow and his short hair is messy like he's been running his hands through it over and over, wondering if he should get out of the car.
He's wearing grey track-pants that hang low on his hips, the band of his underwear visible at the edge and a white t-shirt with some slogan on it I can't make out.
He looks seriously sleep deprived too, which makes me think that he must be the new doctor for sure.
I know all about sleep deprivation. Coffee is my only lover at the moment.
I literally drink it like water.

Said possibly new doctor grabs two suitcases from his car boot, wheeling one in each hand across the red dirt.
His reaction to the dirt getting in his face makes me laugh; he spits it out like it's the most disgusting thing he's ever experienced.
It certainly isn't pleasant, but eating a little dirt never hurt anyone.
It does get under your clothes though, and in your hair, so I understand his frustration.
I had kinda missed the wispy red dirt though when I'd been in the city, as well as the country air.
Breathing it in makes your lungs feel happy, your nostrils clear from the eucalypts scattered around the landscape.

Who needs eucalyptus scented tissues when you can just step outside and breathe it ok?
Ok me, I love those tissues

But I'd missed the country; the city had always been so stifling.
It had too many secrets and held too much pain as it was the place my family and myself always ran to when something went awry.
I'd come back this time, to stay.
I'd come back this time to right the wrongs of my past, and for the first part of that I needed to see Hunter Mackenney.
But I'm truly scared; worried at the prospect of seeing him again.

Scared that he won't want me back and scared to tell him the secret I've been holding onto for years.

(3) Zane

Walking into Ridgehope General hospital, my first day, is like entering a new world, or more an old world.

The hospital is clean, the overwhelming smell of bleach, but it's also quaint and seems like it's definitely going to be my home away from home.

Married to my job is probably still going to be the way.

I walk casually up to the nurses at reception, greeting them warmly, "Ladies, good morning. I'm Zane Rivnay, new surgeon and doctor of all trades I guess."

They giggle at me, eyeing me, from the unbuttoned collar of my crisp white shirt, down to the belt holding up my black slacks.

I give them a friendly wink.

"Good morning to you, Doctor Rivnay. It's lovely to meet you," the nurse closest to me coos, like she's trying to flirt with me.

Sorry hun, you're a little old for me and I'm essentially married.
Ok, that's kind of a lie, I'm separated.

Separated; you separate eggs. It's always seemed like an odd way to describe a relationship breakdown to me.

I know it means to go your separate ways, but if only one person wanted that it doesn't really make sense.

"So ladies, can you point me towards the chief's office?"

One of them stands up, looking as though she's about to curtsy at me like I'm some prince.

I'm starting to think there aren't any eligible bachelors in Ridgehope.

All the nurses are old enough to be my mother and they are practically throwing themselves at me, drooling over me.

I have to admit I actually kind of like the attention.

The nurse that stood suddenly speaks, "I'll take you to the chief."
She sounds like she's popped out of one of those old movies you watch on television late at night.
"Thank you. That would be lovely," I reply, as she comes around the other side of the nurses station.

She looks me up and down again, from head to toe, and I nearly laugh out loud when she actually licks her lips.
This town is definitely in need of some testosterone.

I follow her down the halls of the hospital, trying to take in my surroundings, so as to not get lost later.
For a small country town the hospital is rather large.
There are a number of private rooms down one side of the hallway, the other side with curtained bays, and at the back a large well equipped emergency bay opposite four offices.

The first office has 'Hospital Chief' on the glass, the others appear to not belong to anyone in particular.
The nurse has walked off, not even saying another word to me.
So far I like the attention but at the same time I'm a little creeped out as well.
I knock on the office door, and open it when the chief responds with a friendly, "Come in".

His office is welcoming and very much a Doctor's office, walls lined with medical books and patient files; not to mention a desk that is piled high with papers as well.
He appears to be a Doctor who barely sets foot outside this room.

"Aaah...Doctor Rivnay, welcome. Take a seat," he says directing me to the tub chairs in front of his cumbersome wooden desk.
I feel like a kid at school in front of the principal about to get my sorry arse detention.
"So I take it you settled in all right last night?"

"Yes, thank you Sir," I reply, feeling a damn fool for being so formal the moment the words leave my mouth.

"No sir around here. Herbert is fine by me."

"Zane is fine by me then, Herbert," I say, feeling relief at getting the formalities out of the way.

"Well, Zane, I'm very glad to have someone with your experience and skill set on staff here at Ridgehope."

"I appreciate it. I needed to get out of the city."

"Good, good, get some country air in your lungs."

"Yes, I'm not to fond of the country dirt though."

He laughs, well chuckles actually like an old man playing Santa Klaus at the local mall.

"Yes, it gets everywhere. Shall I show you to your office?" he asks standing from his high back spinning chair.

I grin, hoping there's one of those in my office to.

"Sounds wonderful. But only if I get one of those delightful chairs."

"Yes, yes you do, " he says leading me out the door to the office a few doors down.

He opens the door slowly.

"All yours, I'll leave you to get settled. Whole staff meeting is at ten am in the emergency department."

He shuts the door behind me and like a crazy kid I race over to the high back spinning chair, planting my arse in the seat, leaning back and spinning around in it like mad.

The large clock above the door tells me it's now nine thirty.

Part of me wants to stay in the spinning chair for the next half an hour before the staff meeting, but other than the fact that would make me insanely dizzy I know I need to explore the hospital more.

I actually want there to be a least be some eye candy somewhere in the town. It isn't that I want a relationship with anyone, but not having Amy here, as we are *separated* I need someone to look at everyday.

So leaving my office I head to check out the emergency department and also to find the medicine supply storage as I'd not seen that on the way in.

I've barely walked out of the office however, when I see *'her'*.
A walking wet dream, wearing ridiculous ugly green scrubs and patent white high heels; she seems like a figment of my imagination.
Her long wavy blonde hair cascades down her shoulders, stopping at her breasts and her eyes are blue, ocean blue, so deep you could get lost in them.
One look at her and my heart is pounding in my chest.
She's absolutely gorgeous, insanely beautiful and clearly not my type.
But still I can't help but stare at her.
She obviously works here, given her attire.

Her attire, that I actually kinda want to rip from her body.
Ok Zane, head out of the gutter, you're a professional.

I've always wondered what female doctors wear under their scrubs. And by the looks of her, the delicious woman she is and the way I can see the outline of her nipples against the fabric I don't think she's wearing anything under her scrubs. That thought affects me in a way it definitely shouldn't.

I saunter over to her quickly, as she's about to open the door to the office next to the chief's.
"Excuse me, I'm looking for the medicine supply closet?"
"Near reception," she says abruptly, not even looking at me as she fumbles with the door handle.
"And which way is that?"
She turns to look at me, standing a little to close, her arm brushing mine sending a shiver through me.

What the fuck is wrong with me?
Get a hold of yourself Zane.

"That way," she says pointing down the hallway.

Doctor Attraction

She's most certainly abrupt but I kind of like it.
"Could you show me? I didn't see it on my way in."
She sighs and opens her mouth as though she's going to say something. It makes me look at her lips and I have to think about disgusting things, so as to not lick my lips as the thought of kissing her comes to mind.

I need to get a grip.
I just fucking met her, but fuck she's gorgeous.

Breaking my illicit thoughts she moans her annoyance, "Fine."
Proceeding to walk back down the hallway I watch her arse.

Yes, I looked at her arse.

Sneakily I'm watching the way her hips sway as she walks. It has always fascinated me at how high heels accentuate a woman's legs.
She stops in front of a large wall, pushing against it, and waving me inside.

"Here you go."
She's about to shut the door, with me inside the room, but I stop her, touching her arm.
"I didn't catch your name?" I purr at her.
"Addison Yorke," she says rudely.

And then she's gone, the door slamming shut, leaving me in the dark surrounded by shelves of medicines and other supplies.

Ok Zane, you need to get a grip.
You cannot think about her.
You cannot think about her lips, her arse or any other part of her body underneath those ugly scrubs.

I have never experienced such a deep want for someone in my life.
I want Addison Yorke.

But I shouldn't want her.

I'm a married man, ok, a separated man, but I still love Amy, hopelessly love Amy.

But then she walked out on me and left me heartbroken.

Maybe Addison could fix my broken heart?
No, Zane, she cannot, stop thinking with your daks, you're a doctor, think with your head.

Fumbling for the light switch, I flick on the light and push the door open again. The medicine supply closet is a claustrophobics nightmare. And I desperately need some air, some country air to calm myself and cool down from meeting the luscious Addison Yorke.

I think I'm going to like working at Ridgehope hospital.

(4) Addison

I'd avoided the new doctor, as though he had the plague.
The way he'd looked at me earlier in the week had really gotten to me.
It was like he was undressing me with his dark brown eyes and I felt exposed as
if he had x-Ray vision and he really could see beneath my scrubs.
He'd also been a crazy flirt and he really needed to back off.
He could have used his x-ray vision to find the medicine storage.
I honestly don't like him one bit.

Ok that's a lie, he is kinda good looking.
But who am I kidding, he's no Hunter Mackenney .

I sigh deeply thinking about Hunter.
I've not seen him since I got back a couple months ago and I can't help but think
about whether he's changed.
No doubt he's probably more handsome than ever and is probably still as sexy
as hell.
I'd grown up with Hunter in my life, first as silly kids who wanted to know what it
felt like to kiss someone and then our crazy whirlwind romance.
I should never have left.
If I hadn't rejected his proposal I'd not be here pining after him, but married to
him.

Stupid Addison, why do you keep making the same mistakes when it comes to
males?
Speaking of males, here comes the most annoying one in this hospital.

The new doctor is sauntering towards me, a grin on his face. He's acting like he
runs the hospital and isn't just head surgeon and possible job stealer.

I try to slip away behind one of the curtain bays but he sees me and pulls the curtain back, eyeing me with his x-ray vision again.

"Good morning Addison," he says in his flirty tone.
I feel colour rise in my cheeks and I never blush. He shouldn't make me feel that way. I don't even like him.

"Um...good morning Doctor," I say realising I actually don't know his name.
He laughs, saying his words jovially, "I'm sorry I didn't introduce myself properly yesterday."
He extends his hand to me.
"It's Zane."
I shake his hand, trying not to meet his eyes as I can see from the corner of my eye that he's still staring at me in his annoying I am undressing you in my mind way.
The silence between us is awkward. I have no idea what to say and have forgotten even what I'd left my office to do.
He's the one to break the silence after what seems like hours and I let out a breath of relief, glad I didn't have to pretend to faint to get out of the situation.

"So we have an emergency case on the way. A young woman, unconscious with a severe leg wound and possible internal and other bleeding."

He's so clinical when he speaks about medicine. It makes my head spin.
It's clear I'm no emergency doctor, unless it's something to do with a pregnant woman.
"So is this woman your patient or mine?" I ask, suddenly finding my voice.
"That depends on the reason for her bleeding Addison. Other than the leg wound of course."
I hate how he had to include saying my name in his sentence. It's like he just said it to irritate me. He's certainly rubbing me up the wrong way.

"So, you're telling me, if the bleeding is related to obstetrics you will back off?"
"I didn't say that."

I grunt.

Why is he here?

He wants my job and god knows what else. I seriously hate this man.

"But you implied it."

"Ok fine I did, but let's just wait for the patient to arrive."

"Whatever," I snap at him, heading to the emergency department, hearing the sirens approaching.

Zane appears next to me, when the stretcher with the woman is wheeled in.

The sheets are extremely blood stained and I'm a little shocked.

I'm definitely not equipped for emergency medicine, but being in Ridgehope hospital I'm likely to find myself in the thick of it.

Zane has taken charge of the situation, ripping what remains of her black track pants from her body and cleaning the leg wound to begin stitching the large gash up.

I look at her lower body and know straight away what her other bleeding is from.

I step closer to Zane's side.

"I think we need to take some blood for a HCG test and a possible ultrasound."

"Why?" he asks stupidly.

"She's clearly miscarrying Zane. Are you even a doctor?"

"Well, do it Addison. Why are you standing around telling me what needs to be done?"

God, he's infuriating!

I busy myself with the mystery woman, taking a blood sample to rush off for testing and completing an ultrasound that confirms my diagnosis.

I watch Zane out of the corner of my eye as he stitches her leg up, with ten stitches.

He catches me staring at one point and mouths *'what'* at me. I shake my head in response and tidy up the emergency bay when she's taken to a private room.

Caz May

How am I going to work with him everyday?

(5) Zane

After organising the clinical chart for the mystery woman, I return to the emergency department to find Addison tidying up and restocking the supply trolley.
Approaching her from behind and leaning in close to her side I speak in her ear, "Addison, shouldn't a nurse be doing that?"

She falls against the supply trolley, cursing under her breath at the cold metal against her hands.
I have to fight the urge to not grab her by the waist to turn her around and smash my lips to hers.

Zane, you are thinking with your daks again, head out of gutter.

She forcefully pushes the trolley away, it hits the wall and the items on it fall to the floor.
"Fine Zane. The nurses can do it."
Her eyes don't leave mine and the thought of kissing her is still surfacing in my mind.
I really don't know why she's getting to me so much.
And the awkward silences between us are making me think really dirty thoughts.

Stripping her of the ugly scrubs, kissing her sweet lips, licking her hot skin, oh fuck I have to stop thinking about her.

"Zane, hello, Zane?"
She's waving her hands in front of my face.
"Sorry, what? I was just thinking."
"Of what?"

Wouldn't you like to know, Addison.
"Um you," I say.

Well, I was but there is no way I'm going to tell her the truth of what's going through my dirty mind.

"Oh really?" She spits at me, a hint of flirtation in her voice.
"Yes, I was thinking about assigning you as the head doctor for the mystery woman."
"Ok, but surely you want to do it? Like everything else?"
"I'm only one man Addison."
"A damn cocky one," she mutters under her breath but I heard her as clear as day and my pants feel a little tighter hearing her say, *'cocky'*.

"You should be in charge of her care. You're an obstetrician right?"
She blushes, and it's so damn hot.

Seriously Zane, you have got to stop these thoughts.

"Yeah, guilty as charged."
"Great, I'll leave you to get back to the job that's not yours."
She scowls at me. She's so infuriatingly hot and clearly doesn't like me; and I'll be damned if I don't find out why.

Yeah, I'm technically still married and still in love with Amy but there is something about Addison and her absolute clear disgust for me that is driving me absolutely crazy with desire for her.
Maybe it's partly the fact she's blonde, not a brunette like Amy and maybe the fact that she obviously has an amazing body under her hideous scrubs.

No, Zane, do not think of ripping her scrubs off.
Do not think about kissing her senseless .
God, I have got to get ahold of myself.

Doctor Attraction

I need to sit in my spinning chair.
Rushing to my office I park my arse in the spinning chair, pressing my feet in the floor to spin and make myself go faster.

What would it be like to fuck someone on this?
No I didn't say fuck Addison, but damn.
No, Zane, you definitely cannot think about that.

I slam my palms against the desk to stop the chair from spinning, pushing it under the desk to start focusing on some work but also to hide the crazy lust that is damn ready to burst out of my pants.

How am I going to work with her everyday?

(6) Hunter

Walking into the private hospital room, I don't know what to feel.
I've barely been able to get the mystery woman out of my mind since finding her laying in a pool of blood on my spare bed the day before.
It's silly but I'd brought her a massive bunch of flowers.
I cross the room to her bedside and hesitate a moment, standing next to the bed. Her eyes are closed, but I can tell she isn't asleep.
Her beauty still strikes me and I want her to open her eyes to see what colour they are.
Placing the flowers on the bed beside her I say, "Hi."
I want to say more but the words are caught in my throat.
I want to tell her everything I know about her being found at my place, and tell her I think she's beautiful but it doesn't seem right.

Standing next to her still, I brush her cheek with my hand. Her skin is soft and warm and I smile at her; she appears to stir at my touch.
Her eyes flutter open and she slowly looks me up and down, taking in my outfit and studying my face like she's trying to work out if she knows me.
Her eyes are gorgeous, green with a hint of blue that has a sparkle to them.
I feel as though I could get lost in her eyes.
My thoughts wander to kissing her and I curse myself for even thinking about kissing someone I don't even know. But I feel like I do know her and that scares me.

Looking down at her, I again brush her cheek with my hand.
"Hi, good to see you awake," I say softly.
She looks up at me again ,studying my face as I study hers.
She's truly beautiful, but in a different way to Addison.
Her hair is dark chocolate brown, almost raven black compared to Addison's blonde and she has a sweet innocent look to her delicate features.

A soft murmur escapes her lips, as though she wants to talk.

"It's ok you're safe. Don't speak."

My words come out so softly I don't even think she heard them. She reaches down to tear at edges of the tape of the IV on her arm.

She doesn't even appear to flinch at the pain and I get the sense that she's experienced a great deal of pain in her life.

I shake my head at her to urge her to stop, putting my hand over hers.

She lets out a deep breath, just as the door cracks open and the one person I've been dreading seeing walks into the room.

"Hunter? Is that you?" she asks.

I don't need to look up to know it's her.

"Addison, what are you doing here?"

I know it's a stupid question to ask, considering she's wearing ugly green scrubs.

"I work here Hunter," she announces.

I shake my head. Since when has she worked here?

"I thought you moved to Adelaide."

"I did, but I missed it here. I came back a month ago."

I stand up, pushing the chair I'm sitting back hastily.

"And you didn't think to contact me and tell me?" I practically yell at her.

I don't know why I'm so upset that she hadn't contacted me.

I don't want to speak to her, let alone see her again but obviously that isn't going to happen now she's back in town.

"I wanted to but..." she starts to say.

I don't want to hear her excuses. It has always been the same with her.

When things got tough or she didn't get her way, she had some excuse or ran away.

"Oh, come on, Addison. It's always been about you. What you want, what you need."

I'm almost at the door to leave, but she stops me, standing in the way of the door.

"Please Hunter, let me explain," she begs.

"No, I don't want to hear it Addison, I didn't then and I don't now."

She sighs deeply, touching my arm and nodding to the woman on the bed.

"Um, Hunter, do you know her?"

I shake my head again.

I don't know what to say.

I don't know her but I really want to.

"No, I don't. I found her passed out in the farmhouse."

She seems taken aback that I don't know the mystery woman.

It doesn't make any sense and makes me a little wary about Addison's full intentions for coming back to Ridgehope.

I don't want to get back together with her.

Her words when she speaks again upset me more than they should.

"Oh well um I can't disclose her details to you then."

I don't reply, instead push her aside going straight out the door without another word.

How am I going to find anything out about the mystery woman now?

I want desperately to know everything about her and it's scary how much I want her physically.

Something I haven't felt for years has awoken in me and somehow I'm going to find out everything about her.

I want her, the beautiful dark haired mystery woman.

(7) Zane

Addison had been avoiding me for days like I'm a god damn leper. It's driving me crazy. I want her so damn much and that scares me.

She appeared to have a rather interesting conversation with a guy that came in to see the mystery woman. He seemed as though he didn't really want to speak to her, whereas I would give my right arm to have a conversation with her that isn't about a patient. No woman before has ever gotten to me like her and I barely know her.

Since the only way I'm actually able to speak to her is to talk about hospital patients I head to her office to speak to her about the mystery woman, hoping that I can dig a little deeper and find out who he is as well. She clearly has some connection to him.

Standing outside her office door I take a deep breath before knocking. Her voice welcomes me, "Come in, it's open."

God, even her voice makes me want to...head out of gutter Zane, you're a professional.

I open the door to find her sitting at the desk, scanning some papers in front of her and tapping something into her computer.
"Hi Addison," I start as I walk towards the desk.
She scoffs seeing me in her office. Her eyes show me she still hates me.
"I just wanted to have a chat about the mystery woman."
She glares at me, as though she's trying to say something with her eyes.
I sit in the tub chair in front of the desk, leaning back with my hands behind my head.

"Seriously Zane, you're such a pompous arse."

"Oh, come on Addison. I'm just coming in for a chat about a patient."

"Yeah, ok, Whatever," she says, her eyes slipping to the front of my pants.

"So the mystery woman? Any news?"

"What news could there possibly be? She hasn't said a word and..."

She pauses to slowly run a hand through her hair.

Fuck, she looks so damn sexy doing that, think with head not pants Zane.

"And what?"

"I can't tell you."

"Why the fuck not?"

"Because I don't want to. We're not friends Zane."

That hurts more than it should. Her disdain for me is really upsetting me.

Don't be a pansy Zane.

"I never said we were 'friends' Addison but as a colleague you should be discussing patient details with me."

She lets out a soft laugh. "I wasn't talking about the patient but someone else."

Yes, the man she was talking to, time to make her let down the wall.

"Is it about the man you were talking to outside her room?"

"Yes, how did you know that?"

"I see all Addison," I tease.

"Really? You have x-ray vision?"

"Maybe, so come on tell me about him? You looked pretty smitten with him," I say sitting up.

"He's my ex."

"That's it? That's all you're going to tell me?"

"Yes, you don't need to know my relationship history."

"I do if it's going to affect how you do your job."

"Fine, you want to know?"

Damn right I want to know. I plan to use this information to break down the wall she has built.

"Yes, I want to know Addison."
"He proposed to me and I rejected him."
"Addison, that's heartless. I didn't think you were a a bitch."
"Stop, it wasn't like that. I was scared. I can't talk about it."
"Fine, but you still love him don't you?" I say softly, feeling a little compassion for her creeping in seeing the sadness on her face.
"More than ever. And I want him back."
"And he doesn't want you back?" I ask, hoping her answer is going to be no.

"I don't think so. It seems like there is something going on with him and the mystery woman but he says he doesn't know her."
"Well, Addison I think you're fucked. But hey, do what you like," I say standing up to walk out.

She doesn't say anything as I walk out.
Getting to know her is going to be a lot harder than I thought. And even though she's insanely gorgeous and makes my body feel things it shouldn't I'm not sure what I really want from her.
She seems kind of heartless but at the same time she'd said she's still in love with him.
It doesn't make a lot of sense and I feel like I'm now in a circus not a hospital.

(8) *Hunter*

Not a day has passed when I haven't gone into the hospital to see her.
Even though she hasn't said one word to me, I long to be in her presence.
She smiles and laughs when I tell her about silly things I'd done as kid.
I want to tell her she's beautiful, but every time I try to open my mouth those words get caught in my throat.
Instead I reach out to caress her cheek, loving how she leans closer to my hand, as though she loves my touch and is feeling the same longing as me.
The longing to be with her is becoming harder to deal with.
I honestly don't know why I want her so damn much.
She's not my type at all, but just looking at her makes my insides stir with desire for her.
I want to kiss her so much, to know what it feels like to have her delectable lips on mine. To know how she tastes.

Seriously Hunter, stop thinking about her like that, you don't know her.

As much as I want to stay by her beside I need to get back to farm. I mouth '*I have to go*' to her and she nods before frowning.
I touch her cheek again before crossing the room to the door to leave.
Turning the door handle I bump straight into Addison coming into the room.
I push my hands against her chest to steady us both, cursing myself for touching her a little to high when her nipples rise to attention under her scrubs.

"Hi, Addison," I say trying to remain calm.
"Hi, Hunter. I was just coming to check on her."
"Yeah, cool. Is she going to be released any time soon?"
Addison shakes her head in response.
"Not as yet. She's definitely better, but we don't know anything about her so the chief is reluctant to release her."

"Oh, so you don't know anything about how or why she was in my farmhouse?" I question her, before also adding, "She won't speak to me."

"She's not speaking at all Hunter," she says sternly.

"So can she speak?" I ask, warily.

"We honestly don't know, but she is communicating by writing things down." I glare at her, trying to get her to open up and say something else.

I want to know more, but I also know that professionally Addison can't say anything to someone who isn't family or an emergency contact.

It makes me wonder more about her though, whether she has family back home who are worried about her, or is she running from danger?

"Oh so what has she written then?" I ask, desperate to find something out about her, no matter what it is.

"Her name is Savannah Galison," Addison says shrugging.

Looking back at her in the bed, I whisper her name under my breath.

A smile spreads across her face at the acknowledgement.

My stomach flip flops. I shouldn't have felt that. I want her more than anything.

಄

I think of nothing but Savannah on the way back to the farm. I want to know all about her. I want to find out all her secrets, her past and why she's ended up in Ridgehope of all places.

I'm hoping for a quiet night and I'm just about to sit down to watch some mindless television when someone knocks at the door. Blitz starts barking like a mad thing, which usually means he doesn't like or doesn't know who is at the door.

He follows me to open it.

"Down Blitz," I say opening the wooden main door, looking through the screen door to find Addison standing on my verandah still in her scrubs.

Disgust crosses my face, before I ask, "What are you doing here Addison?"

"I wanted to talk," she replies casually.

"What would we need to talk about?" I ask her, annoyed.

Blitz is snarling at her and I have to stifle a laugh.

"Um...us,"she says softly as though she's trying not to yell.

"There is no us Addison," I say spitefully.

"Please Hunter. Can I just come in?" she begs.

I glare at her.

Why the hell did she think coming here was a good idea?

I've already told her I don't love her anymore but she just can't let go. I don't say anything but sigh and against my better judgement I reach to the handle pushing the door open to invite her in.
Blitz jumps on her, like he's crazy and her whole body tenses up in disgust.
He'd always hated her and part of me didn't blame the dog.
I tell him down and point towards the kitchen for him to retreat.

Addison has headed towards the living room, and after following her I stop in the hallway with my hands on my hips.
She appears to be completely tongue tied and the silence between us is tense.
I have to say something before things get awkward, as I can see a sense of lust in her eyes.
"So why are you here Addison?" I ask again.
She cringes at my words.
"I came back for you Hunter," she declares.
"Why Addison?"
"Because I still love you. I've never stopped loving you."
I shrug. "Seriously, come on Addison, you never loved me."
"How can you say that Hunter? I..."
"Oh I don't know Addison, maybe because you brushed me off twice, ran away to the city and..." I stop mid sentence, not sure if I want to say because *'you rejected my proposal'.*
"And because I didn't say yes?" she asks, reading my mind.
"Ding, ding, ding," I say with a sarcastic tone.
"I'm sorry Hunter. But please just let me explain."
"Whats to explain? You didn't want to marry me. What would have changed?"
"Me, Hunter. I've changed."
Again the silence envelopes us but this time I want to stir things up.
Addison had always been a bit vindictive.
"Maybe you should prove it me," I say again breaking the silence.

Before she has a chance to respond I head down the hallway to the bathroom.

I hear her hesitantly walk down the hallway, towards my bedroom.

The bathroom door creaks when I open it a minute or so later and I call out, "Addison are you still here?"

She giggles, calling back, "Find me."

My bare feet on the floorboards makes them creak. I stop in the door jam of my bedroom, leaning against it.

She's lying down, in a g-string, bra and high heels, butt up, on my bed.

"Seriously Addison? This is your plan?"

"Come on Hunter. You never could resist me."

I slowly step further into the bedroom, closer to the bed and she grabs my hand.

I don't want her but still it sends a rush through my body. Lust is evident in her eyes and lust swells in my jeans.

I inwardly curse myself for being a male.

What the fuck is happening? I don't want this, do I?

(9) Addison

I stand up, my body crashing forcefully against Hunter's. Lustfully I ask, "Do you still want me Hunter?"

I can feel his body saying, 'yes' to my question; his obvious desire for me pressing against my belly.

I want him so much.

No other man has ever made me feel like he does.

Looking directly into my eyes he whispers, "I want you Addison."

His lips crash onto mine and hungrily I respond to his kiss.

Kissing him again makes the longing for him more intense than ever.

I don't want to ever stop kissing him, but he seems a little tense.

I pull away and don't hesitate to lift his t-shirt over his abs before taking it off.

Running my hands down his chest, through the pepper of brown hair across his chest makes my insides stir. Stopping at his belt buckle, I fumble to undo it.

I want this so much and Hunter appears to as well.

He pushes me back on the bed and I giggle at him taking charge. He never was very forceful in bed, so I kinda like him taking charge now.

He quickly takes my mouth in a kiss again as I help him wiggle out of his jeans.

Again I pull back from his kiss, and beg, "Make love to me Hunter."

I reach behind my back to unclasp my bra. The straps fall down my arms and I feel exposed. The look in his eyes has changed from lust to disgust and now I feel utterly rejected.

He doesn't keep touching me, instead he shakes his head, standing up by the bed. I frown, feeling tears stinging my eyes when he speaks, "I can't Addison."

Sobbing I reply meekly, "Why Hunter? Don't you love me anymore?"

"No, Addison I don't love you anymore." My sobbing becomes uncontrollable, the tears streaming down my cheeks and his words cut me deep.

I stand up from the bed then, feeling incredibly hurt. I never thought I'd feel this pain, from Hunter of all people.

Doctor Attraction

It was stupid of me to even come here, to think that throwing myself at him was the answer. It was never about the physical with us at all and I rulned it again by not talking to him.

I lift my hand close to his cheek, about to slap him. But he looks at me with concern on his face, like he's sorry he upset me and I can't do it, instead wiping it across my own tear stained cheek before bending down to pick up my clothes.

I run straight down the hallway, not even looking back.

The stupid dog starts barking when he hears the screen door slam shut.

I have no idea what had just happened. I feel incredibly stupid, exposed and rejected. The man I love doesn't love me.

Sitting in my car for a moment, my head in my hands I sob into the steering wheel. I should have just left straight away but a part of me was hoping he'd come running out, saying he was sorry and beg me to come inside.

Surprisingly, I'm startled by a tap on window. Rolling the window down I giggle finding Hunter standing by my car only in his boxers, shivering.

"What?" I spit.

"I'm sorry Addison. I panicked."

"What?" I spit at him again. I don't know what else to say.

"I'm sorry. I just think we should take the possibility of getting back together slow ok?"

Nodding I reply, "Ok. I can deal with that."

I can deal with that, but I don't want to take things slow.

He leans into the car and presses a kiss on my forehead before he speaks softly, "Goodnight Addison, Drive safe."

I roll up the window after saying goodnight to him and he waves when I drive towards the gate.

Why am I getting the feeling that Hunter doesn't really want me back?

(10) Zane

I seriously don't understand why women cry so much, mainly over stupid things. In the past week I've seen Addison crying more than once and I wanted to tell her to just grow the fuck up. Clearly her ex doesn't want her back and all she does is chase after him, when I'm practically chasing after her begging her to want me.

Stupid I know, but she seriously drives me fucking crazy; I want her so damn much.

This time she's trying to hide the fact she's been crying, sniffing and wiping her arm across her cheeks when she leaves the staff cafeteria, heading back to her office.

I'd seen her talking on the phone earlier and whoever she was speaking to her then wasn't the one who'd made her cry. Shuffling down the hallway I call out to her, "Addison, are you ok?"

She stops dead in her tracks, taking one look at me and the concerned look on my face before she breaks down, into tears.

Through sobs she says, muffled, "Do I look ok Zane?"

She looks more than ok, she's absolutely gorgeous even when she's upset, but I can't tell her that.

I step closer to her, wanting to envelope her in a hug, but I don't think that would be the wisest move to make in the middle of the hospital hallway.

Instead, I reach down, my hand brushing the small of her back to guide her into my office.

She doesn't seem to hesitate or even flinch at the touch and it makes me a little excited, as wrong as that is.

Once in my office, I make her sit in the tub chair and say, "Ok, spill. What's with all your tears?"

She doesn't answer, instead sniffs more, shoving her phone into my hand.

"Why are you giving me your damn phone?"

Doctor Attraction

"Read the messages from Hunter."
I swipe a finger across the screen and it lights up. Pressing the messages app, there is some from Jett and below them Hunter. I feel like I'm prying.
The first message is friendly.

Hunter: Hi Addison. Didn't see you today. How's Savannah?

Her reply is simple and direct, but far from professional.

Addison: Sorry Hunter. Different shift. Savannah is doing a lot better. And I know I shouldn't but I'm going to tell you what happened and what we suspect.

He hadn't replied so she typed more, crossing the doctor confidentiality line further.

Addison: She had a miscarriage. We believe she was about 7 weeks. She also cut her leg in getting to your house. The bruises may have been related to that, but we believe they may be from physical abuse of some kind. Police trying to find out but doesn't help that she doesn't say anything.

Those messages don't tell me anything about why she's upset. Only that she has broken a cardinal doctor rule of not disclosing patient details.
Dropping her phone in her lap I say, "Those messages don't tell me why you're upset Addison."
Wiping her tear stained face she speaks, "Because he doesn't even say anything about our..." She cuts her words off, pain evident in her eyes.
Desperately I want to kiss her, to take the pain away that he has so obviously caused, but I can't do that when she's so vulnerable.
Instead I step closer to her, my legs against hers and my hands on the sides of the tub chair.
"Didn't say anything about your what Addison?"
Her eyes look directly into mine.
"Kiss."
"Should he have?"

47

Anger flares in her eyes. "Yes, I kissed him...well threw myself at him, telling him to make love to me and he rejected me."

Hunter is an idiot, she'd begged him to make love to her and he refused, seriously an idiot.

"I don't understand why you keeping chasing after him Addison."
Pushing her hands against my chest she speaks, almost defensively, "Because I love him. I've never not loved him."
Pushing her back down into the chair, I lean closer to her, my face mere centimetres from hers.
"Sometimes you have to let go and take a chance."
Her chest hitches at my words, her breathing quickening.

God I want to kiss her, so fucking bad.

Leaning back to try to get away from me, the tub chair topples over, crashing to the floor.
She shrieks, waving her arms and legs about in an effort to try and get up.
Obviously my being so close has affected her somehow. I let out a laugh, as she looks absolutely hilarious.

Damn if she had a skirt on, the view would have been rather pleasant.
Zane seriously you have to stop thinking with your pants.

Grabbing her hand I help her up, and she falls into my arms.
Instinctively I wrap my arms around her and to my surprise she doesn't pull away, nor flinches at what I thought would be an unwelcome touch.
Having her so close is making my body rise to attention, especially when I breathe in, my nose capturing the sweetness of her perfume and the scent of her strawberry shampoo.

Seriously, how is she so fucking delicious?

Doctor Attraction

Feeling my obvious desire for her she pulls back from our embrace, looking directly at me when she speaks, "Thanks for listening Zane."

I smile at her. "Anytime, Addison. I'm here for you. Friends right?"

She looks down at my crotch, a smile crossing her face.

"Yeah I'd like that. Friends are few and far between here."

'Mmm' is all I manage to say, watching her walk out of my office, my eyes focusing on her hot arse.

If I had my way now, we'd most definitely not be just friends.

(11) Addison

When he rounds the hallway on his way to Savannah's room I grab his hand in mine. Looking at him lustfully, gripping his hand like a vice in mine I push the medicine storage door open, giggling and pulling him into the room with me. Flicking the latch locked I push his body against some shelving, and pleadingly say, "Hunter, please."

I don't even give him a chance to speak, instead I press my lips to his in a fierce kiss. At first he responds to my kiss, his mouth melting against mine.

I've seriously missed kissing him so much. It sends a rush through me, every time. Reaching down to the waistband of his jeans he flinches pushing me back with his hands forcefully against my hips.

"What the actual fuck Addison?" he questions me.

"I...I missed you," I stammer, still breathless from kissing him.

"Well, ambushing me in the hospital hallway isn't the best way to show me that," he spits at me angrily.

"I'm sorry Hunter. But you've barely spoken to me since you know."

"Yeah, things have been a little crazy. But seriously Addison, I don't know if I..."

He stops mid sentence and I'm afraid of what he's going to say, afraid he's going to reject me yet again. It's breaking my heart, but yet I still love him.

"I can't do this Addison. I can't get back together."

Tears sting my eyes. How can he be so hot one minute and cold the next?

"Please don't cry Addison. I'm sorry but I don't love you anymore."

"But Hunter, please, we're meant to be together."

"No, Addison, we're not. Please just let us go."

He steps away from me, reaching out to unlock the door.

Again I grab his hand, pleading, "Hunter please wait."

"What for Addison? Please just let me go. I only came to see Savannah."

I smile at him and say, "I know."

There's silence between us now and it makes me feel a little claustrophobic when Hunter leaves the room and I'm surrounded by just the shelves again.

I call out to him, "Hunter, please I need to tell you something first."

He turns back towards me and he looks worried.

Stopping in front of the door to Savannah's room I place my hand reassuringly on his arm.

"You know in my text I said about the physical abuse?"

"Yeah, is it true?"

"We don't know Hunter, but that car was registered to a male. Maybe a partner or husband."

He nods when he replies, "I know about the car. Quentin told me. Can we do anything Addison?"

I shake my head. "You need to talk to the chief Hunter. The partner might be an emergency contact but you know if the patient is conscious we need permission to contact them."

He only responds with a soft, "Ok."

He clearly doesn't know what to say and it's evident that for some reason he's captivated by her.

Her arrival had taken everyone by surprise and Ridgehope seems to be turning upside down because of her arrival. Before I walk away I speak again, "And Hunter, when you speak to the chief please don't tell him I told you anything."

"No worries Addison," he says, before reaching out to hug me.

It's just a friendly hug, but still it leaves me feeling an overwhelming longing for him.

Why can't I let go of him, when he's clearly falling for someone else?

I want Hunter Mackenney, but he wants someone else.

(12) Zane

Savannah had made a lot of progress in recovering. She still sported bruises, but her stitches were out and her bleeding from the miscarriage had stopped.

Heading towards her room I bump straight into her. I look her up and down before I speak, "Ms Galison?"
She nods her response.
After screaming that she didn't want her husband to be contacted she'd not said another word. It has made everything about her care extremely difficult.
"I'm Doctor Rivnay. I was just coming to see you to work out your discharge papers," I tell her.
She smiles at me, pointing towards the bathroom.
"Thats fine. Go ahead. I'll just be in the room checking your charts," I say softly.
When she returns from the bathroom she hesitantly sits on the edge of the bed.
I can sense her unease and I know she isn't going to be happy about what I have to say.
"Well, Ms Galison," I begin, "you've certainly been through quite the ordeal."
Her only response again is a nod, so I continue with my observations,
"So, your leg and bruises have healed nicely and we are happy to discharge you, however..." I stop mid sentence knowing she isn't going to like my next words.
She attempts to smile at me, so I let the words out,
"However without being able to contact someone you know we are a bit hesitant to just discharge you."
She bursts into tears.
"I'm sorry Ms Galison. Is there someone I can contact to come take you home?"
She shakes her head and it makes me feel sorry for her.
Without warning her feet make contact with the floor and without looking back at me she rushes out the door.
I race to follow her down the hallways as she desperately tries to find the exit.

Doctor Attraction

I stop at the nurses station, to speak to them, flapping my hands about frenziedly.

I can't believe she'd just run out of the hospital in a backless gown with nowhere to go. There is definitely something up with her for sure.

Turning my eyes towards the front double doors I sigh in relief.

"Oh, thank god," I say exhaling a deep breath I hadn't realised I was holding in.

She's clutching a man's hand and it's obvious to see she's quite taken with him.

He extends his other hand to me in greeting.

"Hunter Mackenney, you must be the other new doc in town?"

"Yeah, nice to meet you Hunter. I'm Doctor Zane Rivnay."

Neither of us speak for a minute, sensing something odd about the whole situation. I look at Savannah and then down at her hand Hunter has a tight grip on.

"So I'm presuming you know Ms Galison then?" I ask Hunter.

"Well, not exactly. She was found unconscious in my farmhouse a month ago and I've been coming in to see her the past few weeks."

I nod when Hunter speaks, listening attentively.

This definitely isn't a normal discharge scenario and I'm not really sure what the best way forward is.

"We haven't been able to contact any family or a partner for her."

"Yeah I'm aware of that," Hunter replies, looking across at her.

"We can't discharge her without knowing her contact details, you know where she will be staying and such."

Hunter nods, giving me a look that shows me he's thinking exactly what I'm thinking. It kinda creeps me out.

He blurts out, a little too eagerly, "I'd be happy to have her at the farmhouse with me. Just for a couple of weeks."

"That's not normal protocol Hunter, but..." I pause, hesitating.

Hunter's offer isn't protocol but I can see that they've become close somehow in the last few weeks and he seems to be a genuinely good guy.

He'd have to be half decent for Addison to be in love with him.

"But I guess in the circumstances we can make an exception," I say.

"Great!", Hunter beams, "So do I just sign the papers now?"

"Yeah, just fill out the details with Maggie and all good."

"No worries Doctor Rivnay."

Hunter still holds her hand when he leads her up to the counter, letting go only to fill out the paperwork. When I turn to walk away, I hope I've made the right decision.

Things are definitely different out in the country. I have a lot to learn and I can only think of one person who I want to teach me the ropes of country life.

It's time to put my big boy pants on and do something to make her fall for me.

(13) Addison

Part of me knows that calling Hunter isn't a good idea. He'd rejected me more than once in the last few weeks and it's clear he doesn't want me like I want him.

It's really getting to me that he appears to be falling for Savannah when he knows nothing about her. She's not said one word the whole time she's been in the hospital.

I do wonder if maybe she'd spoken to him but I highly doubt it. Even though it's foolish for me to still want him.

After finding out that Savannah had been discharged earlier in the day I'm upset that I'm not going to see him come into the hospital and I already miss him.

I just want to hear his voice.

Picking up my phone from beside me on the couch I pull the sleeves of my jumper over my hands.

The night air has a real chill to it.

I scroll through my contacts to find his name, my finger hesitating on the call button. The pressure of my finger against the phone makes it call so I hold it up to my ear, partly hoping it will just go to voicemail and I can hang up and callback again, to hear his voice that way, but on the fourth ring he answers.

"Hi Addison, what's up?" he asks, a happy tone in his voice.

My heart is pounding. I don't even know now why I've even called him in the first place. But I speak anyway, trying to get my brain to cooperate, "I spoke to Quentin about Savannah the other day."

"And you're telling me this because?" He asks with insolence in his voice.

"I thought you'd like to know that he's trying to find out about her husband."

He scoffs down the receiver and I'm a little taken aback at his continued insolence. He's never this rude normally.

"I'm aware of that Addison. You forget Quentin is my brother."

I laugh. How could I forget that fact?

Quentin Mackenney is the most annoying of little brothers , but he'd grown up to be an all right guy and at least had gotten off the farm and gotten a real job as a Police officer.

I sometimes thought he had a crush on me, his behaviour around me when we were younger was quite odd. I'd found him masturbating watching me sleeping in bed with Hunter one night.

It kinda creeped me out, but he's older now and has definitely had his fair share of girls throwing themselves at him.

Stopping my mind from dwelling on the past I shake my head, saying to Hunter on the phone, "And Hunter, you know she's out of the hospital yeah?"

His next words completely shock me and make my heart constrict in pain and anger.

"Yeah, she's staying with me."

"What? Zane didn't tell me that," I spit down the phone angrily.

He appears so calm about it, like it's just something you do everyday; just letting some strange woman stay in your house.

"Yeah, long story. So Addison?" he questions.

"Yeah?" I say feeling guilty from his tone of voice, knowing that I hadn't called to talk about Savannah at all.

"Is that why you really called me?"

I sigh. "No," I say, my chest thudding loudly.

"So why did you really call then?" He says teasingly.

"I miss you Hunter," I blurt out, before I can even think about my words, "And I can't stop thinking about our kiss in the medicine storage the other day."

That amazing kiss I'd spent every minute thinking about, playing it over and over in my mind.

"Oh, right, yeah. Um Addison I honestly don't know what you want me to say," He says coldly.

"Oh, I don't know Hunter, something. I still fucking love you," I declare, feeling the anger at his insolence rising in my chest again.

He's silent. I know what he wants to say, but he can't find the words and instead hangs up, leaving me with my thoughts of how I'd once again fucked things up.

I was too late.

It's too late to make it right.

I should have told him a year ago that I love him instead of rejecting his proposal and running away.

But my emotions when it came to Hunter had always been hard to handle and letting go was harder than I ever imagined.

I just want him to love me back again, but sadly I can see that isn't going to be the case as he's clearly falling for Savannah and if she stays in Ridgehope, Hunter will never love me again.

That's as clear as day and it hurts like hell.

(14) Zane

Meeting and ultimately falling in love with Amy happened so quickly I never felt like I truly let her into my life. She didn't know much about my life before her and it seemed like she didn't want to.

She wasn't a bitch, far from it, but I sometimes got the sense she only married me because of my attractive six figure income, being Head surgeon at Adelaide general hospital. She always said I was married to my job and maybe I was but if it wasn't for my job I never would have met her.

Getting involved with her was wrong, she was my patient and I crossed the line, sneaking into her room after I was off duty and confessing I found her attractive. She seemed almost immediately smitten with me and I was lucky to not get caught in her room by the hospital chief. She had kissed me that first night and she was all I could think about.

Her stay in hospital was only overnight, due to her surgery only being minor, so I slipped her my number on a piece of paper when I was completing her discharge papers the next day. And later on that night she texted me.

I felt a mix of emotions, that what I'd done was wrong. But also she was only my patient for one night so it wasn't a big deal.

But now three years down the line, when she'd found out that I was a complete idiot; who didn't manage my illness well when I was stressed, had run into the arms of my best friend and ultimately decided that it would be better if we split up.

Her betrayal, running to my best friend when I was in hospital wasn't what hurt the most. It was the fact that she promised in her marriage vows to love me in sickness and health and clearly she broke that vow.

I know now I should have been more honest about the real reason for what had stressed me out so much, but I doubt she would have cared, as the blood wasn't on her hands.

She wasn't the one that made the wrong decisions and cost someone their life. And not just any life but the life of a child. It still plagues me to this day.

Doctor Attraction

Ridgehope is supposed to be my fresh start, away from the pain of my career
almost falling to pieces and of losing Amy, but it isn't exactly going to plan.
It isn't as busy as Adelaide general but the day to days are getting to me, and the
absolute disdain from Addison is breaking my heart, even though it shouldn't be
effecting me.
From the moment I met her I'd been struck by her beauty and I'd barely gone a
minute without thinking about her. I'm truly scared of falling for her, knowing
the consequences for my health when things go pear shaped in my life.
It hasn't stopped me thinking about her, wanting to kiss her, to show her I'm not
the pompous arsehole she thinks I am.
Part of what makes her attractive is her naivety, both as a doctor and in general.
I get the sense she's possibly only been with Hunter in a physical sense and she's
scared to be with someone else, to feel that way about someone other than
him.
It kinda seems crazy considering how beautiful she is, that surely guys would
have thrown themselves at her, but she rejects me continually because she
loves Hunter and she's probably done the same before.
I want her and I have to make her see that she might just want me to. I have a
plan to get her to fall in love with me, just as I'm falling for her and the first part
of that plan is getting her to like me, even just as a friend by asking her to the
town fundraiser I've heard everyone talking about.
Hesitantly I knock on her office door, not waiting for a reply when entering.
She looks up at me, disgust crossing her face.
I step closer to her desk, and she speaks patronisingly, "Is there something you
need to discuss Zane?"
I almost chicken out, feeling like a teenager again asking the first girl I liked out
on a date.
"I was just wondering if you wanted to go to the fundraiser with me on Saturday
night? If you're not working of course?"
"Are you asking me on a date?" She teases.
"Um no, I was just um thinking we could go as friends."
She appears to think for a moment, like she doesn't believe me about it not
being a date. She smiles when she replies, "OK but just as friends, no funny
business."

"No worries. I'll meet you at yours at seven."
"Ok, Zane," She says when I turn to leave.

Part one initiated.

I feel kinda giddy thinking about it. To her it isn't a date, but to me it kinda is and I'm going to show her how she makes me feel, by showing her a good night out.

(15) Addison

I'd always thought Quentin Mackenney had feelings for me. He'd never said anything but he'd always acted odd around me, including about a week ago when he'd come to see me about Savannah and he'd looked at me almost lustfully.

He'd pulled me into a hug, and I felt his lust pressing into me. I should have tried to feel something for him—he was the same age as me—Hunter being his older brother, but I can't make myself love him.

Arriving at the fundraiser a little early, Zane has gone to get us drinks and popcorn. Noticing that Quentin is on patrol duty I think I might as well say, 'hello'.

Walking up to him, I can't help but be a little bit creeped out by the way he looks at me in my short sundress.

"Hey Quentin," I say smiling at him.

"Hi," he says, running a hand through his hair, eyeing me as it does it. He's clearly flirting with me and it's kind of cute. But I don't flirt back.

I never have shown the same interest in him, so I don't understand why he hasn't moved on.

"Have you seen Hunter?" I ask, cursing myself for having nothing else to say to him. I always end up talking to him about Hunter and I kind of feel bad considering Quentin's obvious feelings for me.

His reply to my question shouldn't upset me but it does.

"Yeah, saw him with Savannah before, but they left about twenty minutes ago." He hesitates, like he wants to say something else, but when he says nothing after a few moments I speak again, "Is he serious about her then?"

"Yeah, I think he's in love with her. I've never seen him like he is with her."

That answer breaks my heart a little, but it still doesn't make me feel any less for Hunter.

"Oh," is all I manage to say in reply.

I'm not shocked, just upset that he'd said he'd never seen his brother so happy, like he wasn't happy with me.

"I'm sorry Addison, " Quentin says, his head down, looking at the dirt.

"For what?" I scoff.

"I don't know. That he doesn't love you back," He says apologetically.

"It's ok," I say a little confused, before I continue with, "You can't help who you fall in love with."

His reply is a simple, "Yeah, true."

We stand there for a moment in silence. There isn't anything else to say, but something has changed between us since I've returned to Ridgehope.

I'm never going to look at Quentin the same way he looks at me, but I'm kind of hoping that maybe we'll become friends.

"Well, um...I gotta go...um...catch up with Zane," I stutter, trying to break the uncomfortable tension between us.

"No worries Addison. Enjoy the rest of the night yeah?" He says, smiling at me.

"I will, " I say, kissing him softly on the cheek before I walk away.

Turning back to look at him, I notice the blush that has risen in his cheeks, confirming he definitely has feelings for me.

Why can't I love Quentin, instead of Hunter?

(16) Zane

Standing in the line for popcorn and drinks, I scan the surroundings of the football oval. It appears that the whole town and surrounds have come along which I think is really fitting.

Ridgehope is a quaint place, but friendly most of the time. Most people have seemed to welcome me, a few even saying, 'hello doctor' as they pass me, but the one person I want to be friends with still hates me.

Whilst I'm waiting in line she's gone to speak to the local police officer, who appears to be around the same age as her.

Her conversation with him is friendly, but his body language clearly shows that he holds a torch for her that she doesn't return. Still as she walks away she kisses him on the cheek and a blush rises in his cheeks.

I feel sorry for him, pining after her when she doesn't want him, but I also feel quite jealous that she knows him well enough to give him a kiss on the cheek.

Obviously, I want more from her than a chaste kiss on the cheek, but even that gesture of affection would be better than nothing.

Paying for the popcorn and drinks I step out of the line, struggling to hold the bucket and drinks in my arms.

She walks up to me, smiling about something and she laughs when she sees how I'm struggling.

"Let me take the drinks," She offers, grabbing them from my hands, as I try to still manage to keep the popcorn under my arm.

"Thanks," I say when we walk over to find a spot in front of the big screen set up on the oval.

I can't help but stare at her, watching how her dress hitches up a little when she walks. If I wasn't clutching the popcorn strategically I would playfully slap her arse.

She stops walking, close to the front of the screen, where others haven't sat down yet.

"Is here ok?" She asks, a cheeky smile crossing her face.

God, I want her so fucking much.

"Good a place as any," I reply putting the popcorn down on the grass and awkwardly sitting down cross legged next to her. She sits with her legs under her and her dress moves up high on her thighs.

God I want to touch her skin so bad. Head out of gutter Zane. This is not a date. I repeat, this is not a date.

She reaches her hand into the popcorn, putting pieces one by one into her mouth, her eyes on mine.
I need to say something, or I'm going to make a move that I don't think she wants.
"So what's with you and the cop?" I ask.
She sighs and laughs at the same time before replying, "He's Hunters younger brother. I think he's always had a thing for me."
"Really?" I tease, putting a piece of popcorn in my mouth, so I don't say something else stupid.
"Yes, but I can't feel anything for him."
"Yeah because you're in love with his brother."
"That yeah, but he's always been there, like a younger brother even though he's my age."
"You don't have to explain Addison. I get it."
She smiles at me again, before turning her attention to the movie we've missed most of anyway.
The tension between us is really getting to me. Surely she knows that I want her, that I want to get out of the friends zone.
Even now I can't take my eyes off her, watching as she smiles at the movie.
Feeling my eyes on her, she turns to me laughing. "Why are you looking at me like that Zane?"
Shaking my head, suddenly aware she's actually talking to me I say, "What? Looking at you how?"
She laughs again. "With your x-ray vision eyes."
This time I decide it's time to let my guard down and tease her.

"I'm just undressing you with my eyes and well..." I pause licking my lips and she slaps my thigh playfully.

"Seriously Zane, we are just friends."

My heart sinks, once again she's shut me down. But the lustful look in her eyes suggests I'm getting to her and it will only be a matter of time before she gives into me.

Part of me wants to pull her closer to me, right there and now, to smash my lips to hers, but resting my hand on her bare thigh she flinches slightly at my touch. And turning to look at me, she says softly, "Please Zane, just stop. I'm not ready..." She stops mid sentence as though she isn't sure what else to say.

I know she means she isn't ready to let go of Hunter, and she isn't ready to give into how I'm making her feel.

But it isn't a flat out no, and that means that she's possibly beginning to feel the same as me.

(17) Addison

Going to the fundraiser with Zane had been a nice night, but his words and his constant gaze locked on mine were beginning to get to me. The tension between us is definitely thick and the thought of kissing him has crossed my mind, but stupidly I feel like that would be cheating on Hunter, even though we aren't together. I've always loved Hunter and I can't just turn my feelings off, no matter how hard I want to.

Walking into the pub with Zane, he motions to me that he'll grab us a booth and order a round of drinks. I didn't really want to come out with him on what he's presuming is another date, but I never could turn down the invitation for a night of possible drunken stupor. It makes you turn off from being a doctor to live in the moment.

Walking in though, the presence of someone sitting at the bar makes my heart pound. He'd never been a big drinker, especially socially and now when he turns his head slowly towards me when I enter the pub he sighs.

Sauntering up to the bar I can't help but notice that he looks absolutely wretched.

"Hunter, what are you doing here?" I ask concerned.

"Drinking away my guilt, " He responds.

I sit down on the stool next to him, pulling it closer to his legs, in an effort to comfort him.

"Guilt? What did you do Hunter Mackenney?" I say teasing him a little.

"I lost her."

His response shocks me and I laugh, even though I know I shouldn't.

"Lost who?" I ask, even though I'm pretty sure I know who he's talking about.

"Savannah, who else would I be fucking talking about?" He says raising his voice.

My response is selfish. "Oh, maybe it's for the best Hunter," I say, resting my hand on his thigh.

Doctor Attraction

He smacks it away, shoving his hands into the bar and throwing the stool he's sitting on away angrily.

"Seriously, Addison, seriously," He says, even more anger in his voice.

"What Hunter? Why are you so angry?" I spit back at him.

"Because I fucking love her, thats why and she's gone."

There it is. I don't want those words to be true but he'd come out with them, admitting to me he's in love with her and not me.

I stand up from the stool, grabbing him by the shoulders to try and calm him down.

"What are you saying? Gone?" I question him, a little confused.

He looks up at me, and his eyes are focused on me.

Calmly I ask him, "Hunter what are you saying?"

"Didn't you hear the sirens before?" he asks.

"Yes, but whats that got to do with Savannah?"

"It was for arson with a car involved."

He suddenly collapses, falling to his knees on the floor. He's absolutely distraught. Bending down in front of him, I balance on my heels.

"Hunter please, I can't stand seeing you like this."

Wrapping my arm around his shoulder I help him up and usher him over to the booths in the corner.

I slide in across from him, when he sits down.

"So, tell me everything. I'm asking as a friend Hunter."

I touch his hands softly and he blurts out everything; about her seeing her ex-husband at the fundraiser and going to the farm supplies when she had gone to the supermarket. And her not returning because her ex-husband had possibly taken her.

When he stops talking I say caringly, "I'm sure she'll be fine Hunter. She's a strong woman and I'm sure you'll get to tell her you love her."

He smiles at me. "I hope so."

"You will," I say standing up, "look Hunter I have to go meet Zane, but please take care of yourself."

"I will, " He replies, with a smile curving the corner of his lips again. My heart is breaking for him and walking away I stop to look straight back at him when I say ,"And Hunter I'm sorry."

"For what?" He asks.

"You know what for," I reply heading to the other side of the pub and sliding into a booth with Zane.

"You look like you could do with a drink, " Zane says pushing a glass of beer across the table.

Not responding I lift it to my lips, gulping it down like water.

"Woah slow down hun," Zane warns.

Slamming the near empty glass on the table I spit at him, "Don't you dare call me hun, Zane."

"Is that a challenge, hun?" He teases.

I gulp the rest of the beer down, taunting Zane, "Not a challenge, a warning."

He laughs. "I'm so scared."

"You should be, hun," I tease back.

"You have a little froth here," He says reaching to touch the corner of my lips with his thumb, before dragging it across his lips, licking them with a lustful glint in his eyes.

"So what's up with lover boy? He seems pretty pissed."

I sigh, not sure if I even want to admit to myself that I've lost all hope of being with Hunter, let alone admit that fact to Zane.

He'd take it the wrong way, thinking that he might actually have a chance with me. His teasing gesture before had gotten to me a little more than I wanted it to, but there isn't a hope in hell I'm going to tell him that.

"He thinks Savannah is gone."

"What do you mean gone? Like left town?" He asks concerned.

"No...gone...dead," I reply, not sure how I managed to say the words so callously.

"What? Was that the sirens we heard before?"

"Yeah, and he also said..."

"Said what Addison?" He prompts, resting a hand over mine on the table.

"That he loves her."

Tears sting my eyes, the pain of admitting the truth surfacing.

"Any fool could have told you that Addison."

"I know, but actually hearing him say it hurts like hell."

"That's why you need to let go."

"I know."

He's smiling at me with a devilish look on his face.

"How about we get out of here and take the Mustang for a spin down the back roads?"

His eyes search mine for an answer, his question tumbling in my mind. And as crazy and reckless as it seems I ask, "Only if I can drive?"

I'm feeling a little mischievous and give him a wink.

"I don't know about that. You probably can't drive a stick."

I laugh so hard I nearly pee my pants.

"What's so funny? Some girls can't drive manual cars," He replies, a little hurt.

"I'm not just some girl Zane. I'm a born and raised country girl and I can drive a stick car better than most men."

Tentatively I reach down under the table squeezing his thigh, leaning across the table. His face so close he could kiss me, but I ask with a whisper against his lips, "Are you gonna give me the keys or what?"

ZANE

Her teasing gesture of squeezing my thigh, leaning in so close that I'd thought she was going to kiss me has stirred a strange fluttering feeling in my belly.

She has no idea how much she gets to me. I stand up, plucking the keys from my pocket, holding them up in front of her.

She stands up, reaching up to grab them. But I snatch them away, taunting her, "You want them?"

"Yes, Zane. Give me the keys," She demands.

"No, not unless you kiss me."

She scowls at me, scoffing under her breath. "Forget it Zane, I'm not kissing you."

I laugh. "Not even a little one here," I say touching my cheek with my thumb.

"Fine," She agrees, pressing her pursed lips against my cheek.

The simple soft kiss sends a rush of warmth through me. If she'd have kissed me for real I'd have been a goner.

Handing her the keys, she giggles excitedly, sashaying out the door, making a beeline for the mustang. Stopping she leans against the drivers door, cheekily grinning.

God, she's fucking gorgeous.

I step up close to her, pressing my body against hers, my breathing matching hers.
"Are you ready to show me how a country girl drives a stick hun?" I tease.
Her grin turns devilish when she reaches down to the front of my pants, grabbing my dick hard in her grip.
In my ear she whispers, "Damn right, get in."
Her hand is suddenly gone from my groin and she turns her body to open the car door, her pert arse in the air. This time I don't hesitate to slap it and she squeals in delight.

Does she honestly have any idea of what she does to me?

She's in the drivers seat, about to leave me behind. I race around to the passenger side, unlatching the door and sliding in.
She slides the gear knob into reverse, checking around as she backs out into the Main Street. She looks over at me, changing the gears to first and smirking whilst she revs the engine, speeding off out of town. She's changing the gears so smoothly the engine doesn't even have time to protest.
I'm absolutely speechless, watching the Speedo creeping up to one forty.
"Addison seriously slow down," I beg, clutching the door handle.
"What? You scared hun?"
"No, I'm fucking turned on. But I swear a cop car just passed us with sirens on."
"Fuck," She says, braking hard and shifting the gears effortlessly.
She spins the wheel to head back into town.
"I swear Addison, if I get a fucking ticket for speeding you'll owe me."
"Sorry, but this car is a dream."
"You weren't kidding when you said you could drive a stick better than some men."

"Told you so."
She gives me the devilish smirk again.
"The cop was obviously not interested."
"Yeah, so should I gun it back to the hospital?"
I laugh. "As long as I'm not going to be in a hospital bed after, Yeah?"
"Not a chance hun," She teases, causing my insides to stir again.
Her calling me, 'hun' shouldn't get to me; she'd told me were friends but then she teases me, flirting with me and it gets my pulse racing.

I'm fucking falling for her and she's still in love with someone else.

My thoughts are broken, realising we're back at the hospital and she effortlessly again slides the mustang through the gears and into my parking spot.
"Thanks for showing me how to drive my car hun. I'll see you tomorrow."
I leave her sitting in the car, quite aware she still has the keys, but it doesn't matter.
I know where she lives and I highly doubt anyone would steal a car like mine in Ridgehope.

(18) Addison

Watching Zane going inside the hospital, I take a few deep breaths, still sitting behind the wheel of his amazing car.

Driving his Mustang down the back roads of Ridgehope had been the ultimate rush, one that I'd not experienced for years.

Granted, the last time I'd driven a car like that, I'd had Hunter sitting beside me, his hands in a death grip on the dash as I accelerated hard and fast down the highway out of town one night when we'd just gotten our licences.

He was fearful for his life, at my crazy driving, but was also worried that we were both going to be in deep shit when my Dad realised I'd taken his pride and joy out for a late night joyride with my boyfriend.

He never did find out, and everything after that went downhill with Hunter and I.

I'd left for the city to study medicine like I'd always dreamed of, and essentially I broke Hunter's heart. He had always thought it was because I didn't want to be tied down to someone back home, but it was a lot more than that.

The secret I took with me to the city, bothered me so much that even when I returned years later, and Hunter took me back no questions asked, I never told him. But when he proposed to me, that secret from my past, knowing what Hunter really wanted in life, I rejected him, even though I wanted nothing more than to marry him.

Now, to say I'm confused about my feelings would be an understatement.

Hunter is now the one rejecting me. And even though I'm still hopelessly in love with him; I'm confused as well because being around Zane is making me feel something that I never felt with Hunter.

The way Zane teases me—calling me hun—acting like he's about to kiss me any second is driving me crazy. I don't want him, I don't feel anything for him, but still I can't help but tease him back just to get a rise out of him. It's kind of thrilling to get under his skin.

I'm definitely still in love with Hunter, but I also feel a sense of lust for Zane, and I'm scared to give into that feeling.

Getting out of the car—I lean against it—sighing deeply, letting the rush leave my body. Coming from the hospital entrance, I can hear my name being called, "Addison, Addison!"

Turning my head towards the hospital doors, I can see Quentin running towards me.

He stops, standing next to me, trying not to lean on the car.

"Hey Quentin, what are you doing here?"

"Um, long story. Just brought Savannah in."

"What? Savannah's alive?"

"Yes, Addison, but I can't tell you details."

"Um, ok," I mutter, trying to process what he's saying, the reality hitting me like a knife to the heart.

"Um, Addison, this isn't your car?"

I laugh. "No, it's Zane's, but um I..."

Shock crosses Quentin's face and I feel ashamed, knowing it was him in the cop car.

"Addison, who was driving this car before out on Back Ridge Road?"

"I was, and I'm sorry Quentin."

"Sorry for excessively speeding?" he says with a flirtatious tone.

"Yes, but I had to. Hunter confessed he's in love with Savannah and I..." I pause, tears stinging my eyes,"Please don't give me a fine Quentin. Zane will be so pissed."

He laughs, shaking his head. "Addison, I honestly didn't know you could drive like that. And I won't give you a fine if you promise to take me for a drive one day yeah?"

It's my turn to laugh, this conversation further cementing in my mind that Quentin harbours feelings for me, that I'll probably never return.

"Deal," I reply eagerly, "and maybe in a patrol car," I tease, winking at him.

I know I shouldn't have teased him, but a little harmless teasing among friends never hurt anyone.

"No worries, Addison. I'll leave you to it."

He leans forward, again pressing a kiss to my cheek and blushing as he walks away.

I feel so sorry for Quentin. But I completely understand how he feels as well, pining for someone who doesn't love you back.

ZANE

My whole body feels like it's spinning after the wild drive in my Mustang with Addison at the wheel. She's certainly full of surprises and the way she has started to tease me back is driving me wild.

I'd have taken the teasing a step further if I didn't have to head back to the hospital for the second half of my double shift.

It's a downfall of a small town hospital, and like Amy had always said I'm married to my job.

It isn't a particularly eventful day, which in a hospital probably is a good thing. My mind isn't exactly focused on my job either, so it being quieter and uneventful is a definite good thing.

Drawing the curtain back to see who my next patient is a most definite shock. Looking at her concern crosses my face. She appears visibly distressed and Hunter is by her side, the same distressed look on his face.

Glancing at the notes in my hand, definitely shocks me, but I find myself speaking clinically without emotion.

"Savannah we need to take a swab for DNA testing," I declare in a harsh monotonous tone. She gasps, looking towards Hunter for reassurance.

"Let the doctors do what they need to baby," He says to her, trying to calm her. Her response is,"No!" screamed out at the top of her lungs.

"Savannah, it's important we do this," I point out in a much calmer tone than her outburst.

My head is already pounding. I don't need to literally hear her screaming.

She violently shakes her head, again screaming out, "No! I know who it was. What he did!"

Shocked I ask, "Oh, so you can identify the perpetrator?"

She's clutching Hunters hand in hers, squeezing it when she softly replies, emotionless, "Yes it was my husband Dante Haslett."

I now feel concern for her. From what the police have told us, she's possibly run from domestic abuse and I can't breathe thinking about how that must have been for her. She would just want out of the hospital to escape the pain.

"I'm so sorry Savannah. I'll get the nurse to check the wounds on your ankles and we will let you go with Mr Mackenney. Is that ok?" I say, a lot calmer and with more feeling than before.

She nods a yes.

"You will need to give an official statement about what happened, but maybe tomorrow. Speak to Constable Mackenney."

Closing the curtain fully behind me, I practically sprint to my office, planting myself in my spinning chair and yanking the desk drawer open.

Frantically I search for my jellybean supply, the headache becoming more intense, a painful reminder that I've not eaten anything all day and desperately need sugar.

I've also not tested myself for days, not managed my sugar levels at all, too distracted by everything going on in the hospital and thoughts of Addison.

It's stupid—really fucking stupid—but I want to hide my diabetes from her.

I don't want her sympathy and I don't want her help to manage it. My sugar levels are definitely out of control and I know I need insulin badly but I'd left Adelaide without bringing much at all.

Grabbing some painkillers I stumble to the staff cafeteria, dispensing a coke from the vending machine. Cracking it open, I slurp it down like I've never drunk anything in my life and swiftly I down the painkillers in one gulp.

The sugar is sure to rush through me, and to not crash in the middle of the hospital I head to the medicine supply storage.

Flicking the light on, I search the shelves, needing injectable insulin but I can't find any, not even tablets.

Fuck, fuck, fuck, how am I going to get out of this?

The headache is still plaguing me when I knock on Herbert's office door.

He doesn't respond, so I enter anyway.

I try to speak calmly, "Herbert I'm going to head off, got a splitting headache."

"No problems Zane. I'll page you if I need anything."

"Herbert, do you mind checking the medicine supply cabinet? We're running low on some painkillers and there's no insulin at all."
He looks at me both concerned and confused. "We don't normally have insulin on hand."

Fuck, just what I need.

"Well, we should, you never know when you'll need it."
Again he gives me a confused look. "I'll order some Zane. Get some rest, I'll see you tomorrow."
Not replying I leave his office, the headache still gripping me. There's no way I can drive home, so leaving my car in the car park after grabbing the keys from the ignition I stumble home, cursing myself for my self inflicted stupidity.

(19) Addison

Coming into the hospital the next day after the crazy afternoon seeing Hunter at the pub and my joy ride with Zane, I feel a little dazed. Even seeing Quentin has me feeling all mixed up.

I'm essentially an emotional wreck.

In love with Hunter, lusting after Zane and teasing Quentin instead of letting him down easy.

There's literally no chance of getting Hunter back now, but still I want him, still love him.

I really want to find out why Savannah has been admitted to the hospital again and why Quentin is involved.

Zane's mustang is still in the carpark, so I'm not sure if he'd even gone home or if he'd come back.

Practically sprinting inside I race to his office, not even bothering to knock.

Walking in though he's not there and for some reason my heart sinks.

I quickly leave, and thoughts about going to look for him cross my mind, but instead I go to Herbert's office.

Knocking I enter and greet the chief sweetly, "Good morning Herbert. Is Zane here?"

He looks at me quizzically. "No, Addison. He's taken a few days off. Can I help you with something?"

Shaking my head, I reply, "No thanks, Herbert. I needed to speak to him about something personal."

"Is he unwell, Addison?"he asks me.

I'm a little taken aback when I reply, "Not that I know of."

"Hmm, he just seemed off yesterday, asked me to stock the medicine supplies."

"Oh, I'll go talk to him tonight."

"Thanks Addison, come and see me before you leave."

"Ok no problems," I reply worriedly when I walk out the door.

The rest of the day passes pretty uneventful, attending to some older patients in their rooms and an ultrasound for an of town farmers wife. Methodically I do my job, but my mind is elsewhere, thinking about Herbert's question about Zane.

He doesn't appear—as Herbert put it—to be unwell, but I don't even have any idea what he meant by unwell. Zane practically lives at the hospital, so for him to take a few days off doesn't seem right and I just know he's hiding something. I genuinely feel worried about him and I want to see him to make sure he's okay.

Going by Herbert's office at the end of the day he hands me a brown paper bag with some items inside. His instructions are to pass them onto Zane, as he quite possibly needs them.
Walking home, I peek inside and I'm shocked but also angry at the contents of the brown paper bag.

଼

Knocking on Zane's door, I'm a little scared, not sure what I'm going to say to him, worried if he'll even answer.
The door creaks open—a little ajar—and he's standing there in front of me, just poking his head out of the slightly open door.
"Addison what are you doing here?" He asks.
Admittedly, he looks like shit, his eyes bloodshot, bags underneath and his skin is pale.
Shoving the brown paper bag towards him I speak, a little angrily, "Bringing you this."
Opening the door more, he takes the bag from me.
"What is it?" He asks softly.
I take a moment to look him up and down. He's only wearing running shorts and although he's tall and muscular his belly is a little pudgy, bloated.
Underneath his clothes you'd never notice the telltale sign.
"It's insulin Zane," I snap at him.
"Thank fuck," He curses, racing inside, not even closing the door behind him.

Following him into the kitchen, I'm seething. He's begun preparing the insulin for injection, his back towards me. I hear him gasp when he presses the needle against the skin of his stomach.

When he places the needle on the bench next to him and turns to look at me, his eyes are full of regret.

I reach out a hand to him, softly saying his name questionably, "Zane?"

"What Addison?" he spits back at me.

"How come you didn't tell me?"

"Because I'm a fucking idiot ok. I didn't bring enough insulin with me, and I've not been managing it well and I didn't want..." He stops, pressing his hands against the bench biting down on his lip.

"You didn't want what Zane?"

"For you to look at me like you are now."

I was angry before, but now I'm practically irate. "God, seriously Zane. You could fucking kill yourself not managing your diabetes. You should know that!"

His eyes meet mine, the same anger rising in them.

"I do fucking know that Addison!"

"So why get yourself to this point?"

"I fucking told you. I don't want your sympathy. I don't manage my diabetes well and coming here was supposed to be a fresh start to get myself back on track and then I meet you, and I'm..." Again he stops mid sentence.

"Tell me Zane, what have I got to do with this?" I yell, gesturing towards the needle on the bench.

"You really want to know?" he asks, making me a little intrigued.

"Yes, Zane...I want to know why you let yourself get to this point."

"My wife left me, because I ended up in hospital with high blood pressure, complications from not managing my diabetes."

"What? You're married!" I gape, shocked.

"Yes, well, separated. She ran into the arms of my best friend whilst I was in hospital."

I don't know what to feel. I'm shocked, but it's something else I can't place; some other odd feeling that makes me feel like crying.

"I don't know what to say."

"Just forget it Addison, don't pretend you care."

Crossing the kitchen towards him, I step right up to close to him.

"I do care Zane. But tell me what I have to do with how you manage your diabetes?"

He sighs deep. "Because when I get stressed I forget to eat, forget to take my insulin and end up like this."

"What have you got to be stressed about?"

"I'm scared Addison."

"Of what?"

The tension between us shifts when he cups my cheeks in his hands, pressing his forehead against mine before whispering in my ear, "Falling for you."

Stepping back from him, I spit at him, "We're friends Zane. I don't feel that way about you."

He scoffs at me. "Exactly."

"Whats that supposed to mean?"

He laughs this time. "Oh come Addison, you fucking tease me every chance you get. I hid my fucking diabetes from you because I don't want your sympathy and because I want to be with you and not have you run the moment things get too difficult, like my ex-wife did."

Again I step closer to him, wanting to hug him, but he pushes me away.

"Seriously don't even think about touching me right now."

Tears sting my eyes. "Zane I'm sorry, I..."

"Just stop Addison, please. I can't stand it anymore."

I turn to walk away, hearing him take a deep breath behind me. He starts following me, making my heart pound in my chest.

I stop at the door, and he's right behind me. Grabbing me suddenly he pulls me against his body, wrapping his arms around me.

Part of me wants to run from his embrace and part of me wants to melt against him. He'd admitted he's falling for me and I don't know how to feel.

His breath against my ear when he speaks softly sends shivers through me, "I seriously want to kiss you fucking senseless, Addison."

He looks down at me, my breathing panicky when I reply, "I um...please Zane, I can't."

I break free from his embrace, my hand on the door knob, turning it when I ask, "What happened with Savannah?"

He shakes his head at me. "I'm not going to tell you about that Addison. You're in love with Hunter and if you want to know go look at her notes."
Standing in the doorway, he leans against it, his gaze on my lips.
"Um, ok...so I'll see you tomorrow."
"No, I'll be back next week. Can you get my car?" he asks throwing the keys at me.
"Yeah, and I'm sorry Zane."
"Whatever Addison," he says nonchalantly, shutting the door in my face, leaving me dumbfounded on his front porch.

Why can't I give into how he makes me feel?
Because I'm still in love with Hunter and letting go of your first and only love is like forgetting how to breathe.

(20) Zane

Seeing her name and photo on my phone is the last thing I want to face right now. I'm pretty sure before accepting the call exactly why she's calling. And even though I'm not ready to face the reality, I slide my finger across the screen accepting the call and trying to remain calm with my tone of voice, "Hello Amy."

"Zane, I want a divorce."

"Cut to the chase why don't you Ames, no hello Zane, how are you?"

"No, the papers are written up. Just text me your damn address, ok?"

"Um ok, but are you sure Ames?"

"Yes, I'm damn sure Zane."

"Fine I'll text you my address."

"Good."

She hangs up the phone in my ear. And sighing deeply I grab the whiskey bottle from the shelf above the sink, opening the top and taking a long swig.

It isn't good for me—my sugars still all over the place—even though Addison had managed to get me more insulin.

We've barely spoken the last week, since she'd come over and I'd confessed I'm falling for her and want to kiss her.

As usual she'd rejected me, teased me first and rejected me.

It seriously makes no fucking sense.

She obviously feels something for me, but all she ever says is *'I can't, I love Hunter.'*

Like seriously, when is she going to just let the fuck go.

And now Amy wanting a divorce I feel as though because of my own stupidity I'm going to be wallowing in my own self pity forever.

I never seem to learn when it comes to sharing my illness with others, but having it since I was eight I've just dealt with it, hiding it from others because having to prick my finger and inject myself a number of times a day is bad enough but not being able to have a piece of birthday cake or some chocolate with the other kids really got to me. And hitting puberty sent my body crazy and now I still struggle with managing my sugar levels, regardless of what I do to try and control them.

Putting the whiskey back on the shelf my phone buzzes with another call.

"Zane speaking?"

"Hello Zane, I know you're still off but you need to come in now. We have a gun shot victim on the way."

"No worries Herbert. I'll be there in ten."

Quickly I pull on some scrubs, racing out the door to my car, gunning it to the hospital.

Herbert is waiting in the emergency bays for me to arrive, putting me on as head doctor in charge.

Addison is standing across the other side of the room, lost in her own thoughts. I don't really mean for my words to come out so angrily but I'm tense and not a hundred percent prepared for a gun shot victim to be coming in.

I bark at her, "Addison, you need to focus. We have a gun shot victim coming in stat."

She still appears lost in her own world when the double doors swing open, with the ambulance officers and two others at the victim's side.

I'm shocked to see it's Hunter lying on the gurney. Addison has not moved, her jaw gaping in shock.

By his side Savannah and Quentin are both in a complete panic and it's clear they are both involved, somehow. A nurse ushers them both out into the waiting area.

I have to do something about Addison, and her lack of movement.

"Addison?" I ask her questioningly.

Still she's frozen to the spot, looking at Hunter on the gurney. I speak to her again, giving her directions in a hope she'll do something,

"Addison, saline, gauze, seriously now!"

Hunter is put on the bed and I rip open his blood covered shirt, inspecting his wound.

"What?" Addison says softly brushing the tears from her eyes.

I should be more caring in my tone, but her reaction is getting to me.

She definitely isn't an emergency doctor.

"Get over here and do your job," I yell at her.

The tears are pouring down her cheeks now. She still looks completely lost.

"I can't. I can't," She says shaking her head.

"Addison, I'm not asking. We need to stabilise the patient for surgery."

Her breathing becomes panicky.

"Addison, please," I say looking at her questionably again.

"I...c..can't," she stutters, breaking down into uncontrollable tears.

I nod at the nurses to keep preparing Hunter for surgery and look straight into her eyes when I speak, "Addison I'm sorry. I know you're attached to the patient, so I'm going to ask you to step back. Please go out with his family."

Sobbing she turns to walk out of the emergency bay.

Focusing my attention back on Hunter, we start to stabilise his bleeding and wheel him through the emergency department to go to surgery.

I'm not sure if the bullet is still inside as it's too difficult to look for an exit wound whilst he's still conscious.

Savannah rushes to his side, grabbing his hand and pressing a kiss to his forehead. Softly she says to him, "I love you Hunter."

My heart damn near breaks. I have to save his life for her and for Addison.

If he's gone Addison would maybe give into me, but I couldn't ever be with her if I'd not done everything I could to save the man she's in love with.

I'm not heartless and I'm falling so damn hard for Addison Yorke.

If only she felt the same way, as even now she's hugging Quentin and when I push the gurney through the doors to surgery she appears to be leaving with him.

I'm just a little heartbroken.

And all I know now is I have to save Hunters life, without a doubt.

(21) Addison

My body begins to twitch, from feeling him inside me. Throwing my arms behind my head, my climax is overwhelming me and I scream out, "Oh Quentin, fuck!" My squirting release drives him to a hard climax, filling the condom he unnecessarily wore. He collapses against me panting, looking like he's just won the lottery.

I just look at him then, still lustfully. Part of me wants to fuck him again, to escape the pain of the last few months and just enjoy the pleasure of being with someone.

But standing up he discards the condom in the bin by the door when he steps out of the pants still around his ankles. I've gotten comfortable in the bed, and lay back watching him yank off his shoes before he dives at the bed.

Pulling my body close to him, he kisses me softly and sweetly.

I want so much to give into him, kiss him more and have him inside me again.

But he breaks the silence and moment between us, brushing a stray hair from my cheek as he muses in my ear, "Addison, I love you."

I look at him, completely taken aback and shocked.

I knew he had feelings for me but actually hearing him say it is confronting and confusing.

"I'm sorry Quentin," I stammer, feeling like a complete bitch when I continue, "I don't feel that way about you."

I can tell he's angry at me, the pain of my rejection evident in his dark brown eyes.

Getting out of the bed hastily, he grabs his clothes from the floor and turning to leave he spits back at me, "I can't believe you Addison, after what we just did, you still don't fucking feel anything for me."

I reply apologetically, "I'm sorry Quentin, I just can't."

"Yeah, whatever. But thanks for the best sex of my life."

I start to respond but the words freeze on my tongue. I watch him as he tugs his pants back on.

He takes one last look at me sitting naked on the bed before running down the hallway.

The sound of him grabbing his vest from the kitchen table and slamming the door behind floats down the hallway.

A part of me wants to run after him, and tell him that I'm sorry, that I panicked because I didn't expect being with him to feel so damn good.

But the little voice in my head is telling me that's stupid and wrong.

You're in love with his brother, you can't use a guy like Quentin just for sex, Addison.

My head is right; I can't take advantage of Quentin's feelings for me to escape from my own feelings for Hunter.

Honestly I feel rather disgusted with myself. I just fucked Quentin Mackenney!

I'm an absolute idiot when it comes to the Mackenney brothers, but at least there's not a chance of getting pregnant to Quentin like years ago with Hunter.

Thinking back to that time, I clutch my stomach, jumping out of my bed to run to the bathroom.

Vomiting into the toilet is strangely a welcome relief.

I have really fucked up this time, in so many ways.

(22) Zane

Seeing Addison's name flashing on my phone screen is unexpected but excites me a little. She's not spoken to me since I was a complete arsehole to her the day Hunter had been shot.
I'd passed her in the hospital hallways and she didn't even look at me.
I'd wanted to say something but didn't know where to begin.
The tension between us recently has been insane too. I want her so bad, and her rejection and stand offish behaviour is driving me crazy.
Accepting the call I tease her, "Hey hun, missed me huh?"
"No, I didn't miss you. I fucked up Zane. I can't stop thinking about what I did."
"What do you mean?"
"Can you meet me at the pub? I need a damn drink to spill."
To say I'm not intrigued would be a lie, but I also can't help but think the worst.
"Um ok, but I gotta head back for rounds later, ok?"
"Ok so I'll see you in twenty?"
"No worries Addison."

§

Arriving at the pub twenty minutes later I find Addison has already arrived, and she is sitting in a booth at the back of the pub, a beer in hand.
I signal to the barman for a whiskey, and he pours it swiftly, handing it to me before I cross the room and slide into the booth across from Addison.
She looks up at me and I can't read the expression in her eyes. Something is clearly bothering her.
"So I'm here," I start flirtatiously, "what's eating you?"
"I fucked up Zane."
"You said that on the phone Addison. Come on, just tell me. It can't be that bad," I say trying to comfort her.
She lifts her beer to her lips, gulping the rest of it down and swallowing a lump in her throat, signalling the waitress nearby for another.

"Addison, tell me what you did," I beg, wanting her to just spill.

She covers her face with her hands, peering through her fingers when she mutters, "I slept with Quentin."

I was most certainly not expecting that and I'm extremely pissed off, even though I have no right to be.

"You what?"

"You heard me Zane."

"Yeah but fuck, Addison. Have you no self respect?"

She removes her hands from her face, the waitress placing the beer she requested on the table. Again she gulps it down, like it's water.

"I..I was upset about Hunter...and he..."

"He what? Took advantage of you?"

"No, no I wanted him to, but after he..." she starts before pausing and standing up, walking towards the bar.

Following I grab her by the arm, and look directly into her eyes when I beg her to tell me more, "Addison please, he what?"

"He told me he loves me."

Breaking free from my grip on her arm forcefully she walks over to sit on a barstool, ordering a vodka this time.

Stopping beside her and pulling up a stool myself I ask her, "And you rejected him?"

"What do you think Zane?"

"Knowing you, you obviously shut him down with your usual excuse."

"I can't be with him Zane. I can't love him back."

"Seriously Addison, let go of Hunter. He doesn't love you."

She downs her Vodka, signalling for another. I should stop her, as it's clear she's going to drink herself stupid. But a part of me hopes it will make her let her guard down a little.

"I know that Zane, but it's not that simple."

"Why not?"

"Not loving Hunter, letting go of your first and only love is like forgetting how to breathe. I just don't know how to not love him."

I don't know how to respond to her. Her confession that he's her first and only love really gets to me. She's a stunning woman, absolutely beautiful and I can't possibly believe she's only ever been in a relationship with Hunter.

"So tell me this, Addison, you've never had another relationship?"

She shakes her head, replying softly, "No, not really. I've had a few one night stands, a couple dates with guys, but never more than that. No one compared to Hunter."

"Fuck Addison, thats crazy. Surely guys throw themselves at your feet."

She laughs. It's absolutely gorgeous watching a moment of joy cross her face. She's a little tipsy, the alcohol beginning to rush through her body.

"You do," she teases, digging at my obvious want .

"How could I not Addison? You're fucking gorgeous."

She bites her lip, and it seriously takes all of my self control to not kiss her. I've thought of kissing her every fucking second since she'd left my house a week ago.

"Zane please, telling me that doesn't help."

"Well, I don't know what else to say."

"I'm an idiot Zane ok, I'm angry at myself."

"Because of sleeping with Quentin?"

"Yes, because even after that I can't feel anything for him and if Hunter finds out or my brother finds out, they'll both try to kill me."

She signals for yet another drink that she really doesn't need.

"Do you really need another drink?" I ask concerned.

"Yes, I want to forget it ever happened."

"Why? Wasn't as good as you thought? You were thinking about me instead?"

"You wish Zane, and it actually was good, and thats why I'm angry with myself."

"Oh my god seriously Addison, you'd fuck him again?"

A smirk crosses her face and she nods.

"But that's all it would be for me—sex—and I can't do that to Quentin."

She seriously gets hotter with every word that comes out of her mouth. I have to tease her more, to rile her up, just like she does to me. The alcohol she's downing like water is clearly getting to her.

"Fuck me instead then," I tease, winking at her.

She lets out a delicious giggle, grabbing my hand and pulling me up from the barstool.

Her body is pressed against me when she whispers, slurring her words, the alcohol suddenly hitting her, "Z...zane...I c..can't f..fuck y...you."

"Why? Think you'll fall in love with me?" I taunt her.

"N...no..y...your're m...my friend."

"Ok Addison, you're clearly drunk."

"Hhmm...no I...I on...only had one drink."

"Ok, sure. I'll take you home. I gotta go back to the hospital anyway."

❧

Trying to get a drunk Addison home is a challenge. She leans into my side, stumbling up onto her porch, muttering incoherent words.

Once inside her house, I lead her down the hallways to find her bedroom.

Pushing her down on the bed, I take her shoes off first, about to pull the skirt that is clinging to her hips off when she sits up throwing her arms around my neck.

Gasping at the contact, my hands find the hem of her blouse, about to lift it off her when I feel her soft lips against my neck, kissing and licking me.

The unexpected contact sends a shot straight to the front of my pants. I push her back towards the bed, my body over hers, looking down at her.

God she's fucking gorgeous, but I can't, not when she's blind drunk.

Her sudden words completely shock me, "Fuck me Zane!"

Oh God, she did not just say that, and God do I want to but no.

I brush my hand across her cheek, whispering softly, "God knows I want to Addison, but I can't."

She grunts angrily, shrinking back from me further, onto the bed, pulling the sheets to her chest.

"Get some sleep," I say softly, turning to walk out the door.

Doctor Attraction

She throws a pillow at my back as I leave, mustering all the self control I have to walk out the door and head back to the hospital.

જ

Back at the hospital I try to focus on rounds. My head is definitely not focused on the job. I have to get the thoughts of Addison out of my head. It's crazy that she'd slept with Quentin a week ago and then gets drunk throwing herself at me.

Stopping outside Hunters room, I decide to knock. Savannah has literally not left the hospital all week, and I don't doubt they've probably gotten up to something in the bed. I'd done that with Amy, and I barely knew her at the time.

When I open the door, it's clear they've been making out. Savannah's lips are red from the stubble on his chin. I stifle a laugh, and discuss Hunters discharge details with him.

He's damn lucky to be alive. If he'd been shot any higher or the bullet had been lodged inside he would have no longer been here for sure.

Walking back to my office I can't help but feel jealous of their make out session and jealous of Quentin for sleeping with Addison. It'd been too long since I'd gotten any action, and even my last time with Amy was pretty much *'just get the fuck off me'*.

She'd have much rather been fucking my best mate Max anyway so I don't even know why I'd bothered. I'd taken her out for dinner, and a movie, trying to salvage what was left of our marriage after my hospital stay but she wasn't really feeling up to having sex and practically just lay underneath me, as I thrust into her. I felt terrible, barely getting off. Sex had never been like that before and even though she tried to tell me that she'd only kissed Max I didn't believe her for a second.

And after she'd left, hearing of the post to Ridgehope seemed like exactly what I'd needed, but I hadn't counted on meeting Addison.

I can't tell if I want her purely because I'm missing being with someone or because she gets to me like no one before ever has, and I'm falling in love with her.

Since Addison had thrown herself at me a month ago I'd been the one to avoid her. We just existed, at times working side by side, but not daring to even glance at each other. I'm not sure if she even remembers her drunken advances but I sure as hell do and it has made me lust after her more, but also keep my distance because I know I'll not be able to control myself if she's that close to me again.

Now walking past her office after seeing her running down the hallway in tears I have to know what's wrong. I startle her by knocking on her office door.

Opening it, when she doesn't respond, worry crosses my face when I look at her sitting in the chair by her desk.

"Addison, are you ok? You look like someone died?" I say concerned.

"Yeah, me."

"Sorry what?" I ask crossing the office and standing at the side of her desk with a hand on my hip. She looks me up and down, eyeing the white button down shirt open at the top and the black slacks and black belt I'm wearing.

A sweet blush rises up her cheeks and she stutters, "I...um...feel like a part of me died today."

"How so?" I ask, again a little worried.

"Savannah is pregnant," she blurts out.

"And what's that got to do with you?" I question in a tone harsher than I mean.

"It's clearly Hunter's," she states.

That's it, I cannot take this any longer.

I lean closer to her, so close our noses are nearly touching, and looking directly at her I whisper, "He doesn't love you Addison. Move on."

I give her no time to reply, instead I grab her cheeks between my palms smashing a hungry kiss to her lips. She responds, melting into the feeling of my lips finally one with hers. When I pull back from the kiss, she lets out a little moan than drives me crazy, but I stop myself from kissing her again.

I damn well want to grab her from the chair and push her against the desk, to kiss her, taste her and fuck her until she forgets all about the Mackenney

brothers, but instead I smirk at her, licking my lips, before walking out the door.
"Have a good night Addison, I'll see you tomorrow."

God that kiss was fucking hot, the way she melted at the feeling of my lips on hers.
God I want her so fucking bad.

(23) *Addison*

Watching the image flicker on the ultrasound screen, my heart constricts. She's only about six weeks along so a stomach ultrasound is going to be unlikely to show anything, but I start with that anyway.

I speak softly, "Can you just lift up your top first?"

"Um...ok," She replies hesitantly.

I prepare the wand, rubbing the icy clear gel over her stomach. And waving it across her skin when I speak, "I'm not sure if we'll see anything."

Continuing to wave the wand over the skin of her belly, just as I thought nothing on the screen is clear. She's pregnant—definitely—but I can't show her clearly enough.

Stopping suddenly, not wanting to say the words at first, I stutter, "Um...I...will have to do a vaginal ultrasound instead..."

I look up then, my eyes meeting Hunter's. He's practically seething at me, upset at my insolence towards Savannah, but he has no idea that this is the hardest ultrasound I've ever had to do. I should have been the one on the bed, whose hand he was clutching, about to see our baby on the screen. But I'm not and it's the most painful rush of emotions I've ever felt.

Tears have started dripping down my cheeks and I blurt out suddenly, "Sorry...I can't do this...give me a minute."

I practically bolt out the door, the tears breaking free the moment I turn to walk away.

Rushing down the hallway to Zane's office, I barge in, not knocking and through my sobs I scream out, "I can't do it!"

He stands up to meet me in the centre of the room, putting his hands on my shoulders when he looks at me, asking, "Can't do what hun?"

"Savannah's ultrasound."

Concern crosses his face when he replies,"because of Hunter?"

"Yes, that...but..."

The tears are streaming down my cheeks now. Zane wraps his arms around me, pulling me against his chest. In my ear he says, "But what Addison? You need to tell me the truth."

I pull back from his embrace a bit to look up at him.

"It should have been me."

"What?"

Freeing myself from his arms, I turn away, not wanting to look at him whilst I'm falling apart.

I've never told anyone my secret, not even my parents or Jett.

"When I left for Uni...I was pregnant."

"To Hunter?" He asks, touching my arm to urge me to turn back to him.

"Yes...and I was scared he was going to hate me. We'd used protection but the condom broke and I..."

"I'm sorry Addison, but you should have told him."

"I know but I wasn't sure if I wanted to even keep the baby and I know he would have...so I left and we'd pretty much broken up."

"So what happened? Did you end up going through with an abortion?" He asks with care in his tone.

"No...I had a miscarriage at about ten weeks and..."

"And what? Something is still upsetting you."

"I needed a D&C and I ended up with an infection so bad that now my Fallopian tubes and uterus are so damaged I will likely never fall pregnant."

He pulls me towards him again, kissing my hair, not replying. He doesn't need to.

After a moment just melting into his comforting embrace, he follows me to the door of the room Savannah is in. I speak to him briefly and he touches the small of my back drawing me close to his side, pressing a kiss on my tear stained cheek before he walks into the room and shuts the door behind him.

Walking back to my office I feel a pang of affection for Zane. I've barely been able to get his kiss from a few weeks ago out of my mind and part of me actually wants to kiss him again, to give into the lust I'm beginning to feel for him.

But I'm also beyond confused.

My reaction to Hunter having a baby with Savannah is further proof that I'm clearly not anywhere near being over him and that all I'm feeling for Zane is lust. Having him admit he's falling for me is making the lust harder to not give into.
I kind of want to run back to Quentin, to fuck him again to make my mind blank for a while and just give into the pleasure, but as enjoyable as that would be for both of us, I know being with Quentin physically again would be an even bigger mistake than the first time was.
I care about him too much to use him. And crazily enough I'm starting to care too much about Zane to think about using him as well.

Waking up the day after I confessed to him about sleeping with Quentin, I was in my underwear and recalled throwing myself at him, begging him to fuck me.
I know he didn't and that made me happy, but it also scared me.
Even his kiss on my cheek just before is making me feel something for him that has me truly scared.
Evidently there is lust between us, after the way his kiss has stirred my insides and made me actually want something more, but I know from his confession and his care towards me that he is falling in love with me. And no matter how much I want to I can't let myself fall for him.
I can't deny he's hot—gorgeous even—especially with his usual five o'clock shadow, but he's definitely not Hunter Mackenney hot.
Hunter had gone from gorgeous, sweet boy next door to insanely handsome.
His baby with Savannah is sure to be the most gorgeous kid ever, inheriting the Mackenney genes.

God, I seriously have to get over Hunter .
But I don't know how, not even sleeping with his brother made me forget about him.
I'm a lost cause.

(24) Zane

A large white envelope is sticking out the front of the letterbox by the fence.
There's no doubt it's the divorce papers Amy had needed to send to me so urgently that she showed absolutely no care for how I feel at all.
It isn't that I want to still be married to her, quite frankly I'd be happy for my life to be free of her, but signing them and setting myself free is a completely different thing.
Signing them means that I'm technically single and free to be with whoever I want.
And I want Addison.
Her opening up to me about her past, and her reasons for not being able to let go of Hunter are making me fall for her harder. I want to be with her physically for sure, but I want more from her than that. I want her to fall for me too.
I've only kissed her, a sweet sensual kiss and it has been all I've been able to think of for weeks.

Fuck it, I need to see her, get blind drunk and see what happens.

Throwing the envelope on the kitchen counter I grab my phone from my pocket, typing her a teasing text.

Zane: hey hun...wanna go get blind with me?
Addison: Fuck yeah...I could do with a stiff one

Oh god, that text made something else stiff, seriously Zane calm down.

Zane: maybe a slippery nipple is on the cards?
Addison: or Sex on the beach?
Zane: don't tempt me hun. Come over when you're ready...

Even though I'm expecting her, I'm startled by Addison knocking on my door twenty minutes after I texted her. I was expecting her to take a lot longer to get ready, considering that she always looks done up to the nines, no matter what she's doing.

Tonight is no exception. Opening the door I scan her outfit, my eyes focusing on parts of her body I know I shouldn't be looking at. It isn't exactly my fault, taking into account that she clearly could have had more clothes on.

Her spaghetti strap little black dress hugs her hips, drops into a scoop neckline at her cleavage and sits high on her thighs. My mind wanders to what she's wearing underneath; it possibly being nothing as the dress is practically a second skin and I can't see any visible underwear lines.

On her feet, extenuating her long lean legs she has patent black high heels. Her makeup is flawless, natural with a hint of mascara on her already long lashes and red lipstick that I ache to kiss off.

God she's fucking gorgeous.

"Fuck Addison, you're smoking hot tonight hun."
She blushes bright red, almost the colour of her lips. It makes her even more gorgeous.
Her eyes scan me before she speaks teasingly, "Not looking to bad yourself hun."
Laughing I say, "Well thanks, but this isn't a date you know?"
"I know hun," she says back, giving me a wink.
"Ready to go get blind? I've been thinking about that slippery nipple."
Shutting the door behind me, I follow her down the garden path.
One good thing about living in a small town is the fact you can literally walk everywhere. The pub being about a twenty minute walk away from our houses down the back streets.
We begin slowly walking towards the pub. The tension between us since our kiss has shifted into high gear, and my body aches for her, especially as she keeps stealing glances at me.
"Are you undressing me with those looks hun?" I tease.
"No, but you look hot Zane," she muses, biting her lip.

"Don't tease me Addison."

"I wasn't. I was just stating a fact."

"Really? A fact...ok."

We're close to the pub now, and I'm starting to feel a little giddy at the prospect of getting drunk with her. I'd not taken advantage of her last time she was drunk, but now I don't know if I'll be able to control myself.

My fingers brush against hers, sending a shiver straight through me when she grabs my hand tighter in her grasp, leading me inside the pub whilst looking back at me with a delicious smirk on her lips.

Fuck, I want to kiss her so bad right now, calm down Zane, get a drink and calm down.

At the bar, she pulls out a stool, taking control when she orders our drinks,

"Mike, two slippery nipples please."

Her gaze turns to me sitting beside her when she utters *'nipples please'.*

My jeans feel tight at the way those words roll off her tongue. I lick my lips, thinking about tasting her nipples instead of the shot that's slid down the bar to me. I down it in one gulp, my eyes locked on hers as she downs her own.

Slamming the shot glass down on the bar top, I keep my gaze on hers, ordering,

"Mike, two Cocksucking Cowboy shots, yeah?"

It's her turn to lick her lips, and that teasing gesture after I've just ordered a drink with a name that I want her to do to me, the strain in my pants increases.

Downing the shots again, we repeat the same process as before, except instead of licking my lips I thrust my tongue against my cheek.

The tension between us has definitely increased, and it seems as though no one else is in the pub.

She leans in closer to me, her breath in my ear, "In your dreams hun."

I whisper back, "That and more hun."

"Mmm," she whispers back, before turning her attention to Mike.

"Tequila shots, Mike."

Fuck, fuck, fuck, tequila always goes straight to my head.

"You ready, hun?" she taunts when Mike slides the bowl of lemon wedges and the salt shaker down the bar with the Tequila shots.

"Whose taking the shot first?"

She presses her forehead to mine, her breath against my face, "You hun."

"So I get to lick the salt off you then?"

She doesn't reply, instead holds out her arm, shaking a line of salt across her wrist.

Looking straight into her eyes, I bend down over her arm, keeping my eyes locked on hers. I press my lips against her arm, licking all the way down from her elbow until the salt strikes my tongue. It's bitter compared to the sweet taste of her skin.

Keeping my eyes on hers I down the tequila and suck the lemon wedge between my teeth.

Whispering in her ear I say, "You taste fucking good hun."

"Mmm," she muses again, further torturing my desire for her.

"And hun, you're not licking the salt from my arm."

Grabbing the salt before she has a chance, I tilt my head back, pouring a thin line of salt down my neck, right at my Adam's apple.

I hear her gulp, and then her tongue is at the my collarbone and slowly she licks up over my Adam's apple and up my chin. Her tongue sweeps across my lips before she pulls back downing her shot and sucking the lemon wedge in her mouth.

Fuck I should have kissed her, that was so fucking hot.

"Fuck Addison, that was hot."

"Mmm, you taste good too hun."

Fuck, she's killing me, make a move Zane, man up.

Her gaze has not left mine, still she's unconsciously licking her lips and driving me utterly crazy with want. Standing up, leaning close to her I whisper, "Dance with me Addison."

She stands up, her body pressing into mine.

"We can't dance to this song."

Grabbing her hand I pull her even closer to me, her back against me.

"Really, because I happen to think this is the best kind of song to dance to."

The music beat is steady, slow and rhythmic.

Following the beat I run my hands down her sides, and across her belly, urging her to push her back into me.

I can feel the curve of her arse against the strain in my jeans. Feeling my desire for her, she starts grinding against me; to the slow beat.

Leaning against me more, she throws her arms back wrapping them around my neck, before licking my collarbone towards my chin again.

When her licking reaches my lips, I tease her back, kissing her hard and lacing my tongue with hers.

She lets out an exquisite moan and grabbing her waist, I urge her to turn and face me. Her body against mine, I grab her arse forcing her closer against my obvious desire for her.

Slowly I begin licking her neck, tasting her skin and loving the little moans she can't keep in. My lips lick further down, across her collarbone, up her neck and across her lips. Her sweet lips that part the moment my tongue caresses them. She murmurs, so deep and longingly.

Grabbing her cheeks between my palms and looking directly into her lust fuelled gaze I smash my lips to hers again, a kiss more fierce and demanding than the first I'd shared with her.

Her whole body is melting into me, her kiss intoxicating and wild when her tongue again laces with mine.

Breathless she pulls back from our kiss. "Stop Zane, I can't do this. I still love Hunter."

The moment those words leave her mouth, anger rises in my chest.

She's teased me all night, made me want her so desperately and the minute she starts to feel something and give into the lust between us she pushes me away.

Turning away from her, I slam my fists against the bar.

"Fuck Addison, seriously you tease me all night, and fuck that kiss was hot as and..."

"I'm sorry Zane."

"Just stop. I don't want to fucking hear it!" I scream, my hand swiping the glasses on the bar, smashing them to the floor.

"Zane, please, I just can't..."

"I can't deal with your shit anymore. You drive me fucking crazy!"

Tears are stinging her eyes and she lets out a little whimper, biting down on her lip. The anger is further rising in me, partly because of the alcohol.

I grab the wooden bar stool in front of me and crazily smash it against the floor.

"Woah Zane, mate. You need to calm down," Mike says from behind the bar.

"How can I calm down when she literally drives me insane?" I yell pointing towards Addison.

"Look mate. I can't tolerate that behaviour in my pub. The cops have been alerted."

"Great, just make my night even more fucked up."

Addison is still standing in the same spot, completely dumbfounded. I feel a pang of guilt for my reaction, but her constant rejection of me when it's clear she feels the same as me is infuriating.

"Sorry mate, but you'll need to stay until they arrive. Sit in the booth over there and calm down."

Following Mike's direction I sit in the booth, running my hands through my hair and looking at Addison.

Her back is turned; she can't even look at me.

I've really fucked up this time, and I'm cursing myself even more when the cops arrive and none other than Quentin Mackenney is on duty. The fucking traitor runs straight to Addison to comfort her.

We both know what him comforting her leads to.

(25) Quentin

Getting an alert from the pub always freaks me out a little. You never know what you're going to walk in and see, what fight or altercation you'll have to break up.

But tonight is different. The pub is eerily quiet, only a few customers and two of them I know well. My heart sinks seeing Addison near the bar, her back turned away from the door. Zane is sitting in a booth near the door, an angry scowl on his face.

Sam goes straight to him, sliding into the booth across from him to ask some questions. Walking up behind Addison I tap her shoulder gently. She jumps at the touch and turns to face me. She's sobbing but a slight smile crosses her face when she sees me.

"Addison," I say softly, a hand on her arm, "what happened? Did he hurt you?" She shakes her head but doesn't respond with words.

I nod to Sam, calling out, "I'm going to take her home. Catch you tomorrow for the details."

"No worries Quentin," She says, nodding at me and going back to her conversation with Zane.

Grabbing Addison's hand I lead her out to the patrol car, opening the front passenger door for her to slide in. She starts giggling, and mumbling, "I'm in a cop car."

It's obvious she's had a bit to drink and I can't help but feel annoyed at her. She's a grown woman and can do whatever she wants but we both know she's a bit of a Cadbury when it comes to alcohol.

Thankfully the drive to her house is only five minutes because her incessant giggling is getting to me. I need to get her inside, sober her up with some coffee and water, before grilling her about the cops being called to the pub on a quiet night.

Pulling up in front of her house, I sigh helping her out of the car. She's stumbling a little, leaning into my side when I take her into the house.

Once inside she looks at me with a lustful glint in her eyes, and again starts giggling.

"Remember last time you were here?" she asks, her giggling increasing and annoying the shit out of me.

"Like I could forget Addison," I muse at her, memories of our night together flooding my mind.

"Wanna repeat?" she teases.

"No, actually I don't. You need to sober up."

"Fine. Coffee sounds good."

I leave her standing by the front door, discarding my bulletproof vest on the table before depressing the boil button on the kettle and grabbing two cups, putting coffee and sugar in them. The kettle starts bubbling wildly, when Addison stumbles into the kitchen, stopping behind me at the kitchen counter. She wraps her arms around me, and I turn to her. Sneakily she kisses my cheek, before looking straight at me and licking her lips.

"Come on Addison. Stop yeah."

"Don't you want me?"

"Not when you're drunk, Addison."

The kettle pops, and stepping aside from her I pour the hot water into the cups ,filling them to the brim before handing her one.

"Sit and spill, Addison."

She sits at the table, stumbling a little, but managing not to spill her coffee. Slowly, she sips a bit and I give her a moment for it to sink in and sober her up a bit.

Pulling up a chair in front of her I ask, "So Addison, whats going on with you?"

Putting her coffee on the table, she starts blurting out words, "Well Savannah's pregnant and..."

I cut her off, touching her thigh when I ask, "What? She's pregnant?" I'm shocked, and annoyed that Hunter hasn't told me that news himself.

He's been a little distant so obviously he's been hiding that news. It doesn't make me any angrier, but I'm definitely annoyed.

"Yeah, she's pregnant, like six weeks and they are engaged too," Addison continues, tears beginning to sting her eyes.

"How do you know this? I can't believe my own brother hasn't told me."

"I was her doctor."

"Was?" I prompt confused by her past tense language.

"Yeah, was...I couldn't deal with it so asked Zane to take over."

This conversation is really getting to me. She's so nonchalant and staring at me with the oddest look in her eyes.

I want to put the past behind us and be friends but she's making it difficult when she looks at me like she wants to undress me slowly and kiss me senseless.

"So whats really going on with you and Zane?"

"Nothing, Quentin."

"Really Addison? So nothing happened at the pub tonight?"

She shakes her head, pursing her lips together.

"Addison, you need to tell me. We don't get called to the pub for no reason."

"Ok, ok, fuck," she curses loudly, pausing and looking down at the floor, before continuing, "We were doing shots, kind of teasing each other and then he asked me to dance."

"Ok, and then what? Did he hurt you?"

"No, we were dancing, teasing each other and he kissed me."

"And let me guess, you rejected him?"

"Yes but I..."

I stand up from the table, not wanting to believe the words she's saying, the constant excuse that always comes out of her mouth.

"Seriously, Addison, you can't keep throwing yourself at every fucking male in town and then get upset when they want you!"

She lunges towards me, an odd look in her eyes. "But I love you Hunter."

"I'm not Hunter, seriously Addison, get a grip."

"But I..." she stutters.

"Hunter doesn't love you, Addison," I chastise, my hands on her shoulders, "And right now neither do I!"

Grabbing my vest from the table I turn to leave, hearing her beg behind me, "Quentin, please, I'm sorry. I'm an idiot."

"Yeah, and I've had enough of your shit!" I scream at her, leaving her shocked when I storm out, slamming the door behind me.

Anger is coursing through me, my heart pounding.

I'm angry at Hunter for not telling me his news and angry at Addison for her constant idiotic behaviour.

I still love her, but I certainly don't like her right now.

(26) Addison

Quentin's words are ringing in my head. I hate that I made him angry. Things haven't been the same between us since we slept together and even though I know that was inevitable I hate the wretched feeling.
My night out with Zane should have been fun, getting drunk and blocking out my feelings but instead it turned sour.
I'm incredibly stupid when I drink. And sobering up I'm cursing myself for my actions and thoughts tumble in my head.

Why can't I love Quentin instead?

Did I seriously just call him Hunter?

I know I did and the way he yelled at me, rushing out of the house again really hurts. We can't even be friends, the tension between us is always going to be there. But the tension that's getting to me the most is definitely between Zane and I. He's definitely on my mind, his kisses, the first one in my office that was sweet, filling me with warmth and tonight's teasing and steamy kiss that made me really want to give into him.
Desire had rushed through me, soaking my underwear feeling his reaction against me, and when his lips smashed against mine that desire had me scared. It's something I've never felt before, not even with Hunter and that scares me more than anything.
I want Zane, but I'm scared to acknowledge that wanting him means letting go, giving in to what he makes me feel and opening my heart.
That thought makes fear rise in my chest, especially thinking back to his reaction to my rejection. The way he smashed the bar stool was violent and I feared he was going to hit me.
I can't give myself to him, and subject myself to the possibility of pain like that.

I'm definitely fearful, but a part of me still wants him, if only I can truly get myself to let go of Hunter.

(27) Zane

Tonight had gone from awesome to fucked up in a matter of minutes. Just when I thought she'd finally come to her senses and was going to give into how I make her feel, she rejected me again, with her same sad excuse.

It literally shattered my desire hearing her say those words yet again, after the hottest kiss I've ever experienced in my life.

The cop is sitting across from me in the booth, muttering something that my spinning head can't handle.

"Sorry what?" I question rubbing my eyes that feel a little blurry.

"We aren't going to press charges Doctor Rivnay, but you will have to pay for the damages."

"Ok I can do that."

"And you're also not to set foot in here for three months."

"Oh, great," I snap, annoyed and frustrated.

"Yes, I'm sorry. If you do then you will be arrested."

She leans across the booth to whisper, "We wouldn't want a local doctor to be the subject of town gossip."

"Um yeah, true," I mutter under my breath.

I'm probably already on the town gossip radar if anyone had witnessed that kiss.

"Do you need a lift home?"

Shaking my head, I respond, "No thanks Constable. The walk will do me good."

"You'll need to come by the station tomorrow to write up the order for the damages and some paperwork regarding the ban."

"Ok no worries," I reply, sliding out of the booth, a little unsteady on my feet when I walk out, crashing through the double doors. The fresh air hitting me in the face is refreshing.

Walking home takes longer than normal, partly because I'm still a little drunk, but also because my vision is super blurry. And the ground at my feet appears to be like mountains I need to climb as I walk.

I must look like a right idiot. I sure feel like one, as thinking back over the last few months I've certainly not been thinking straight.

Going out drinking, not eating well and neglecting to take my insulin is for sure going to catch up with me, but drowning in my own self pity is all I feel like doing.

I've hurt Addison, my violent outburst obviously effected her, but her rejection is hurting me more than she realises. The kiss was hot, sensual and the most amazing feeling I've ever felt rushed through me.

For her to reject me after that, when she appears to feel exactly the same way makes my heart ache.

I want her. I'm falling in love with her.

&

Arriving home the divorce papers on the kitchen counter are a reminder of how I feel. Amy doesn't love me, Addison doesn't love me either. Tears are stinging my blurry eyes.

Man up Zane, you're being a fucking pansy.

I open the envelope, and try to focus on what I'm actually looking at it. It's legal jargon, that makes absolutely no sense at all. My head is already spinning and looking at the words on the page is making it worse.

Slapping them back down on the counter, I cross the kitchen and grab down a bottle of whiskey from the shelf above the sink.

It's rather stupid of me to have so much alcohol in the house, so easy to reach for when my mood is down, but right now I just want to escape the pain.

The pain of Amy throwing the life we'd once shared down the proverbial toilet and the pain of Addison's constant rejection.

No one, not even Amy has ever made me feel how Addison does. Just thinking about her, her image in my mind, sends desire rising in my pants and makes my stomach flip flop.

Feeling her lips on mine was nothing short of amazing, sending an electric shock feeling rushing through my veins. I want so much more than that heart stopping kiss. I wanted to bring her home, strip her of the little clothes she had on and taste her all over.

Just licking her arm, that one taste of her skin and I desperately crave more of her. She literally has no idea how much I want her, what I want to do to her. Collapsing against the couch I down the rest of the whiskey.

The whole room is seriously spinning now, the alcohol and lack of food hitting me hard. Closing my eyes I let myself slip into sleep, knowing that my dreams are going to be wicked, thinking of Addison, of making her mine.

(28) Quentin

Hunter had been a little distant since he was shot by Dante. It had been a traumatic event for us all, but I thought he'd at least have called me to check in with me. We'd gotten closer again recently and I miss my older brother.

Leaving work I race home, grab a beer out of the fridge the moment I walk in the door and flop down on the couch. Taking a few sips of the beer I let it begin to seep into my veins, before standing up to strip off my uniform, leaving only my boxers remaining.

Of course that's the moment Tiberius has to make his presence known at the front door with his incessant miaow, as though he's going to die if he's outside for another minute.

Jumping up off the couch, I edge the door open just enough for him to slink through and wrap himself around my ankles in greeting. He'd been a good confident in the past couple of months since I'd found him on my doorstep skin and bones, starving hungry and desperate for love.

No one knew I had him, not that it was my intention to keep his existence quiet but having a cat wasn't the best for my image as a tough young cop.

Still I love the crazy bugger and it's good having someone to talk to, that doesn't talk back to tell me I'm an idiot for still being in love with Addison or for making the mistake of sleeping with her.

Picking him up, I cuddle him close to my chest, my cheek against his soft fur.

"I should probably call Uncle Hunter huh buddy?"

Uncle Hunter, god does that sound weird, but so does Uncle Quentin.

Tiberius' response is a loud miaow, but he's more than likely hungry and not responding to my question at all. He jumps out of my arms, slinking across the kitchen and pawing at the fridge. He knows his kangaroo meat is in there and if I let him he'd climb in the damn fridge to get it. He's still miaowing like crazy, so it's best to feed him to shut him up before I call Hunter.

After feeding him and listening to his contented purr, I again flop down on the couch, grabbing my now warm beer, sipping a little before digging out my phone from my discarded uniform and dialling my brothers number.

He answers straight away, "Hey Quent."

"Hi, Hunter," I say with an unenthusiastic tone.

"Is something wrong Quent?"

"You could say that Hunter."

"Quentin seriously, what's up with you?" He asks concern in his tone.

"Oh, I don't know, maybe that my older brother didn't want to tell me that his girlfriend is having a baby, and that she isn't just his girlfriend now but his fiancée."

He's silent for a moment, only his breathing on the line as he's thinking of what to say.

"I'm sorry bro, but we wanted to keep it quiet until Savannah was twelve weeks and we're going to have a double celebration."

"But you could have told me Hunter. I'm your fucking brother and after everything with Savannah you know."

"I know Quent, I'm sorry, but hey who told you anyway?"

"Addison," I reply quickly, knowing Hunter is going to be upset.

"Of course she fucking did," He replies angrily. I can practically hear him seething.

"Hunter?"

"Yeah bro?"

"I'm worried about her."

"I know Quent. I'll try to speak to her, but things aren't the best between us."

I sigh, wanting to tell my older brother everything, but I know it isn't the time.

"Yeah, so um I guess I should say congrats big bro. You deserve to be happy."

"Thanks Quentin, so do you."

"Does Mum know?"

"Yeah told her a couple of weeks ago."

"Nice, don't be a stranger now big brother yeah?"

"I won't Quentin. Chat soon, love you."

"Love you to Hunter," I say when he hangs up.

It feels strange to tell my brother I love him. It's not that I don't obviously feel that way about him, but since Dad had fallen ill and his death we never really express our feelings to each other. The pain when loss comes about is always too difficult when feelings are expressed.

The way Hunter had reacted to Addison telling me his news has me worried as well. Something is definitely going on with her and Zane and I feel insanely jealous of anything that has or is happening between them.

I shouldn't feel jealous though, she's not my girlfriend and we are barely even friends, but I still can't quell my love for her.

Sleeping with her a few months ago, even though she'd blatantly rejected me, has stupidly made me fall for her more. Being with her was so much better than I'd ever dreamed and it hurts like hell that I'll probably never get the chance again.

Now she appears to be feeling something for Zane, even though all she ever says is she that she's still in love with Hunter. If she truly loves my brother like she says, she'd not be able to even look at another guy. I'm sure I love her that much and since being with her after pining for her for years I've not even given anyone a second glance, not even Samantha who everyone at the station knows has a major crush on me. I should try to move on, but that's definitely one thing Addison and I have in common; neither of us knows how to let go of our first loves.

(29) Addison

The tension between Zane and I after our night out has been even harder to deal with. He passes me in the hallways, and occasionally looks up at me, with a sad look in his eyes.

The kiss we'd shared that night was nothing short of amazing, filling me with longing and desire that I've never felt before. I wanted to give in so much to how he made me feel, but every time I think about the possibility of doing that, the panic rises in my chest, thinking about his violent outburst that night.

We've barely spoken, not even a text and we're constantly working around each other in the hospital on eggshells.

I know the tension is getting to him as well. I'm finding it super hard to even focus on my job, and today doing an ultrasound on an out of town farmers wife is incredibly difficult. I love my job, but the reality of not being able to experience pregnancy myself is hitting me harder these days.

After she'd left, I'm tidying up the curtained bay. Zane's voice is in my head about it not being my job, but it's calming me and taming the melancholic thoughts that fill my head.

Tears are stinging my eyes and I try to sniff them back, but they break through into sobs. It's crazy and I'm not thinking straight when I climb up on the bed, clutching my stomach, the tears flowing down my cheeks.

My body flinches when I hear his voice from the other side of the curtain, "Addison, are you ok?"

I don't reply. Part of me wants to speak, to say, 'no I'm not ok' but the words won't come out. He slides the curtain across, looks straight at me and I see his heart break when he takes in my curled up body on the bed.

"Addison what's wrong?"

He's at the side of the bed now, touching my cheek with his hand.

"Speak to me Addison."

"I...c...can't."

"Please Addison, I know I've been avoiding you but it doesn't mean I don't care about you. We needed space."

"My job Zane...it's too hard."

He doesn't respond, instead leans down and kisses my cheek. The simple gesture makes my temperature rise, heat rising in my cheeks that makes me feel like they're on fire. He's looking at me with care and longing in his eyes.

"Zane, please...kiss me," I say lustfully, almost begging him.

Again he doesn't use words, but presses a soft sweet kiss to my lips. I moan when his lips leave mine, knowing that drives him crazy but not being able to stop myself.

The look in his eyes has changed to the longing lustful look. I sit up on the bed, and he steps closer to me, not saying anything before he grabs my cheeks between his palms, kissing me fiercely.

I give in for a moment, his kiss intensifying when he licks my lips with his tongue, forcing me to smile against his mouth, giving him entrance to tease my tongue with his.

My hands find their way into his hair, my fingers entangling in it, and forcing his body closer to mine. Abruptly he pulls back from the kiss, groaning, "Fuck Addison, I'm sorry I..."

I'm speechless. He'd kissed me speechless.

"Say something Addison, for fucks sake."

"I..I..that.."

He looks at me like I've just stabbed him in the heart, turning to walk away. Looking back at me, licking his lips sends me a signal that he'd not only enjoyed kissing me, but didn't want to stop at just a kiss.

Watching him walk away, the only thing I can think of is that I've once again fucked up big time.

Why did I practically beg him to kiss me? Do I want more from him than just a kiss?

ZANE

Walking away from Addison after another hot desperate kiss is insanely difficult. The only reason I'd even pulled back was the fact of being in a curtained hospital bay in the middle of the day.

She has no idea that I wanted to push her body back down onto the bed, kiss her more, taste her skin and discard her of the scrubs that envelope her until she was mine for the taking, completely.

Sitting down at my desk, sighing and running my hands through my hair that she'd moments ago had entangled in her hands, does nothing to calm my body's reaction to kissing her again.

I hate myself for constantly taking advantage of her when she's vulnerable, but it's in those moments that I feel the most for her. It's those moments when she needs someone that she lets her guard down and lets herself feel.

Breaking me from my thoughts of reliving the kiss, a knock sounds on my office door. I don't answer and she walks in, looking absolutely gorgeous, her lips still red from my kiss.

"Zane?" she says softly, my name both a whisper and moan on her lips.

"Yes, Addison?"

"I'm sorry, I shouldn't have told you to kiss me but I..."

Pushing my chair back, I start to get up when I speak, "What Addison?"

"I...I.."

My hands grip the edge of the desk. She's walking further into the room, the desk the only thing between us. I want to throw her onto it, pull off her scrubs and show her crazy she makes me feel.

"I know you liked it Addison, and if you seriously come any closer to me right now I won't just stop at kissing you."

My breathing hitches in my throat when she walks around to my side of the desk, pressing her body against me and wrapping her hands around my neck, pulling my mouth to hers in a desperate kiss.

The desire in my pants is rising, she deepens the kiss more with her tongue. And my hands have a mind of their own, running up her sides underneath her scrubs. She moans against my mouth again and I pull away breathless.

"Fuck Addison, your kisses are hot."

"Mmm...so are..."

I don't let her reply, instead I kiss her hard, again, grabbing her by the waist and pushing her against the edge of my desk. She gasps at the contact, but her lips don't leave mine.

Running my finger along the edge of her scrub pants I can feel her skin heat with the contact of my hands against the sensitive skin of her hips; that she pushes against my desire for her.

Slowly I edge my hand down across the lace of her knickers, lower until I can feel they are soaked through with want. She pulls back from our kiss, breathless, panting. Her eyes are full of want and teasingly I ask, "Do you want me to touch you, Addison?"

She nods a reply; I gaze straight into her eyes, pushing the lace of her knickers aside and inserting my finger into her waiting body. Pushing it in and out, I keep my gaze locked on hers.

Her breath grows raspy when she gives into the pleasure.

Pressing another kiss to her lips, I push another finger inside her, teasing her sensitive bud like my tongue is teasing her mouth. Her hot moans begin to break through our kiss and pulling away I whisper in her ear, "Come for me Addison."

I lock my eyes on hers again, watching her as her pleasure increases and her hips buck against my fingers inside her.

Pressing her palms into the desk she screams in idyllic release, collapsing back onto my desk when I remove my fingers.

"Fuck, Addison that was seriously hot."

She sits up, looking at me. I lick my fingers clean, smirking at her.

Not being able to help myself I again take her cheeks in my palms, kissing her hard, licking her lips so she can taste herself on me.

Panting she pulls back. "Zane that was...but I can't believe...I can't."

Before I have a chance to respond, to pull her back to me and silence her with another kiss, she pushes her hands into my chest to move me aside. And without another word she runs out the door of my office.

Once again I'd let my lust get the better of me, sending her running again. But I'll not soon forget making her come so hard it dripped down my fingers.

I'll not soon forget tasting her after making her come, and sharing kisses with her that damn near set me on fire.

Doctor Attraction

God, I want to kiss her all over, and make her come over and over screaming my name.
I'm a fucking goner.
I'm falling head over feet in love with her and I want all of her.

(30) *Hunter*

The last months have flown by. Savannah has tried to continue helping around the farm, but it got to difficult when her beautiful pregnant belly started to show.
I love how she giggles when I kiss it every night before holding her close.
Even making love is difficult and I miss being intimate with her more than anything. That's part of the reason we decided to hold off getting married, because we don't want anything to make our wedding night less than perfect.

This morning the sun is beginning to make an appearance around the corner of the blinds. It's warming my body up, but I've been awake for hours, excited for the day ahead. Propping myself up on a pillow I watch Savannah sleep for a bit, before kissing her hair softly. She stirs, turning her head to look back at me.
"Morning, handsome fiancé," she says to me happily, making my heart swell.
"Morning, gorgeous mother of my child."
I smile wide at her. "Hunter you know that makes me teary."
"Sorry baby, but you know what today is?"
She presses a soft loving kiss to my lips.
"Yes, baby Daddy. Time to find out if we're having a boy or girl."
"Yeah, I'm thinking boy."
"Me too Hunter and I bet he'll be a spitting image of his gorgeous Dad."
"Thanks baby," I say lifting up her night shirt and kissing her belly, blowing raspberries against her skin.
"Hunter, stop, that tickles."
"Oh really, should I do it more then?"
"No stop please." She laughs, squirming around on the sheets.
"If you don't stop Hunter I'm seriously going to pee my pants."
Stopping I stretch up to kiss her, taking my time to savour the feeling of her lips on mine.
I whisper in her ear, "I can tickle you somewhere else if that would be better."

My hand rubs the side of her thigh, her arms grabbing my cheeks to kiss me before she responds, her words not a threat but an invitation, "You wouldn't dare Hunter Mackenney."

"Oh really? I wouldn't dare huh?" I tease, my fingers brushing against the elastic of her knickers.

"Hunter, please."

"Please what Savannah?" I ask, lifting up the night shirt again to kiss her belly. She doesn't respond with words, instead lifts her hips up when my kisses rain over the lace of her knickers.I edge a finger into the top yanking them down to her knees, teasing her for a moment with my finger.

Her fists are grabbing the sheets, and teasingly I ask, "Does that tickle baby?"

"Ummm....yes...Hunter...oh."

Her moan drives me wild when I press my lips to her waiting body, licking and tasting all she has to offer. The taste of her is insatiable, a drug I'll never get enough of.

Her breathing is becoming faster, her hips bucking against my mouth whilst I continue tickling her with my tongue.

"Oh Hunter, fuck," she moans loudly, coming hard over my face.

I lick my lips, looking down at her. "Baby, that was so hot."

"Mmmm...that was amazing Hunter."

"I aim to please, baby, " I say, pressing a kiss to her forehead before standing up to get off the bed.

Grabbing my hand, she says with a wicked smirk, "Its my turn now."

"Baby, you don't ha..." My words are caught in my throat when I feel her grab my erection through my boxers.

"Oh yes I do baby," she teases, pushing my boxers to the floor and grabbing my length in her grasp.

Looking straight up at me, she glides her hand up and down my throbbing length, before letting out a delightful giggle when she takes me into her mouth. Teasing the tip with her tongue, she licks and sucks, hard and fast making my moans increase.

Grabbing her hair in my hands I push my dick deeper into her mouth, making her let out an 'mmm' that drives me wild.

"Oh Savannah I'm gonna come baby," I say huskily.

She pulls back slightly, just when I blow my load into her mouth. She swallows hard, licking her lips to collect every last drop and she stretches up to wrap her arms around my neck, looking at me with her delicious smile.

"Baby, that was amazing."

The words of reply are caught in our throats, instead our lips meet in a hot kiss, our tongues entwining to taste each other. She lets out a little moan, her fingers entangling in my hair, pulling me closer and deepening the kiss.

Kissing her truly sets me on fire every single time. I can never get enough of her. Breathless she pulls away.

"I love you, Hunter Mackenney, so much."

"I love you to, Savannah Mackenney."

Playfully she punches me in the chest, laughing softly when she replies, "Thats not my name yet, Mr."

"I know baby, but I love the sound of it."

"Me too. We should probably get ready to go."

"Definitely, I'll just help you get undressed," I reply laughing and smirking at her, my hands grazing the edge of the night shirt.

She giggles, her hands stretching above her head. Lifting it off her, I kiss her belly again, before trailing kisses higher, across her breasts, teasing them for a moment with my tongue. My kisses continue grazing her collarbone, up along her neck, where I lick and suck her skin, leaving my mark against the sensitive spot.

She smacks a hand against my chest, taunting me, "Hunter, you bad boy."

I laugh, kissing her lips softly. "Sorry baby, but you're mine. Just marking you, so the rest of the world knows whose baby is in your belly."

"Yes, I am yours, but we have to get dressed."

"I know, I'm sorry. I just can't help myself," I say teasingly, pulling up my boxers from around my ankles, watching her pull up her knickers.

From the drawer I open, I throw a bra to her, to catch. I watch her when she puts it on, jumping off the bed to find her other clothes.

I put my jeans on, and stretch a t-shirt over my head. Savannah is rummaging through the drawers, grunting in disgust. I step up behind her, wrapping my arms around her waist.

"Whats wrong baby?"

"Nothing fits me Hunter. I'm so freaking huge."

I lean closer to her, to whisper in her ear, "You're not fat Savannah. You're growing our baby and you're beautiful."

She turns in my arms, her head against my chest. "But I have nothing to wear."

Kissing her hair I say softly, "How about that pretty yellow maxi dress? You know the stretchy one?"

Pulling back she looks up at me. "I guess."

Her expression is sad, and I want to make it better. "How about we go to Adelaide during the week, go to Baby Bunting? And get you some new stuff from Ripe as well?"

"Really?" she says, a little happier.

"Anything for you, baby. We need to start on the nursery soon anyway."

"Oh Hunter, I'd love that."

"I know baby, I know," I muse, kissing her forehead softly, before I let her go to finish getting dressed.

෨

Seeing our baby on the ultrasound screen is the most amazing sight ever, no matter how many times throughout Savannah's pregnancy that we've seen the sight.

In the room now, I laugh watching her squirm when the cold gel is spread across her belly. She clutches my hand, grinning at me before turning to the screen.

For a moment I think back to making her squirm in pleasure before we left the house, and the last time we were in this very room.

Doctor Rivnay doesn't seem himself today though. He's yawning, and his eyes are bloodshot. He fumbles a little when he prepares the wand and I don't want to say anything to upset him when he seems on edge, so keep my lips shut, my eyes on the screen.

My heart leaps when our baby appears on the screen, all other thoughts disappearing watching our baby wriggling on the screen.

Doctor Rivnay speaks methodically, "All is good, heartbeat still strong and the gender, you want to know?"

"Yes, we want to know," I squeal, squeezing Savannah's hand.

He points towards the screen, speaking, "Well you can see here, it's most definitely a boy. No doubts about it."

"Did you hear that Hunter? A baby boy!"

"Yeah, Savannah," I say, leaning down to kiss her forehead.

"I'll just finish up and print some pictures for you. And I'll see you again in a few weeks."

"Thanks Doctor," I reply keeping what I really want to say in.

Once everything is finished, I take Savannah's hand in mine and we start to walk out of the hospital, feeling giddy.

The giddy feeling is crushed though when I bump straight into Addison when she's walking into the hospital. I don't really want to talk to her, but after the conversation I'd had a couple of months ago with Quentin, I've avoided her at all costs and it's time to face her.

"Savannah, baby, I actually need to speak to Addison. Go wait in the car, yeah?"

Savannah looks at me, with fear in her eyes.

"Um okay," she says, biting down on her lip worriedly.

"Savannah, trust me baby. It's just some family stuff."

She doesn't speak, instead nods her head before walking out of the hospital to the car.

Addison has stopped dead in her tracks. She seems off, a little excited when I ask, "Can we chat in your office?"

"Yeah, sure Hunter, follow me."

I follow her hesitantly towards her office at the back of the hospital.

When she ushers me into the office I try to quell the anger that's rising in my chest.

Shutting the door behind us Addison crosses the room and sits in the chair behind her desk.

"So, Hunter, you needed to talk to me about something?"

I can't even sit down, I'm so angry and anxious. Seeing her has brought up the feelings from the conversation with Quentin.

"Cut the crap Addison!"

"Sorry Hunter, I don't know what you mean."

"You fucking told Quentin about Savannah being pregnant," I yell at her, my hands balling into fists.

"I didn't tell him that."

Those words make me feel even more angry, knowing that my brother would never lie to me.

"Don't lie to me Addison!"

"Ok...ok...I was drunk...it just kinda came out."

"You're so vindictive! How dare you try to get my own brother angry at me!" I scream at her.

She has the gall to beg, "Its not like that Hunter, I still love you!"

God she makes me so angry!

"Stop fucking telling me that Addison. I don't give a shit anymore!"

"But Hunter…"

"I'm engaged to Savannah, I'm having a baby with her and you need to let go, " I plead angrily, desperate for her to finally hear the words.

"Hunter please…"

"Stop, Addison, I can't deal with this anymore. Get with Quentin because for some fucking reason he still loves you."

Turning to leave, I can't even look back at her, even though I can hear her beginning to sob.

About to turn the handle, I feel her behind me.

"Addison please just let me go."

"But Hunter you never let me explain why I rejected your proposal."

I turn to face her then, not liking how close she's standing next to me.

"Whatever it is Addison, it's too late. I don't want to know."

Pain crosses her face, the tears streaming down her cheeks, but at this point I'm done with her. I've had enough of her excuses, enough of her trying to tell me why she'd broken my heart.

I do have my suspicions about why we'd broken up when she left for Med school, because the first time we'd slept together the condom broke. But I couldn't be sure because she'd never mentioned anything when she came back, and I'd stupidly taken her back, falling for her again to the point of proposing to her.

But it's all in the past and I don't want to think about it.

Addison is my past and Savannah is my future, that is all that matters now.

(31) Addison

The tears that had been threatening to fall the moment Hunter raised his voice in anger at me, crack through when he slams the door leaving me dumbfounded.

Knowing I'd upset him to the point of him showing anger and disdain towards me makes me feel truly wretched.

He's not one to ever get angry, even in the most dire of situations. My words have caused his reaction though and I don't think I'm ever going to be able to tell him the truth now. I always wondered if he possibly knew and never said anything, that maybe even though he proposed to me he didn't love me as much as I thought. I've seen the way he looks at Savannah and I can't recall him ever looking at me like that.

Two other people in my life look at me that way, one whom I've broken the heart of and the other I'm too afraid to let in, afraid he'll break my heart. I don't think I could deal with another heartbreak.

Still, I find myself standing up from my chair, walking out my office and straight into his without knocking on the door.

We've barely spoken, barely even dared to look at each other in the past few months since I'd come undone on his desk.

He looks up at me now walking into his office in tears with genuine concern on his face. He doesn't say a word when I cross the room and sit in the tub chair in front of the desk.

"Zane, um, can I talk to you about something?"

"Yeah, I'm all ears. I hate seeing you upset."

"Well, um, I saw Hunter before, and he got really angry at me about telling Quentin their news."

"Um, yeah, ok. I kinda understand that. It wasn't yours to share."

"I know that," I say, raising my voice, "but I thought he'd at least let me finally explain."

"And he didn't?"

"No, he just shut me down, again."

"He doesn't know anything about the pregnancy?"

"I don't know, maybe but he's never said anything."

"I don't know Addison. Is that honestly why you rejected him & went back to the city?"

"Yes, I couldn't bring myself to tell him, I didn't want him to experience the pain like I did. It broke my heart."

"And you thought it was better to break his heart by rejecting his proposal rather than telling him you lost his baby?"

"Yeah is that crazy?"

"No, Addison, thats not crazy. But you still should have told him."

"I know."

He comes around to the front of the desk and sits in the other tub chair next to me, just looking at me, not sure what to say. He looks a little shocked to be honest and I feel guilty.

It was stupid not to tell Hunter, but I'd honestly thought he'd not love me and now I don't want to crush his happiness with Savannah with sadness of the past.

He'd said something else to me recently, about us not being meant to be together and I'd heard a hint of pain in his voice.

I know there's something about my family's past that connects to the Mackenney's and when Hunter mentioned us not being able to be together I started to wonder about it more.

Zane breaks my thoughts by caressing my cheek softly with the back of his hand.

"Addison, is there something else? Is that why you're so upset about Hunter and Savannah?"

"Yes, all I ever wanted was to be with Hunter."

"Really?" he asks me oddly as though he's not really sure of what he's asking me.

"Yeah, even when we were kids, you know we played in the paddocks."

"And?"

"He was my first kiss, but that's not what I remember the most about that day."

"What do you mean?"

"Something happened that day with my grandfather. He was sent to jail, I don't even know why, what actually happened but we left to go live in the city for a while."

"How old were you when you left?"

"I'm not sure, maybe twelve or thirteen. And we came back a few years later."

"And that's when you really fell in love with Hunter?"

"Yeah, my family came back to run the general store, much to most of the towns disgust."

"Thats interesting," he says not really concerned about my family, "So, what happened with you and Hunter?" he asks, trying to get me to open up.

"He became friends with Jett again, they were inseparable even though our parents didn't really condone them being friends and we were at a party one night when I was about seventeen."

"Why didn't your parents want them being friends?"

"I honestly don't know. Something to do with my grandfather I think, but yeah I kinda passed out at this party and woke up lying on Hunter's lap, with him looking down at me with teenage lust in his eyes."

"And thats when you got together?"

"Yeah, I kinda threw myself at him, kissing him." I laugh, the memories of that night crashing into my mind. I'd certainly not stopped that childish behaviour.

"Of course you did." Zane laughs with me.

"And well you kinda know what happened after that, a year or so later when we slept together and I left for Uni."

I can feel tears dripping down my cheeks and wipe my arm across my cheek. I've never told anyone the full details of my past.

Not Jett, not Quentin—no one—not even the so called friends from Uni that promised to keep in touch, but practically disappeared off the face of the earth the minute we'd graduated and gone our separate ways.

The pang of attraction for Zane hits me again. The fact that he's listened and not judged me is nothing short of amazing and I know I have to tell him soon how I really feel, when I work out how I feel that is.

"Thanks for listening. I've never told anyone," I say softly into the quiet, thick with tension air.

He puts his hand over mine on the edge of the tub chair, not saying a word, just looking at me, with a look of shock in his eyes, but maybe a hint of something far deeper, something that I'm not sure I'm ready to acknowledge.

(32) Zane

My heart is constricting in my chest, hearing Addison tell me about why she truly can't let go of Hunter. He was her first kiss, first time and first love. And she'd never let anyone else in.

It seems crazy that a woman as beautiful as her has never opened herself up to loving someone else, comparing everyone to Hunter. I can barely remember anything about my past relationships before Amy, not intentionally blocking them out, but they seemed insignificant and I'd thought Amy was my forever. But forever was never part of her plan, and it truly hurts still.

It made me wonder so many times if she did love me or if it was all about my money. Addison clearly doesn't care about money in her life, happy to be a small town obstetrician and in love with a farmer.

From what she's said though her rejection of Hunter's proposal was because she couldn't give him a family but I get the feeling that she'd not wanted to spend life holed up in his farmhouse. She definitely doesn't seem like the type to give up on her career.

Sitting across from me now, after she's spilled more about her past I'm taken aback. The tears are dripping slowly down her cheeks, and her breathing is slow, sniffles breaking through as she tries to calm herself.

Leaning closer to her I brush the tears away with my thumb, speaking softly and looking straight into her eyes when I speak, "Oh Addison, I can't believe how much you guys have been through together."

She sniffs, muttering, "Yeah I...I.."

"Its ok," I coo, my hand cradling her chin in my palm, "I get it now, but still you've got to let go, for you, no one else."

Leaning into my hand, she speaks again, through sobs, "I don't know how to not love him, I always have."

Leaning even closer to her I press a kiss to her forehead, looking straight at her again.

"Addison, you will love him until you don't, until you fall in love with someone else."

She appears to ponder my statement, her head falling a little to one side when she looks straight into my eyes. Of course I'm hoping she'll fall in love with me, just like I'm falling for her. Her moments of vulnerability make my heart ache.

"Zane...I...um..."

"Its ok," I say standing up from the chair to stand in front of her, "come here. You need a hug."

Standing up she leans into my chest, sideways to not press her body into mine. Wrapping my arms around her, I pull her as close as I can.

Desperately I want to tell her how I feel, that her opening up to me has made me long for her to be mine, to take away all the pain of her past, but I know it isn't the right time.

After a couple of minutes, she pulls back from the embrace and looks up at me, smiling and speaking softly, "Thanks for the chat."

"Anytime gorgeous, " I reply, watching the delicious grin spreading further across her face at my calling her gorgeous.

"Zane...don't say that."

"What? That you're gorgeous?"

"Yes."

"Come on hun. You know it's true. I'm not going to lie about that."

"I know...um Zane..."

"Yeah?" I ask, my hand brushing aside the stray hairs leaping out of her ponytail when I look at her face.

"K..k..." She starts to say the words, not able to form the word I know she wants to say, the demand she makes that always gets to me.

Part of me knows it's wrong, but I can't help myself. If this is the only way to get her to open up, to get her to feel and fall for me then I'm going to take it.

"Are you sure Addison?"

She doesn't reply, instead fiercely crashes her lips to mine, turning her body to press closer into mine. Her hands wrap around my neck, her fingers once again entangling in my hair whilst she kisses me like never before.

This kiss is passionate, full of pure want and need. I grab her ponytail in my fist, wrapping it around my fingers, yanking it as I bite her lip softly.

She lets out a deep moan, before licking my lips when she kisses me deeper and more fiercely. The desire is rising in my pants again, this kiss sending me higher and making me fall deeper.

She teases my tongue with hers, moaning ever so softly, and even more so when I grab her arse with my other arm, pushing her against my body more.

I'm literally melting into her when she pulls away, completely breathless, her face red from the stubble on my chin. She looks straight at me, the lust disappearing from her eyes.

"Zane...I..oh my God I can't believe I just did that...I'm sorry."

I want to grab her hand, to pull her back for round two, to make her not sorry but she rushes out the door, as though she was never even in the room with me and I'd just imagined another illicit kiss, that is going to be sweet torture in my mind until I kiss her again.

Slumping back against my desk, I let out an exasperated sigh. I can't fucking believe she'd run after kissing me again. I'm starting to think it's something to do with me, but the way she responds to kissing me—every time— proves otherwise. The only explanation is her fucked up past, that she doesn't know how to let go of the only man she's ever loved.

I'm going to do everything I can to be the one to make her let go, in heart and body.

I want her so fucking bad.
Ive fallen in love with her haven't I? Bad Zane, you can't, you can't do that.

But it's already too late.
I have fallen in love too deep to let go.

(33) Addison

Sitting on my couch, with a coffee between my palms I'm stupidly reliving my kiss with Zane in my mind. It's stupid to continue throwing myself at him, kissing him absolutely senseless until I can't breathe and then running when I actually begin to feel like I want to give into him.

He wants more from me, that's blindly obvious and I've still not been able to quell the feeling of fire that burns in my belly when I think back to him touching and teasing me on his desk.

I've never come so quick—or at all—from just being touched. Surely that has to mean there's something deeper between us, but I'm just too scared to face it.

He's been so sweet about my past, not judging me for the choice I made to not tell Hunter about our baby. And every time I open up to him about my past, the choices that haunt me, he looks at me with so much longing and care in his eyes that it makes me forget, even just for a moment and I give in, just for a moment before the flood of emotions of what giving in truly means and I run.

Sometimes it feels like I'm falling for him, but acknowledging that feels like I'm betraying myself, as crazy as that seems.

And I've not been able to stop thinking about his violent outburst at the pub either. His reaction when drunk truly scares me, and I wonder about his temper normally, as he's gotten angry at me before and then is all of a sudden calm.

My head is spinning just thinking about him, the attraction I feel towards him, that I can't deny has been there from the first day he sauntered into the hospital like he owned the place, but it's that same attraction that has me completely scared and wanting to run down the back roads to escape. I cannot feel that for someone I don't love.

Sighing and contemplating the word love, I place my empty coffee cup on the table and grab my phone. I need a friend right now, and I really don't want to call him, but there's no one else.

Doctor Attraction

Dialling the number I wait for him to pick up, partly hoping it will go to voicemail, but after a couple of rings I hear the click and his voice on the line, with a happier tone than I thought he'd have after our last conversation.

"Hey Addison, whats up?"

"Hey Quentin. I just need to chat."

"Yeah, ok, not for long though. I'm just at work."

"Thats ok. I'm just scared about something."

He's breathing down the line.

"Scared? Whats going on? Did Zane do something to you?"

"Oh no, nothing like that. Quentin um?"

"Yeah Addison, what?"

"Can we go out for a drink?"

"Addison I don't know about that."

"Please Quentin, just as friends?"

Again he's silent for a moment, pondering my question.

"Yeah ok Addison, but things are pretty hectic at the moment. In a few weeks yeah?"

"Ok, text me then."

"Sure I'll let you know."

"Thanks Quentin."

"No worries. Are you still going to Savannah's baby shower on the weekend?"

"Um yeah I guess. Is Hunter going to be there?"

"I don't think so Addison. Girls only."

"Ok, I guess I should go then."

"It will mean a lot to Savannah."

"I know. Text me later about that drink."

"I will. Bye, Addison. Take care of yourself."

"I will Quentin. I promise. Bye."

He hangs up after hearing my goodbye.

Part of me still wishes I could love Quentin like he loves me. Even when we slept together and he told me his feelings, I was shocked but I kind of always knew he was in love with me.

When I'd been with Hunter and was over at their house, he'd constantly be staring at me, smiling and looking away if I looked at him. And there was the masturbation incident that I've never let him forget, but thinking back now it was kinda sweet in a weird way.

Maybe I should have broken up with Hunter then and gotten together with his little brother, but I still wouldn't have loved him. I was already in love with Hunter long before that, from the moment he'd kissed me in the paddock, so innocently, but a kiss that opened up my feelings and awakened my teenage hormones. There was no going back from that.

Speaking of hormones though, whatever is going on between Zane and I is definitely doing something to my hormones, because even though it sounds crude just being in the same building as him is making me feel things in my body that have long been dormant. Just kissing him makes me so wet with desire and I honestly can't imagine what actually giving in and sleeping with him would do to me.

I'm too scared to explore that spark, because I feel I might just burst into flames.

Am I falling in love with Zane?
No...I can't...I can't love him can I?

(34) Samantha

The police station feels stifling today, sitting at my desk trying to focus on anything but thinking about him. We haven't been assigned to any other cases or call outs together since the incident at the pub with the local doctors a couple of months ago, and not being around him has made me pine after him more so than usual.

It's silly to feel the way I do, I know that; some crazy school girl type crush. But I can't help it.

From the moment I'd walked into Ridgehope police station six months ago and met him I've felt something for Quentin Mackenney. It isn't just the fact that he's a few years older than me, it's his presence.

He has a sweet sophistication about him, not to mention his good looks, his mop of dark hair that's always unruly on his head like he never brushes it and his chocolate brown eyes that make me feel like melting.

He'd introduced himself, sauntering up to my desk, extending a hand for me to shake, that made my eyes focus on his arms, that are tanned, and muscular. I'd felt a spark rise up my own arm when shaking his, and had to force myself to look up at him instead of the floor.

Looking at him though, made me want the floor to swallow me whole. He was grinning at me, looking me up and down. I'd had to shake thoughts from my head of kissing him—as I completely transfixed on his lips—the deep philtrum at the top of them that makes his lips look utterly delectable.

I don't even know anything about him, and I'm already falling for him.

Now sitting at my desk months later I'm chewing on the end of my pen, so deep in thought I barely notice him walking up to my desk. He stops right next to my chair, one hand resting on the desk when he leans against it.

"Hey Sam," he says huskily, causing a fluttering in my belly.

I have to force myself to speak. "Um, hi Quentin," I say awkwardly wondering why he has sauntered up to my desk. I'm feeling a little flustered with him standing so close to my chair, so close that I could stand up and our faces would be close enough to kiss him.

"Did you end up sorting out the paperwork for the pub incident?"

Stupidly, I feel heat rising in my cheeks from him just talking to me, about work no less.

"Um yeah, it's um right here," I say flustered shuffling through some papers on my desk.

He places a hand on my shoulder and I feel like I'm going to self combust at the simple touch.

"Sam it's ok. I was just going to follow up on the dates. Get the pub to sign off on everything."

"Um, yeah ok. I'll find it and give it to you later?"

"No worries. Are you ok though? You seem a little out of it."

"Um, yeah. I'm fine."

"Good. I'll catch you later."

Watching him walk away I look at his butt. His tight slacks hug his the peachy curve outline of his butt and thighs. My mind wanders to being between his thighs, wondering what it would be like to finally take that step with someone, instead of running when things get to heated, like I had with Seth.

I'm a twenty-three year old woman for fucks sake.

I should just get it over with.

I want him to be that someone, as crazy as that is. But something about Quentin gives me the sense that he's had his fair share of women in his bed though and that he'd not even give me a second look in that department.

He looks at me like I'm his little sister, and it makes my heart ache. I want him to look at me the way he looks at the blonde doctor. I'm sure he's in love with her, but I also know they aren't a couple.

Some would say that means I could have a chance to be with him, but in my eyes it doesn't seem possible. He's never going to look at shy little me that way, no matter how much I want him too.

Maybe I should ask him out...no...no, Sam...you could never have the guts to do that

You'd self combust...but what if he says yes?

Doctor Attraction

Come on Sam...do it...take a chance.

Taking a deep breath, grabbing the papers he'd needed from my messy desk, I stand up clutching them to my chest when I walk over to his desk.
Slapping the papers down, telling myself to breathe and open my mouth I stutter a little, "Um, is t..that all of them?"
He picks the papers up, flicking through them with his hands.

I want those hands to touch me...no Sam, don't think like that now...ask him out.

"Looks like all of them," he says, looking up at me, his eyes meeting mine.
"Cool, and um Quentin?"
"Yeah Sam?" he asks casually and with the usual huskiness that makes me feel weak at the knees.
"Would you...um?" I start, my throat suddenly feeling dry. His eyes are still locked on mine, and I gulp hard to try and soothe my dry throat.
I rush through my next words, hoping they aren't to jumbled, "Go out with me sometime?"
His hand brushes mine, and I feel the heat rising up my body, concentrating in my cheeks that are now on fire.
"Yeah, sure. I'd like that," he replies, setting the butterflies off in my belly.

He said yes...oh my god..he said yes.

"Cool. Tell me when, yeah?" I say, a slight giggle in my tone.
"Ok, I will Sam. I gotta get back to work, but we'll chat later."
"Ok," I reply when he swivels his chair around to face his desk.

↊

Of course I'm on cloud nine for the rest of the day, not believing that I'd had the courage to ask him out and I'm also wondering if I'd actually heard him correctly when he'd said yes.

My question is answered though, when at the end of the day when I'm tidying my desk he again saunters across the room, resting both hands on the desk, and looking straight at me.

"Sam?" he starts, an odd tone in his voice, "About that date?"

My heart falls to the floor at the tone in his voice. Clearly he's having second thoughts.

"Yeah? It's ok if you don't want to," I mutter.

He's shaking his head. "I didn't say that Sam."

"Um, ok, so um."

"Sam," he says softly, "is Saturday good for you?"

"Um yeah."

He reaches across the desk, touching my cheek softly, sending the blush rising up my face.

"Good. I'll see you at the pub at seven."

"Ok," I mutter, trying not to grin like the cheshire cat.

He turns to walk away, winking at me as he leaves.

I have to sit down for a moment, plonking myself back in my chair. I'm going on a date with the hottest guy I've ever laid eyes on.

How in the world did that happen? And what in the world am I going to wear?

Slinging my bag over my shoulder, I walk out of the police station, feeling absolutely giddy.

Saturday is two days away, and I'm both excited and scared. It has been years since I've been on a date and I want this one to be perfect, just like Quentin is.

I think I'm falling for Quentin Mackenney. Oh god...I can't...can I?

(35) Quentin

It was a little insensitive to accept the date with Samantha, knowing that she has a crush on me, but that knowledge is why I knew I couldn't say, 'no' either. She's so sweet and shy and it'd clearly taken her a lot of guts to ask me out.

Waiting outside the pub for her I think back to when I asked a girl out for the first time who was a checkout chick at the supermarket. I'd been so nervous, a pimply faced scrawny teenager asking out a pretty blonde girl. She'd said yes—much to my shock—but that first date never amounted to anything and growing up a little more after that I became more flirtatious and was never without a date or bed buddy.

I'm not proud of the number of girls I've been with, but I only really went down that path because I couldn't have Addison. I'd never had the guts to ask her out, and she always seemed to be around Hunter. It's obvious she's loved him since we were kids.

Now, even though I slept with Addison, and still love her, I know she'll never fall for me. Moving on from her is hard though. I've tried so many times, never actually letting anyone else in, preferring as idiotic as it is to just sleep with whoever's willing, rather than let myself feel any real emotions.

Leaning against the wall outside the pub, I run my hands through my hair. It's crazy that I'm actually feeling a little nervous.

Honestly, I don't find Sam attractive, but she's pretty in a sweet innocent way. My eyes focus on her walking towards me, a sweet smile on her face.

She's actually wearing a dress, a far cry from her usual Tom boyish work attire. The dress brushes the top of her knees, dipping low across her cleavage and I can't help but stare at her. She has coupled it with a dark denim jacket that she's tugging at the sleeves of in nervousness.

Stopping in front me, she looks down at the ground, muttering a sweet, "Hi."

Putting a hand around her back, my hand brushing against her jacket, I kiss her cheek softly.

A sweet blush rushes up her cheeks. "You look great," I say to her, an attempt at calming her nerves, and mine.

"Thanks. So. Do. You," she replies stumbling on the words and a little breathless.

"Ready to go inside?"

"Yeah, Ok."

Following her I sneakily look at her butt, watching the fabric of the dress hitch up when she walks. She turns a moment to look back at me, pointing towards a booth near the back of the pub.

Sliding into the seat she props her elbows up on the table.

Sliding in across from her I look at her, speaking softly, "Relax Sam. I promise I don't bite."

She sighs softly, like she's trying to let go of her nervousness, and I tease her, "Unless you want me to."

Her elbow lifts and she playfully grabs my arm.

"Haha, Quentin, not funny."

"Sorry, just relax yeah?"

Her innocence is so endearing and not what I'm used to, but it intrigues me somewhat.

"I need a drink, " She blurts out suddenly, cutting the odd tension surrounding us.

"What's your poison?" I ask winking at her.

She appears to ponder my question for a moment before replying, "Um...I'll have a.."

"Don't tell me you like those girly drinks? Like Cruisers?"

She laughs, and screws up her nose when she replies, "No ick..."

"So a beer then?"

"Yeah thanks."

Walking over to the bar, I keep my eyes on her. She's fidgeting with a ring on her right hand, deep in thought. I really don't know what to make of her. Her shyness, and innocence is so sweet. I've never met anyone with such innocence and the fact that she wants me kind of tugs at my heart.

Grabbing the two beers from the counter I slap the ten dollar note on the bar top, before going back to the booth and sliding back in.

I lift my glass up, and doing the same we clink it our glasses together, whilst I tease her, "Drink up Sam."

I watch her when she takes a slow sip, before quickly gulping the rest down like it's water.

"Woah, slow down girl. I don't want you getting drunk."

She laughs, slamming her glass back down on the table.

"I'm no Cadbury, thank you."

"Good to know." I laugh, taking a long gulp of my own beer.

"Thanks for saying yes," She says innocently breaking the silence that has again taken over.

"Why wouldn't I say yes to a date with a pretty girl?"

"I don't know...cause you're hot and...I.."

"You think I'm hot huh?" I tease, making the blush rise in her cheeks again.

She gulps down the rest of her beer and giggles.

"Yeah I..uh."

"Sorry Sam I'm just teasing you."

"Well, stop it yeah?" She says defensively.

I've upset her and feel like a tool. "Another drink or a dance?"

"Drink then dance."

"Good thinking. The band is really good tonight," I inform her, standing up to get another round from the bar.

This time she follows me and sits on a barstool. Again she gulps the beer down, a little froth lingering at the corner of her mouth.

"You have a little froth here," I tell her, trying to show her where by touching my own mouth. She licks her lips to try and get it off, but her eyes are locked on mine. It oddly makes my breath hitch. I barely know the girl and she's not my type, but her innocence is getting to me in ways I know it shouldn't be.

"Did I get it?"

"Um, no, here," I say, brushing my thumb against the corner of her mouth and licking it clean. She lets out a 'huh' sound, like her breath has caught in her chest.

There's definite tension between us, not attraction per se but something and I feel a little guilty for wanting her, for wanting to break down her innocence. Swallowing hard I gulp down my own beer, fully aware of her gaze on me.

"How about that dance now the band has started?"

"Um, ok. But I'm not a very good dancer."

Taking her hand I reply laughing, "That makes two of us then."

She laughs sweetly when I lead her towards the dance floor that is filling with people.

This band always gets the pub pumping and tonight is no exception. Sam has begun to dance, swaying her hips to the music, her arms above her head, throwing them casually from side to side. I've admitted to myself that I don't find her attractive but watching her dance, her dress hitching higher up her thighs, exposing more creamy skin has my mind wandering to wicked thoughts. Following her lead for a moment I dance like a damn fool, gulping hard when her eyes lock straight on mine and a delicious grin spreads across her face.

"You said you couldn't dance."

She laughs devilishly and I swear my jeans suddenly feel a little tighter. The band has changed to a slower tempo song, and she sways her hips slower, more rhythmically. Edging a little closer to her, I extend an arm around her waist, pulling her closer to me.

For a moment she melts into me, grinding her hips against my body, wrapping her arms around my neck. I would be lying if I said I'm not throughly enjoying the sensation of her grinding against me. I've not gone out dancing or a date in general in too long and it feels damn good.

The song has once again stopped, and she's still standing close to me. Brushing a stray hair from across her cheek, I say softly, "Thanks for that gorgeous."

A sudden frown crosses her face and she grabs my hand away from her back before rushing out the door, not even glancing back at me.

Quickly, I run after her finding her sitting on the bench outside with her head in her hands, her elbows on her knees.

"Sam, I'm sorry. I didn't mean to upset you."

She looks up at me when I sit next to her.

"Don't Quentin. Don't tease me."

"Sorry, but I wasn't teasing you Sam."

"You..you...c...c..called me..."

"Gorgeous?"

"Yes," She spits back at me.

Yes, I hadn't been thinking that at the start of the night, but having her dance with me, letting her guard down was so sweet I couldn't help but see her in a different light.

"I meant it Sam."

"But I..I'm not the type of girl that..."

"That what?"

"A guy like you wants."

I don't reply, instead brush my hand across her cheek, leaving it lingering in place when I bend down to kiss her lips. It's a sweet kiss, soft and innocent, but still she murmurs softly, kissing me back a little deeper.

I pull back, apologising, "Sorry Sam, I shouldn't have done that."

The blush rises in her cheeks again and she licks her lips like she wants me to kiss her again.

"Now who is being a tease," I jeer, poking her arm.

"Sorry, but no one has ever kissed me like that."

"Lucky you then huh?" I say with a laugh, grabbing her hand to pull her up with me.

"Thanks for tonight," She says, still holding my hand.

"No worries, it was fun," I reply bending down to kiss her again, a little harder than before. Her lips are soft and she tastes sweet. I love how her lips seem to melt into mine, but her kisses are still so innocent compared to what I'm used to.

Pulling away again, I caress her cheek. "Lets get you home huh?"

"Thanks Quentin but I only live around the corner. I'll be ok."

"Are you sure? I can walk with you."

"No, that's ok. Goodnight and thanks again," She coos, pressing a kiss to my cheek before she walks away.

I sit back down on the bench seat, a little lost at her sudden departure. Kissing her was never part of my plan for the night at all. I'd actually just wanted the night to be causal—a just friends date—but her sweet innocence had stirred something in my guts. I'd had to tell her she's gorgeous and tell her I meant it. Honestly, I actually think I do mean it, and although kissing her hasn't sent blood rushing through my veins it was definitely good and for the first time in forever I feel like I could let someone in. Whether that someone is Samantha I'm not sure but she likes me and maybe we could be just what the other needs.

I wander back into the pub, ordering another drink from Mike.

"What did you do to the poor girl Quentin?"

I laugh when I reply, "Thought with my pants, not my head."

He laughs and replies with his jovial fatherly tone, "Good work son. She seems sweet. I'd tread carefully with her."

"Yeah I know," I reply, nodding my head and quickly downing my beer before heading home.

My head is spinning, even though I've barely drunk anything. It's going to be a long night, thinking about the predicament I've put myself in with Sam.

Next time I need to think with my head, not my pants.

(36) *Savannah*

Hunter had made himself scarce after collecting his Mum from the rest home to bring her out to the farm for the day. She won't stop fussing over me, her absolute delight not leaving her face.
It makes me truly happy I'm going to be soon giving her the gift of a grandson. She's made me feel so loved in the short time I've known her.
Losing Mum is something I'll never get over, as I've always wondered if Dante had played a part in causing the car accident they'd had on the way to the restaurant the night we got married.
The investigative team ruled it was due to a poorly maintained vehicle and unforeseen driving conditions, but I always knew that wasn't true. My Dad looked after his car like it was another baby, and yes the road would have been slippery from the recent rain, but Dad was a careful driver, no history of any accidents until he ran through the traffic light that night, colliding with oncoming traffic and stopping across the intersection hitting the light post so forcefully there was not a chance they could have survived.

My guests have started arriving, and Grace has not let me move from the couch. She's gotten a bit of strength back lately and is no longer using her wheelchair to get around, instead using a walking frame. She totters over to the door when we hear knocking.
The person at the door shocks me a little. I wasn't expecting her to come at all, because she's made it pretty clear she's not happy for me and Hunter at all.
She speaks softly, greeting Grace, "Hi Grace."
"Hello Addison," Grace replies with a hint of disdain in her voice. "Come in dear, Savannah is in the lounge." Her tone a little lighter when she steps back for Addison to come in.
Addison is definitely feeling uncomfortable when she comes into the room.
"Hi Savannah, um...I'm sorry if you didn't want me to come but..."

Awkwardly I stand up, my hand on my back to quell the pain that rushes through my body every time I move. Most of the time I feel like I'm growing a baby elephant inside me.

"You don't need to be sorry Addison. I'm glad you're here."

"Really? I mean I've just been a complete bitch to you about everything with Hunter and the baby."

"Yeah you have but I get it Addison, I do."

My stomach juts out with a kick. "Shit, oww."

Pain crosses her face, worry even.

"Are you ok?" She asks.

"Yeah, the little devil kicks pretty hard sometimes."

"Oh ok," She replies, the pain on her face still evident.

"Do you want to feel his kicks?"

A smile crosses her face then and I grab her hands pressing them against my belly. He kicks hard against her palms and her smile spreads wider.

"Oh, Savannah that's amazing. Is it really a boy?"

"Without a doubt. A little footy player I think."

"Yeah he'll be gorgeous just like his Dad." She laughs. I can still sense the pain in her voice though.

"Addison, I'm sorry yeah."

"Why?"

"I just get the sense that there's something you've not told Hunter about your past together."

She sits down on the couch, and helps me sit beside her.

"Um yeah but I don't want to upset him. He's so happy with you and delighted to be having a baby."

"I don't understand."

"Savannah, I don't know if I should tell you."

I touch her hands lightly, leaning close to her. "I won't tell Hunter if you don't want me too."

"I don't know. I don't want Grace to hear either. She already hates me."

Slowly I stand up, grabbing her hand. "Follow me, I want to show you something and we can talk there."

I lead her down the hallway to the room across from mine and Hunter's.

It was once the study, that Hunter never used, so we'd cleared out the furniture, only leaving the wall to wall to bookshelf on the wall facing the window.

Hunter had painted the remaining walls a pastel yellow, and around the edges we'd placed a 'Lion King' trim, decking the room out with a Safari theme.

Next to the bookshelf is a wooden change table, a large sleigh cot and a rocking chair closest to the window with cushions on it.

Over the cot I hung a mobile that plays lullabies when it spins around. On the other side of the room is a chest of drawers, that I've begun filling with cute baby clothes for my little man.

I tried not to go crazy in Baby Bunting, but it was seriously cuteness overload and my heart was bursting at being able to buy him things. Hunter was again like a kid in a candy shop, wanting to buy every cute item of clothing we saw, as well as every baby item under the sun that we clearly don't need.

Getting home, his giddiness didn't decrease, as he raced to get everything inside and put together as though our baby boy is going to be here any second.

It warmed my heart to see him so excited, and I can feel the tears stinging my eyes now as I look around the room.

Addison's eyes light up the minute we step into the room. "Aww Savannah, it's gorgeous."

"I know. Are you ok?"

"Yeah, its just I'll never get to do this."

"What? What do you mean?"

She breaks down into tears, and I can't help but break down to. I'd thought she was so heartless, hated that she was still in love with Hunter, but seeing her upset tugs at my heart.

"I can't have children, Savannah and I..."

"Oh Addison, I'm so sorry. Here I am rubbing it in your face."

"No, no...don't be sorry. I'm so incredibly glad that you can give Hunter a family. He's always wanted a family of his own."

Putting an arm around her, I say softly, "Addison, is there something else that upsets you about my being with Hunter?"

"Well, yeah, but it hurts to say it out loud."

"You don't have to tell me, but Hunter was upset when I asked him about your past together. He won't tell me anything."

"He doesn't know everything Savannah," she pauses, my heart constricting at her change in tone.

"Do you really want to know Savannah, really?"

"Yes, I do."

"Fine," she says, sitting down in the rocking chair.

"When I was like eighteen I fell pregnant."

My jaw drops, hearing the words coming out of her mouth shocks me, and I ask, even though I'm sure of the answer, "To Hunter?"

"Yes, it was our first time and the condom broke...and I didn't want to tell him. I was so scared."

"Oh my God Addison, I'm sorry but you said you can't have kids?"

The tears are pouring down her cheeks now. "No not now I can't. I went away to Uni without telling Hunter, we'd kinda broken up and I..."

"Its ok. You don't have to tell me."

"No...no I have to..." she stops a moment, wiping her arm across her face, "I had a miscarriage and got an infection that led to permanent damage."

My heart literally breaks for her. I'd not liked her at all, but her pouring her heart out to me makes me see a completely different side of her.

"So you never told Hunter when you come back from Uni?"

"No, I couldn't and then he proposed...and I just couldn't do that to him knowing he always wanted a family."

"Oh Addison, I'm so sorry. I honestly am."

"Thanks Savannah. It means a lot. And you know what?"

"What?" I ask, extending a hand to help her up from the rocking chair.

"I'm really glad you came into Hunter's life. He adores you."

"Thats really sweet, thanks."

"You're welcome."

I smile at her, knowing that we are never going to be best friends, but can at least be civil. Being in love with the same amazing man is of course a wedge between us, but I feel for her more now, understanding the deep connection she had with Hunter before I came into his life.

"We better get back to the celebrations, cake and presents are calling," she says eagerly.

"Yeah that they are. And Addison?"

"Yeah?" she says looking straight at me when I start to head back down the hallway to the kitchen.

"Thanks for telling me. I promise, this is just between us girls."

"Thanks Savannah. I really mean it."

Back in the kitchen, Grace has spread the kitchen table with an array of baked goods, cupcakes with blue icing, biscuits and slices. Looking at it all makes my mouth water and I lick my lips in delight.

"Wow Grace, it looks wonderful. Thank you."

She totters over to me, pressing a kiss to the side of my head. "Anything for you darling. You've made my son so happy. And I love you."

My heart melts, tears of joy stinging my eyes; the emotions of my soon to be Mother in law telling me 'she loves me' hit me deep.

My own Mum not being able to share this joy me is overwhelmingly hard, but having Grace by my side makes it all better. I wrap an arm around her, pulling her as close as I can with my baby bump in the way. "I love you too Mum," I tell her looking straight at her and watching the absolute joy cross her face at my calling her 'Mum.'

It feels amazing to be part of a family again, so amazing that I sigh, letting the happiness rush over me. Only one thing will make my life more complete, and he will soon be here, my sweet baby boy.

(37) Samantha

Avoiding Quentin since our date has been a little torturous. He's tried to talk to me, but I've completely ignored him, turning away or standing up from my desk to run off.

I still like him, even more so since our date and can barely stop thinking about his lips on mine for a second. His kisses were hot, sensual and made my body ache for more. I've never had a feeling of warmth rush through me like when Quentin kissed me.

I felt like I'd never actually been kissed until that moment, when his sweet lips pressed against mine. I'd kissed Seth so many times before but it was never that earth shattering, on my god kiss.

I want to be brazen, and take a chance on something more with Quentin. I've been fantasying about so much more than kissing him for months. But I was taken aback by his flirtation with me, him calling me gorgeous. It set butterflies off in my belly and it scares me.

The thought of someone as gorgeous as him actually liking me and thinking I I'm gorgeous too is overwhelming.

It's not that Seth isn't gorgeous either, but he's more boyish and the fact we'd gotten together when we are only sixteen. He was my first boyfriend, and he was sweet and caring, but our break up hurt a lot.

He'd planned a special night together for my nineteenth birthday, his parents away for the weekend and knowing what he really wanted from me I panicked when I came out of the bathroom to find him naked on his bed.

Our argument is still in my head, the words he'd said that literally yanked my heart out.

If you love me you'd sleep with me Sam.
You don't know how good you've got it.
I could have anyone.
I can't be your boyfriend anymore if you won't have sex with me Sam, its not fair.

Doctor Attraction

The last words hurting the most, 'its not fair'. Those words made me feel like I meant nothing to him, that the three years we'd spent together were nothing. He wasn't prepared to wait for me to take that step.

And now after coming to Ridgehope for my first official posting as a police officer I'd hoped to leave the past hurt Seth caused me behind, to not feel anything like that again, but I'd not counted on meeting Quentin Mackenney. Speak of the devil, he once again is crossing the room towards my desk. Tears are stinging my eyes. I can't cry in front of him, so sniffing them back I get up from my chair to escape his gaze on me.

But he instead grabs my arm, his fingers brushing my skin causing heat to rise all over me.

"Sam, please don't run off."

I don't say a word, instead yank my arms back, crossing them against my chest. I bite my lip nervously. Just being this close to him is making me feel warm over, and I have to focus on my breathing to stay calm.

"Look Sam, I'm sorry ok?"

"Sorry for what?" I spit at him, upset.

"For accepting your date, and for kissing you."

I bite my lip again. "Well, Im sorry for asking you out. I thought you were a nice guy, but you're not," I snap at him defensively, feeling like a stupid innocent school girl.

"Oh Sam, that hurts. I really am sorry. I didn't mean to hurt you."

"Well, you did, I...li." I snap my mouth shut.

Don't tell him that you like him Sam, are you crazy?

"Let me make it up to you."

"How are you gonna do that?"

"Go out with me again," he asks me.

"I don't know Quentin...I don't think..."

"Please Sam, don't make me beg."

"I'm not going to make you beg, but at the moment, no, I don't want to go out with you again."

"Fine. If thats what you want," he states, leaving the office without turning back to even look at me.

Why do I like him so damn much?
Because he's hot, and makes you feel like you're melting Sam, thats why you like him.

꙳

I've thankfully not had to see Quentin for the rest of the day, as I'd had to go out of the station with the Sergeant to investigate an incident in the next town.
My mind still can't focus on anything but Quentin though, and I hate how he's getting under my skin, hate the way he looks at me with his dark eyes that make me want to melt.
The sergeant is trying to make small talk with me on the way back to the station. I try to shrug him off, but he's persistent like a father.
"You ok Samantha?"
"Um...yeah. Just thinking about someone."
He nods, still focusing on the road when he speaks again, "Wouldn't be a certain younger cop who seems to have taken a liking to ya?"
My cheeks flush. "Um...I don't know who you mean."
"Be careful Samantha. Quentin is a great cop, but he's not known to be a one woman man."
I don't know what to say to that. Everyone in Ridgehope knows Quentin is in love with one of the local doctors, but I've not heard anything about him being the type of guy who sleeps around.
I'm cursing myself now for asking him out, for thinking that he'd ever want to get involved with shy little Samantha.
Back at the station, I sneak back in to grab my handbag before leaving for home.
My eyes scan the items on my desk first, and seeing them makes my heart pound.
In the middle of the desk, right where I would see it, is a single pink carnation with a card, the writing on the front scrawly calligraphy that reads, 'I'm Sorry'.
My heart is leaping in my chest from the sweet gesture.

Doctor Attraction

One look at Quentin and I melt, and now he isn't even in the room, and I'm melting.

Picking up the card, I flick it open and my heart swells reading his thoughtful words.

Samantha
I'm sorry
Please let me make it up to you
Saturday @ my place 6pm
15 Burrows Lane
I'm cooking
And come as you
You don't need to impress me by wearing a dress
I like you already
Quentin xoxo

I hold the card to my chest, against my pounding heart, picking up the carnation and inhaling the musty aroma. Grabbing my handbag, I walk out of the station, a feeling of cloud nine rushing over me.

Quentin Mackenney is full of surprises for sure and I know as unsettled as I am about our date, and his kisses I'm falling for him.

I'm ready to strap myself in for the ride, this time I can see my innocence being unraveled and I'm ready for the rollercoaster.

(38) Quentin

It's been a week or so since Addison had called to ask me out for a drink. I'd accepted then but since I'd gone out with Samantha and I'm a little worried she'll find out.

Her innocence isn't a dealbreaker, she seems really sweet and I kind of feel a bit of an ego boost knowing that she likes me and doesn't just want to fuck me like most of the single girls in Ridgehope who know me.

Even when I'd gone to the Police Academy in Adelaide I'd gotten a bit of a name for myself, as the go to hot quick fuck. I wasn't proud of it at all, and it had created a rift between Hunter and I for a while, but he'd thankfully forgiven me. Our relationship hadn't always been the best, because even though I looked up to him I'd always been jealous of his relationship with Addison and when they broke up I still never got the guts to actually be with her, except for fucking her months back. Nothing had hurt me more than her reaction after that, but it doesn't make me love her any less.

Hunter falling in love with Savannah though is the best thing for him, they're so sweet together and I actually envy my older brother again. I want what he has with Savannah but with Addison. It still seems as though it's never going to happen and I need to move on.

Despite not wanting to go out with Addison on what I'm sure isn't a just friends date I end up in the pub with her, sliding into a booth near the front door.

"So Addison what's up?" I ask casually.

"I don't know how to tell you Quentin."

"What do you mean Addison?"

"Well, you know after we slept together. You probably hate me already."

I took a gulp of the beer in front of me. "I could never hate you Addison, seriously."

She takes a sip of her own beer and I can't help but watch her lick the foam from her lips. It makes me want to kiss her so bad, because her kiss wouldn't be sweet and innocent like Sam's.

Addison breaks my thoughts when she starts speaking again, "I don't know what to do about Zane."

"What do you mean?"

"Well, we've kissed a few times and he..."

"He what? Did you fuck him?"

She punches my arm. "No, Quentin we've just kissed...but..."

"But what? Did you like kissing him?"

My heart is pounding in my chest, I have to lighten the moment, so I jeer, "Was it as good as kissing me?"

Again she punches my arm, laughing a little. "No..." she starts, a smile on her lips that makes my leap, "but yes it was different to kissing you."

"How so?" I ask, a little confused.

"I don't know how to explain it Quentin, it was like my lips were on fire, and I just couldn't get enough...couldn't get close enough and wanted more, like a drug."

Again my heart is pounding in my chest, the words she's staying are exactly how I feel when kissing her.

"That's how it feels when I kiss you Addison. You're in love with him."

She laughs, flicking her lush golden hair back when she speaks, "Not a chance, you know I still love Hunter and..."

"And what Addison?"

"I don't know Quentin. He scares me...you know the outburst when you came here that night."

"Yeah I know Addison, but I don't think he's a bad guy. Maybe there's another reason for his behaviour."

"Yeah, maybe."

She appears a little forlorn, thinking about something she doesn't know how to say or doesn't want to tell me.

"But hey why don't you forget about him and Hunter...get with me instead," I say in a joking tone, even though I'm dead serious.

She lets out a half hearted laugh, like she's actually considering what I'd said.

"Surely you can get used to kissing me," I tease her, winking.

But then she shatters any hope I had left of being with her.

"Quentin, stop, yeah. I'll always love you but not that way...and I'm really sorry for everything."

It literally feels like my heart is breaking, but I can't let her see that.

"I'm sorry to Addison. I shouldn't have fucked you that day. It was selfish to take advantage of you when you were upset, but I gotta admit it was damn good being with you."

She blushes a little. "I can't deny that either, Quentin. We shouldn't have gone there but it was definitely good."

My ego isn't quite as bruised hearing her admit that she actually enjoyed fucking me, and even though I know it's wrong, thinking about my new relationship with Sam, I find myself suggesting, "We could be fuck buddies?"

She smiles. "As fun as that sounds Quentin, I can't do that to you."

"I know Addison but..."

"There's no but Quentin. You deserve to be with someone who loves you; not someone who can't get over your older brother."

I feel sorry for her, but completely understand. She's still in love with Hunter, and we're just friends. To me it's evident that she's falling for Zane, even if she doesn't want to admit it and for all I know maybe I'll finally be able to let someone else in.

"Yeah I guess you're right. Did you walk?"

"Yeah but I can walk home. It's fine."

"That's ok. I'll take you home, but first you need to take me on that joyride you promised."

She laughs, touching my hand lightly. "Ok. And Quentin thanks for tonight."

Standing up, I take her hand, not feeling the rush touching her normally gives me. "No worries Addison, we will always be friends."

"Thanks Quentin. That means a lot."

"Ready to show me how to drive?"

"Damn right," She says, walking out of the pub to my patrol car.

I sigh, watching her slide into the drivers seat.

Finally, I feel ready to let go of her. I actually feel like I could let someone else in and that maybe fucking her wasn't a mistake after all, but a way to let go and heal my broken heart.

(39) Zane

My breathing is shallow. It's stupid of me to keep pushing myself so hard, but running is my only escape to block things out for a while. The sound and feeling of my feet hitting the hard ground courses through my body, giving me a sense of euphoria.

Exercise is crucial in managing my diabetes, which I know I've not been focusing to well on again. My sugar levels are still sky high, and I've had to dose myself up with even more insulin and it's not really helping.

So running is my last resort to try and use the excess sugar in my body.

I round the corner of Masters Street, stopping to rest a moment against a tree, a few doors down from home.

My heart is pounding and I need to steady my breathing. Addison's house is the second from the corner, and my heart drops when I see her walking inside with none other than Quentin Mackenney.

I feel sick watching them, Addison laughing, playfully punching Quentin in the arm as she flicks her luscious hair over her shoulder. He's smiling at her, a wicked smile, and before walking inside he runs his hands through his hair in the flirtatious way I'd seen him do at the fundraiser.

The jealousy hits me hard in the chest. I don't really have a right to be jealous. It's not like Addison is my girlfriend, but I've thought that there's something between us, especially after she'd told me more about her past and kissed me like she couldn't get enough of me.

That kiss is all I've thought about for weeks. Just thinking about it, the rush of lust and emotion courses through me and my body responds. I want more of Addison, I need more of Addison.

I've also not stopped thinking about making her come, when she lent back on my desk either. If she'd come like that from my just touching her, I'd fucking love to see how hard she'd come with my mouth on her instead, or even better when I'd fuck her.

Doctor Attraction

Shaking my head—noticing they're no longer on her porch—I race back to my house, slamming the door behind me.

Yanking my tank top off I throw it on the floor, taking a few deep breaths in and out to calm my jealousy and my raging libido. Thinking about fucking Addison is damn good, but so bad at the same time.

Only one thing would block out the jealousy though, and I know I shouldn't go down that path, especially with my sugar levels out of control. The heart palpitations I've been having should stop me too but I reach for it, grabbing the clear glass bottle down from the shelf above the sink.

Unscrewing the top, I throw it on the counter and skull a quarter of the clear warm liquid. I quite like the burn of skulling Vodka. It really does block out all the pain, the physical and the mental.

Taking the bottle to the couch, I flop against it, taking another long swig. Pressing my heels against each other I slide my sneakers off and lay back further on the couch.

Thoughts of Addison in her house with him come to mind. I can see them together, and it makes bile rise up in my throat. She isn't his.

She's not yours either Zane.

She isn't mine. And just the thought of that makes my heart constrict hard in my chest. I take another long swig, holding the bottle after, realising I've actually downed half of it already and I still feel oddly sober, far from numb like I want to be.

Stumbling up from the couch, drawing the blind across I peer out to see his car driving away.

Skulling the vodka again, I unlatch my front door, fumbling with the lock, whilst clutching the now near empty vodka bottle against my chest.

Going to her house is pretty darn stupid, but I'll drown myself in alcoholic stupor if I don't confront her about him.

It's true she isn't mine, but there's not a chance I'm going to let him have her, when I'd give anything to be with her.

Stumbling out my front gate, I down a little bit more vodka, only a splash is left in the bottom now. I don't even care I'm only in my running shorts.

Reaching her door, still clutching my vodka in one hand I pound my fist hard against the wooden door, trying to think of what I'll say when she opens the door.

(40) Addison

Quentin had just left, giving me a chaste kiss on the cheek. It'd been a great night, finally both of us admitting that we are better off being friends, than lovers. It's evident though that despite the admission of us just being friends, that he's still in love with me. There was pain in his eyes whenever he said the word 'friend'.

But I know I could never feel that way about Quentin. He's like a little brother to me, even though he's six months older than me. I've always seen him that way though, because I'd been closer with Hunter. In relationships though, age never really mattered to me.

I'm still feeling awake, but an early start at the hospital is looming and I know I need to head to bed if I'm going to get up, but I need something to settle my stomach. Grabbing the milk from the fridge, I get out a saucepan to heat up some milk for a hot chocolate.

I nearly drop the milk, when a loud banging comes from the front door. I'm expecting it to be Quentin, telling me he'd forgotten something, even though I know he hadn't.

But opening the door my mouth falls open, finding Zane standing on my doorstep, wearing only his running shorts.

No shirt and no shoes.

He looks dishevelled, his hair unruly and his face flushed. My heart skips a beat seeing him almost naked, but I shake my head, waving the thought away when I look down to the item he's clutching in his fist. It's clear he's drunk.

"Zane what are you doing here?" I say pissed off.

His response shocks me a little.

"Are you seeing him? The cop?"

"No, he's my friend, Zane," I try to say calmly, even though I'm feeling angry at him for asking.

"But he was...he was touching you," Zane stutters.

I'm even more angry at him now, for thinking he's the only person who can touch me.

"We have a past together Zane. You know that!"

His next words make me seethe in anger, "Are you fucking him?"

I snatch the vodka bottle from his grip, before I speak again, anger in my tone, "Seriously, Zane, No! Quentin is just a friend."

"Yeah, blah, blah!"

"Seriously, Zane, how dare you..." I stop, not sure what I'm going to accuse him of.

But when he continues I'm seething, "He's just another guy you throw yourself at. You tease, flirt and reject! You're a fucking cock-tease!" He spits at me, slurring the words but they still come at me like knives.

Inside I know his words are true, and I hate myself for that fact. Hate myself for not being able to let go of Hunter and for hurting Quentin by just using him for comfort, when I know deep down how he feels about me. And now seeing Zane in a drunken stupor, clearly upset at me, hurling words at me like spitfire truly hurts.

There's no way he meant those words but they still hurt.

He's glaring at me now, waiting for an answer I don't have. Most likely waiting for me to throw myself at him, like I always do. But instead I slam the door in his face, yelling, "Go home Zane!", before turning back to the kitchen to continue making my hot chocolate, that I now need the comfort of more than ever before.

(41) Zane

Stumbling back home from making a damn fool of myself on Addison's doorstep, the vodka hits me hard. It rushes through me, and combining with a lack of sugar my head is pounding.

It's beyond stupid to do this to myself again and again, knowing my history, but I just want to block out the pain of constant rejection. Needing to not focus on anything for a while, but getting home with a pounding head isn't helping me block out anything.

Nausea also churns my stomach, partly because I've not eaten, instead filling my stomach with nearly a whole one litre bottle of Vodka. That's absolutely moronic of me to consider drinking so much.

Hitting the walls when I walk to the bedroom, my head pounding and spinning and stomach churning is nothing compared to the sudden gallop feeling of my heart in my chest. My heart literally feels as though it's going to burst out of my chest. My heart is beating so fast and irregular.

Falling against the bed, closing my eyes I try to shut out the pain, both mentally and physically, but it's overwhelming.

Drinking so much is definitely not a good idea, and inwardly I curse myself as my body slips away.

৵

Waking up after what feels like mere minutes, not hours my stomach is still churning, the urge to vomit rising in my chest. Springing off the bed, I race to the bathroom, hurling into the toilet bowl, hoping desperately for relief. But relief doesn't come.

The churning is still in the pit of my stomach, and I feel woozy. I wrap my arms around the cold porcelain, to try and quell the heat of my skin.

Resting my head on the toilet seat I again close my eyes, too afraid to move and too tired to care that I'm sleeping with my head practically in the toilet.

Again I wake, to an overwhelming pounding sound reverberating in my head. It sounds far away, but also like it's right in my head. It's a knocking sound. Slowly lifting my head, I try to focus on the knocking to work out where it's coming from, when I hear a voice calling my name, "Zane, Zane. Open the door Zane!"

Pressing my hands into the floor I force myself to stand up, to move but my chest constricts—the pounding irregular heartbeat feeling rising again—with a pain so sharp I feel like something or someone is squeezing my heart in a fist. Clutching my chest I stumble out of the bathroom towards the front door, but I stop in the lounge room when I see a figure standing in my house.

The pain is so overwhelming I haven't even registered the fact that she'd let herself in.

Shock is plastered on her face; she hasn't moved an inch since I'd come into the room. Clutching my chest tighter I start to walk closer to her, wanting to lean against her for support.

"Zane...I um.."

She starts to speak but it's though she has no words to say seeing me looking like I've been run over by a bus.

The pain increases and I scream out, "Ohhh, FUCK!"

She moves closer to me, about to reach out to pull me closer when she asks, "Zane what's wrong?"

"My chest fucking cains!" I scream again.

"What do you mean? Are you..."

That's the last words I hear from her mouth, falling at her feet and the world disappears into blackness.

(42) Addison

Having only come over to Zane's to apologise for being a bitch the night before I'm beyond shocked to walk into his house to find him in overwhelming pain.
Fear rushes through me, I know what is happening the moment the words leave his mouth and when he falls at my feet blacking out, the panic and déjà vu hits hard.
It's like the feeling of when Hunter came into the hospital, but this time I'm the only one here. No one else is going to step in and take over.

Breathe Addison, breathe, you're a doctor, you know what's happening, do something .

I shake my head, trying to make my brain focus. Bending down next to him, I brush a hand across his cheek, sighing, acknowledging the thought in my head.

Yes, you feel something for him, Addison, get it together or you'll never get to tell him.

Stretching I dig my phone out from the pocket of my jeans, dialling Herbert's number.
I don't even let him answer when he picks up.
"Herbert! I'm at Zane's," I blurt out, the panic increasing when I continue, "I think he's had a heart attack!"
"What? Addison, seriously?"
"Yes, He was clutching his chest in pain and he just collapsed," I say, breathing slowly.
"Is he breathing?" Herbert asks concerned.
I lean an ear closer, resting a hand on Zane's lower chest. "Yes, shallow breaths but yes."

"I'll dispatch the ambos, get Mark out ASAP. Stay with him Addison. Let him know you're there."

"Ok thanks Herbert," I reply before hanging up, dropping my phone to the floor and wiping a hand across my face, tears dripping down my cheeks.

Time seems to stop whilst waiting for the ambulance. The reality of possibly losing him hits me hard.

I'm not sure if I'm in love with him, but there's no way I can even think about losing him. He means something to me, as scary as that is to admit to myself. It's like I had to face the possibility of losing every person I love, to realise how much they mean to me. I feel like this is punishment for rejecting Hunters proposal and not telling him about our baby.

Karma for being such a bitch.

"I'm sorry Zane, it's going to be ok," I tell him, kissing his cheek softly, hearing the approach of the ambulance.

They rush inside, pushing me aside to check his breathing and pulse. Their words are muffled and I can't focus on them, instead I watch when they lift him onto a stretcher before wheeling him out into the back of the ambulance.

Mark nods at me when I climb in the back with the other officer. She places an oxygen mask over his face and his breathing becomes less shallow.

"Are you ok Addison? Did you find him?" The officer asks.

"Um yeah kinda," I reply, not looking up, but instead focusing on Zane.

Clutching his hand in mine I squeeze it, hoping to maybe wake him up.

Abruptly he stirs, looking around the back of ambulance and lifting the oxygen mask off his face in disgust. Looking straight at me he murmurs, "Oh hey Amy."

My heart sinks. I try not to think anything of him saying her name, but it actually hurts that he would think of her in a time like this.

But despite the hurt, I play along.

"Yes, Zane I'm here. You're gonna be ok hun."

I brush a hand across his cheek—and want to kiss his cheek too—but the ambulance officers eyes on me make me feel a little uneasy.

Arriving at the hospital, they rush Zane into the emergency department, pushing me aside, telling me I'm not on duty and my presence is no longer required.

It makes me feel useless and hopeless. I need a listening ear, so walking through the hospital I go out to the courtyard, sitting on the bench seat before I dial his number. It nearly rings out before he answers.

"Hey hot shot doc," he greets me happily.

"Hi Jett."

"Addi, what's wrong?"

I can feel the tears stinging my eyes.

"Sorry Jett, I just needed to talk."

"I'm all ears Addi," my brother says comfortingly.

"Everything is going wrong here Jett."

"What do you mean?"

"Well, you know what happened when I tried to get Hunter back and now he's engaged and having a baby."

"Woah, that's a lot to take in."

"Yeah and I've been kinda seeing the new doctor."

"That's great though Addi isn't it?"

"Well, yeah, I mean we've kissed a few times and I don't know, it makes me feel something...but he did..."

"What Addi?"

"Oh, it's nothing. It was my fault. I rejected him after he kissed me."

"And he didn't like that?"

"Yeah...but I can't stop thinking about the kisses we've shared Jett and..."

"What Addi? I'm not going to get upset with you."

"He's in the hospital right now. I think he had a heart attack," I say surprised I even managed to say the words before the sobs began.

"Oh, Addison that's terrible. Is he ok?"

Through sobs, I speak slowly, "I don't...know...they wouldn't let me stay...but Jett I...c...can't lose him!"

"Addi can I be honest sis?"

"Yesss," I stammer sniffing back my tears.

"I wish I could be there with you, but honestly I think you're falling for him."

"But...I c...can't Jett...I..."

"Addison if he is ok, if he pulls through, then give him a chance for both your sakes."

"I guess."
"I'm sorry Addi I have to go. Chat soon. Love you little sis."
"Thanks Jett. Love you to big brother," I reply quickly before he hangs up.
Tucking my phone back into my pocket, I can't hold back the tears anymore.
They flow down my cheeks, and my heart is pounding.
I'm not sure if Jett is right that I'm falling for Zane, but I definitely feel something for him and most of all I'm desperately afraid of losing him.

(43) Zane

Waking up in a hospital bed is a cruel case of self inflicted déjà vu. The pads attached to my body for detecting my heartbeat are incredibly itchy and I want to rip them off. Everything else on the monitor screen seems normal considering the last twenty-four hours. The last thing I remembered was collapsing at Addison's feet.

The door cracks open, and my eyes tried to focus on who's entering the room. Rubbing them a little helps, and I can hear the click clack of her heels on the floor to. She stops next to the bed, glancing at the monitor and then at me.

The look on her face is a mixture of emotions that I can't decipher.

She starts to open her mouth like she's going to speak but nothing comes out.

Instead I laugh when I speak, "Oh hey you, are you my doctor?"

She doesn't laugh, and appears to be unhappy with me.

Her tone when she speaks is filled with anger, "No Zane I'm not your doctor!"

Her disdain really hurts. "What's wrong Addison?"

"How come you didn't tell me about your full medical history? The recurring hypertension?"

I shake my head, feeling guilty for not opening up to her more like she'd done with me.

"It...um kinda didn't come up again Addison. I didn't want to burden you."

Clenching her fists I can see her anger at me increasing, heat rising in her cheeks when she yells at me, "Seriously Zane! You're a diabetic, prone to high blood pressure!" She stops, taking in a few breaths before lowering her head in shame when she continues, guilt evident in her tone, "I made you go out and get drunk with me and the vodka you drank to, because of me! God, Zane you could have fucking died!"

Her words are true, all of them, but her tone irritates me and I find myself screaming back at her, "What do you care?"

A smile tries to cross her face but she turns away, muttering to, "I'm ff...all..."

Again she pauses, the same angry tone present when she turns back to look at me, "I don't care Zane."

I can't help but wonder what she was going to say. It seemed like she was about to say she's 'falling for me' and I should be elated, but I can't shake the feeling that she's lying to me.

Trying to lighten the mood, I tease, "Not even a little bit?"

"No, Zane! You should have thought about your health! Obviously for some fucked up reason you let your diabetes get out of control again, even though I tried to help you." The anger in her words hurts like a knife to my already stressed heart.

She sighs, turning away but I grab her hand, pulling her against the bed.

"Yes, I did ok. I put myself here, in this fucking hospital bed because I couldn't deal with how my life has gone to shit again."

"What the fuck do you mean?" she spits at me, still angry, "Oh and who is Amy by the way? Is she your wife?"

It's my turn to sigh. I've told her some of my past, but not everything and still I'm not sure if I should truly open up and relive the pain of the events that drove Amy away.

"Yes, Amy is my wife. And she cheated on me with my best friend when I..."

"You don't have to tell me Zane. I'm sorry."

"No, I need to tell you. I...um...killed a child."

Absolute shock crosses her face. "Not like that Addison, seriously."

"But?"

"She came in for appendicitis, and there were complications and she passed on the table. It really stressed me out. I was a wreck and started drinking, not managing my diabetes and blood pressure."

"And thats when you ended up in hospital the first time?"

"Yes, and Amy didn't understand. She wouldn't even talk to me about what happened, and instead ran into the arms of my best friend and it all went to shit between us. She barely looked at me after I got out of the hospital, and I tried to get back on track with everything. But I had bad days, when I drank too much or didn't take my insulin."

I pause, taking in another deep breath, knowing that this time I have to focus on the now.

"She left me then and I heard about the post to Ridgehope. It seemed like the perfect fresh start and then I met you and..." I pause, my heart pounding.

Her eyes turn to look at the screen, watching my increasing heart rate on it.

"What Zane?" she asks with upset in her tone, worry that my increasing heartbeat is a bad sign.

"I met you Addison, and..." I pause, cursing myself for a moment.

I have to get the words out, I have to tell her.

"I'm in love with you Addison."

She starts to open her mouth, but the words die on her tongue. I knew she'd have nothing to say back. I'd expected nothing less.

"And all you do is reject me for Hunter and he's getting married to someone else."

She takes a deep breath before she speaks, "I can't make myself love you Zane."

"I'm not asking you to, but it's just so fucking unfair."

"What? Unfair? Whats that mean?"

"Amy wants a fucking divorce! You don't love me and I just can't escape from all the shit."

"I'm sorry...I don't know what to say Zane," she replies with a hint of concern, that seems half hearted.

"You never do Addison."

She mutters 'sorry' again, as though just uttering that word will fix things.

Shocking me she bends down closer to me on the bed, pressing her lips to my cheek, her lips lingering there.

Reaching up I cup her cheeks in my hands, and pull her lips against my own, kissing her softly. She moans against my lips, and I lick her lips to get her to open up to me. It's a kiss like none we've shared; it's soft and loving.

Addison pull back abruptly from the kiss, causing a whimper to escape from my mouth when the door cracks open and a voice roars, "Who the fuck is this Zane?"

Addison looks completely shocked, not even able to look at me. She wants to say something but her mouth opens and closes in tongue tied shock.

Addison rushes out the door and I look up at the new person standing in the room. She's the last person I want to see right now and I wish the hospital bed would swallow me whole.

(44) Amy

The blonde woman rushes out of the room, obviously having some idea of who I am. But I don't know her and she was kissing my husband.

Stepping closer to the bed I seethe, "Care to explain Zane?"

"What are you doing here Amy?"

I reach out to try and take his hand, but he snatches it away.

"The chief called me Zane. You know, emergency contact and all. He said you had a heart attack!"

His gaze shifts from glaring at me to the shy little boy clutching my other hand. The guilt of not telling him suddenly hits me.

"Oh um, say hello to your son," I say, urging him forward.

"What? You weren't even pregnant when you left me!"

"Yeah, I was Zane, about six months actually but you were so blinded by what happened at work and with Max you didn't want to know."

His mouth falls open, the shock of my words hitting him when he speaks with a confused tone, "But you didn't look pregnant?"

Now I'm a little pissed off. He's being so nonchalant.

"Come on Zane, you barely looked at me, didn't touch me much, if at all. You were always at work and plus I carried it well."

It feels like I'm making excuses, and even though I'd sent him the divorce papers I'm feeling a little regretful. When he speaks again, his words hurt.

"How do you even know he's mine? He's probably Max's!"

His words make me fume, and I spit at him, "How many times do I have to tell you? I never slept with Max! It was just a kiss!"

He doesn't respond, instead looks up at me and down at his son.

"Plus, look at the kid Zane! He's clearly yours."

"So you think you can just come here with my son and everything is going to be okay?"

Again his words hurt, and my regret increases.

"Well, you didn't sign the divorce papers, dumbass!" I spit at him, instantly regretting the name I called him.

"You kinda sprung that on me."

"Seriously Zane! I can't deal with your shit over and over again!"

"Well, don't then! You can leave!" He almost screams the words, pointing towards the door.

There's no way I'm leaving now. I'd not done right by Zane, but he's still my husband, and in some ways I still love him and want to make things right between us again, for our son's sake more than anything.

There's something I need to know though, so I ask, "Who was that blonde kissing you?" I hope I'm not going to regret the answer to that question when I hear his answer.

He doesn't respond straight away, and colour rises in his cheeks.

"No one," he mutters, turning away from my intense stare.

"Didn't look like no one Zane. She was kissing you back."

"What's it to you anyway?"

Why is this so hard? Maybe I don't want this?

"I was..um..hoping to get you to come home...make things better."

He doesn't say a word again, doesn't smile, just glares at me like he's pondering what I'm saying.

Grabbing our son by the waist, I holster him up to sit on the edge of the bed, before I bend down to him, and speak softly, "Say hello to your Dad, Zach."

Zach lets out a delightful giggle, clapping his hands before leaning closer to Zane on the bed with his arms outstretched. Zane doesn't move at all and the expression on his face remains unchanged.

I never should have left.

I'm thoroughly confused. Tears are stinging my eyes. I've really messed up and I'm not sure if I actually do want out of my marriage now, but it seems as though Zane does.

He finally breaks the silence, "Go and stay at my house. When I'm out we'll sort this mess out."

"Um, ok. But I can't stay long."

"Amy I don't care! Work it out!"

"Ok...I'll um see what I can do," I reply a little taken aback by his tone. He does raise his voice at times, especially when he's been drinking, so it shouldn't get to me, but it does.

Grabbing Zach off the bed, I leave the room, not saying anything to Zane or anyone else when I leave the hospital to go and find his house.

Kicking up the red dirt into my face makes it feels like I've entered hell. And maybe I have, because it seems as though my decision to stay this time—for Zach—is going to be literal hell on earth.

(45) Addison

Rushing out of the hospital room, again tears sting my eyes. It's crazy the amount of tears I've cried in the last few months, crazy the amount of tears I've cried because of Zane. It's true no man is worthy of your tears, but this time he's done nothing wrong to cause my tears.

He should be the one upset with me, not only for my constant rejection but for not letting him in, to allow him to open up to me about his wife and the real reason he's in Ridgehope.

But he blindsided me, confessing he's in love with me. Those words tugged at my heart and I'd desperately wanted to kiss him, but still I'm afraid of letting him in after he'd told me everything.

It's stupid, I want to be there for him, like he'd been for me, but something is still holding me back.

Kissing his cheek was meant to be a caring gesture, but as soon as he pulled my lips against his my insides melted. The way he kissed me showed that his confession was definitely true.

If we had not been interrupted I'd have kissed him harder and told him how I feel. My heart is pounding as hard as his was on the monitor screen.

But when his wife entered, clutching the hand of a little boy, my pounding heart sank to the floor. I couldn't look at him, didn't want to see the reaction to their presence on his face.

As per usual, I panicked, the tears increasing when I ran out the door, not looking back or ahead, on autopilot racing towards my office.

My hands over my face, just trusting my feet to take me away and I bump straight into a tall figure who comfortingly wraps his arms around me. I know as soon as his arms wrap around my body in a hug that it's Hunter.

Stepping back from his hug, I wipe my sleeve across my cheeks. He doesn't say a word, instead just looks at me like he's waiting for me to speak.

"What are you doing here Hunter?" I ask worriedly and through sobs.

"Savannah has just been admitted for preeclampsia."

A look of pain and confusion crosses his face.

"What seriously? Is she ok?"

"Yeah we just came in, and another doctor is just doing some tests. I just came to grab a drink."

"Oh um.."

There are no words to say. I've been so hung up on the fact of Savannah being pregnant, so jealous of what she has that I can't have and now she's back in the hospital with a serious medical condition. I'll have to get my head out of my arse, and be the doctor she needs me to be.

Hunter touches my arm, noticing my unease.

"Seriously Addison, are you ok? You look like you're going to pass out."

"No, I'm not ok...but I'm not going to pass out I promise."

"Are you sure? I can get you some water or something."

"I'm fine Hunter, please just go be with Savannah."

"Are you going to be ok?" He asks again, a firm tone to his voice.

"Yeah, thanks Hunter I will. Let me know if you need anything," I tell him, walking away and trying not to cry.

Savannah doesn't deserve this. After everything she's been through, she deserves happiness.

I can't say the same for myself. Not only had I lost Hunter, but I have a feeling that I may have lost Zane too. All because I was too afraid to give in to how he makes me feel, to afraid to put my heart out there, in case of heartbreak but it doesn't matter, because my heart is shattered anyway.

And there's only one person now who could put it back together.

(46) Hunter

Something has definitely changed with Addison. I can't quite put my finger on it. She seems to be closer to Zane, and I know about what had happened between her and Quentin.

Bumping into her in the hallway, seeing her in tears tugged at my heart and I had to hug her as a friend.

Surprisingly she didn't hug me back and didn't melt at my touch like she'd normally do, which definitely means something had changed.

I'm not sure if that means that she doesn't love me anymore or whether she's just accepted that I no longer love her.

Grabbing a coffee from the machine in the reception foyer, I head back to the room Savannah is in. The hospital sadly feels a bit like a second home for us, we've spent so much time there and now looking at Savannah in the bed as I sip my coffee, I know it's going to be just that again.

"Whats wrong baby?" I ask her, even though I know the answer.

"I have to stay here Hunter, until he's born."

"Oh, baby, that's no good."

"It's horrible Hunter. I hate being here!"

"I know, baby, I know, but we have to do whats best for our little boy."

"Yeah, but I...I'm only like thirty-two weeks Hunter. It could be weeks before he's born."

Pressing a kiss to her forehead I softly say, "He'll be here before we know it baby."

"I hope so," she muses softly, closing her eyes.

I down the rest of my coffee, dropping the cup absentmindedly on the floor. Brushing a hand against Savannah's cheek I lean closer to her and whisper to her, "I love you, Savannah and our baby boy."

Her eyes shoot open, gazing at me with longing in her eyes, like the very first day she'd seen me when she awoke in the hospital nearly a year ago.

"I love you too handsome."

"I love it when you call me that Savannah."

"You know it's true Hunter. I thought you were handsome the moment I first woke up in this hospital bed and looked at you."

"Oh, baby, thats so sweet. I thought you were gorgeous from the moment I found you in the farmhouse and when you opened your eyes and I saw the blue sparkle in them I knew I'd never met anyone as beautiful as you."

Tears are stinging her eyes, happy, emotional pregnancy tears.

"Hunter, you're making me cry," she says, giving me soft punch to the arm.

"Sorry baby, but it's true. No one is as beautiful as you," I muse, leaning closer to kiss the tears from her cheeks.

"Remember last time one of us was in a hospital bed?"

"Mmm...how could I forget?"

"Kiss me Hunter," she demands sweetly.

Scooting up the bed, trying not to get tangled in the monitor wires attached to her body, I press a soft kiss to her lips. Her hands wrap around my neck and she pulls me closer, entangling her fingers in my hair when she deepens the kiss by licking my lips with her tongue.

It drives me wild when she takes charge of a kiss, and I find myself moaning and breaking away breathless.

"Savannah, baby, I love it when you kiss me like that."

She lets out a delightful giggle, noticing the desire for her evident in my pants.

"Sorry, about that," she says laughing, pointing towards the front of my jeans.

Laughing I reply, "Its ok baby."

A cheeky smile spreads across her face, her eyes blinking furiously when she tries to fight the urge to close them.

"You need to get some sleep, baby. I'll come back first thing tomorrow once I sort some stuff out at home, ok?"

"Ok, baby," she mutters, her eyes closing as she slips into sleep.

Pressing a kiss to her forehead, I pick up my discarded coffee cup and leave the room to head back to the farm for the night.

I'd almost gone back to see if Addison was okay, but decided against it.

It isn't a long drive back to the farm, and despite the fact I've had a coffee sleep is definitely on my mind.

Doctor Attraction

Cranking the radio up loud, 'Kiss Somebody' comes blaring through my speakers, and in effort to keep awake I sing along, thinking back to my first kiss with Savannah.

The first kisses we'd shared made me long for her, and truly made me fall in love with her.

Honestly I'd loved her from that first day finding her unconscious in the farmhouse. Her beauty struck me, igniting a fire in my heart that only burnt harder when I finally kissed her, when I made love to her the first time I knew she was my everything and to think that from that first time together, joining us together we'd conceived our son.

It's truly amazing. Savannah is the person I'm meant to be with. I know that for certain, and reaching the farmhouse tonight I can't help but think of something my Mum had told Savannah.

'Mackenney men fall hard and fast for the woman they are meant to be with.'

And I had done just that, I'd fallen hard and fast for Savannah, but I love her more each day. She's my world, my everything and will soon be my wife.

It doesn't get much better.

Crawling into bed, after I stumble into the farmhouse exhausted, I pat the sheet next to me. "Come on Blitz, just for tonight buddy," I say to him, laughing at the eagerness of his wagging tail.

He jumps on the bed next to me and stroking his fur gently I let myself slip into sleep, to dream of Savannah.

(47) Addison

After Hunter left me I slowly walk back to my office, with a little more composure than before.

He'd always had a sweet way of making me feel better when I was upset, his caring nature extended to anyone, even me now when he probably hates me for all I put him through.

But being honest with myself, the love I have for him is less than before. When he hugged me, I hadn't wanted to melt into his embrace or pull him closer, nor kiss him.

My mind is replaying the kiss with Zane, the sweet kiss that had left me tingling all over and made me question my feelings.

Even Jett had sensed my feelings, but I still can't admit them to myself, let alone admit them to Zane.

I'm questioning myself now though, questioning how Zane feels about me too.

He'd confessed he's in love with me, but did nothing, said nothing when his wife walked in the room.

It literally yanked my heart out. My heart is shattered.

Grabbing my phone out of my desk drawer I type a message, hoping he still cares enough.

Addison: Hey are you busy tonight?
Quentin: kinda busy all weekend Addison
Addison: oh...I just wanted to go and get blind
Quentin: no can do...but why?
Addison: um...
Quentin: tell me Addison
Addison: Zane had a heart attack
Quentin: wtf! When?
Addison: yesterday...and he...

Doctor Attraction

Quentin: is he ok?

Addison: yes it was mild...but he told me he loves me

Quentin: and that's a bad thing?

Addison: I don't know...but he kissed me and his wife turned up

Quentin: shit...did you know he was married?

Addison: yeah but he said they were separated

Quentin: oh Addison I don't know what to say

Addison: I'm heartbroken Quentin

Quentin: why? Are you in love with him?

Addison: I don't know...but what does it matter...you don't want me anymore and he probably doesn't either

Quentin: I never said that Addison...but I'm kinda interested in someone else

Addison: :(but I'm happy for you...do I know her?

Quentin: it's Sam

Addison: the new cop?

Quentin: yeah...look Addison I gotta go...Sams coming over...but we can catch up soon...

Addison: Thanks Quentin xo

Quentin: no worries x

Putting my phone down on the table I sigh. Even Quentin is moving on and I'm still alone, wallowing in my own self pity. The fact I'd brought it upon myself doesn't make it any less painful. There's one last thing I need to do tonight before I head home, and I know it's going to shatter my broken heart even more.

Knocking on the door she doesn't respond. I enter, trying to not make any noise when I check her charts and the monitor with the heartbeats of her and the baby beeping on it. Stirring in her sleep, she mutters, *'no, don't...you'll hurt him.'* My heart definitely shatters, and I have to wake her.

Shaking her softly, I whisper, "Savannah you need to wake up."

Sitting bolt upright, she holds back a scream, looking at me worriedly. "I...uh...what."

Touching her arm, I softly say, "Its ok Savannah, I'm here. It was a dream."

She wipes a tear from her cheek, stammering, "Addison, it was...he was alive... and he..."

I sit on the bed next to her, tears stinging my own cheeks when I speak, "He's gone Savannah. Dante is gone. He can't hurt you or your baby."

"But it was so real...he was here...and..."

"Come here," I say, pulling her against me in a hug.

Since her baby shower, I can't hate her. In fact I've never hated her, and completely understand why she fell in love with Hunter.

Getting to know her more, I understand why Hunter had fallen for her too. She doesn't hold a grudge against anyone, and even after all she's been through with Dante she's still so caring and loving towards everyone she meets.

She could hate me, for being in love with Hunter too, but she treats me as a friend, not the enemy.

And now hearing her having nightmares about Dante really tugs at my heart.

"Do you want me to call Hunter?" I ask pulling back from hugging her.

"No, I don't want him to worry about me."

Her words break my heart more. "Savannah, he loves you."

"But these nightmares will break his heart."

"Yes, but only because they are breaking you Savannah."

"Look, how about I finish checking you and give him a call? Even if it's only to hear his voice?"

"Ok...I'd like that."

Checking things over again, she seems to be handling things ok, but squeezing the blood pressure sleeve tells me her blood pressure is still slightly elevated, from the preeclampsia as well as her nightmare.

"Well, Savannah, I'm not exactly happy about your blood pressure. But both your heartbeats are fine."

Tears are still stinging her eyes.

"Can you call Hunter now?"

Thankfully I'd slipped my phone into my bra, so extracting it I dial Hunter's number.

I don't expect him to even answer, seeing my name flashing on his screen, but he picks up almost straight away.

"Addison!" He screams into the phone, "Is Savannah ok?"

"Yes, she's fine but wanted to speak to you."
Handing the phone to Savannah I stand up from the bed and slip out the door.
I try not to listen to their conversation but find I can't help myself.
"I miss you baby."
"Yes, I'm ok...but I had a nightmare."
"It was...horrible."
"I know...I love you to Hunter."
I can only guess what he's saying to her on the other end of the phone, but her responses and the way her heartbeat steadies shows me that his comfort, just hearing his voice makes the pain disappear and the evidence of their love is as plain as day.
"Bye handsome," She says softly, dropping the phone on the bed next to her.
She looks at me sweetly when I come back into the room.
"Thank you Addison. I feel better."
"No worries. And Savannah?"
"Yeah?"
"I'm honestly really happy you and Hunter found each other."
"Oh Addison, that's really nice of you to say."
"You deserve to be loved by someone as special as Hunter."
"So do you...maybe Zane?"
"He told me loves me."
Her eyes light up and I smile.
"Yeah but I can't say it back...I don't know how I feel."
"Give him a chance. He's definitely smitten with you."
"I can't...his wife came back."
Her cheerful expression disappears, and her whole face scrunches when she speaks again, "He's married? I can't believe it."
"I know. I guess we just aren't meant to be either," I say sadly, the emotion of what I'm saying hitting me hard in the chest.
"Anyway, I need to be getting home. Get some rest."
Softly she grabs my hand. "I have a feeling that you're meant to be. It will work out."
"I hope so. I'll see you tomorrow. Goodnight, Savannah."

"Goodnight, Addison," She replies, as I'm leaving and closing the door behind me.

Hunter has definitely found his perfect woman; sweet, accepting and loving just like him.

I never deserved Hunter's love. And maybe I don't deserve love at all; doomed to be alone forever.

Walking out of the hospital my mind again wanders to Hunter mentioning about our families past. Something is still bugging me about it and I want answers, because now more than ever I need to move on, from Hunter, Quentin and sadly Zane. And running back to the city is not the answer, but finding out about my family's past is.

If only I knew where to start.

(48) Hunter

Savannah had to stay in the hospital, her blood pressure not stabilising and her legs were so swollen she couldn't move from the bed. I'd not been able to go in to see her as much as I'd wanted to and it was breaking my heart to see her in pain, but also bored out of her brains.

Walking into the room, I find her asleep, thrashing her arms about and screaming out, *'no, no Dante, no!'*

My heart shatters, that I wasn't here for her when she's caught up in another nightmare. She's been having them on and off for months since Dante's death, and it's usually when I've not been in bed with her, having needed to get up early to go out droving or when I'd come back late and she was already asleep. My heart shatters for her again, but also swells knowing that I'm her comfort and make her feel safe.

Dropping the flowers I'd brought for her at the end of the bed, I sit on the edge and brush her cheek with the back of my hand.

"Savannah, baby, I'm here. Wake up baby, you're safe."

Her eyes slowly open, and focus on me. "Oh Hunter...he...was...here."

"No baby...he wasn't. It was a dream," I sooth, bending down to hold her closer. Kissing her forehead I softly say, "Baby, I think you need to speak to someone about these nightmares."

"I'm scared Hunter."

"Why baby?"

"Maybe the last months are the dream...that he's not dead and is going to come back for me."

Tears sting my eyes. My heart is breaking for her, my beautiful fiancee. She's opened up about her past to me, let me in and has fallen in love with me, as I have with her, but even in death he's still plaguing her.

"Savannah, he's gone. That was not a dream. You're safe with me. I love you, and no one will ever hurt you again."

"I love you to Hunter, more than anything in this world."

"Oh, baby, thats so sweet. What did I do to deserve you?"

"You saved me Hunter."

Tears are dripping down my cheeks now, and she reaches up to wipe them away with her thumb, not saying a word. I lean closer to her again, and kiss her softly.

"I miss having you at home with me, baby."

"Me too, Hunter. This bed is like a plank of wood."

"I know, but hopefully you çan come home soon. Has the doctor been in today?"

"No, but I'm not sure who my doctor is. Addison was so good when I first came in, but now that Zane is back on deck from whatever he was away for, she keeps pawning my care off to him."

Grabbing the flowers, I hand them to her. "Sorry baby, these are for you. I'll go and see whats going on."

"Ok," she replies, sniffing the flowers and smiling.

I race down the hall to Addison's office, knocking hard on the door.

"Come in," she calls out.

The expression on her face is unreadable and her words are almost callous, "What can I do for you Hunter?"

"Are you Savannah's doctor?"

"No, Zane is. He's been back on deck for nearly a week, I've filled him in on Savannah's case."

"I'm sorry Addison, but I..."

"Hunter, I'm not her doctor. I have not been her doctor at any point of her pregnancy. Please go and speak to Zane if you need to know anything."

"Addison, is something wrong? Did something happen between you and Zane?"

"Please leave Hunter."

She turns her attention to her laptop, her eyes not looking at me when she told me to leave. Her constant change in attitude towards me has me throughly confused. I do as she asked, leaving her office to head back to Savannah, but I'm not going to let her insolence go unnoticed.

Even though I no longer love her, we have a past and I still care for her. Something is bothering her and I will find out what it is, even if that means telling her about our families past. I have my suspicions it has something to do with that too.

Walking back into Savannah's room, I find Zane fumbling with changing the bed pan and checking Savannah for bed sores.

"Zane, are you ok?"

"Yes, Mr Mackenney. Just doing my job."

He looks at me with disgust, as though I'm the rudest person on the planet.

"I'm perfectly capable of doing my job, Mr Mackenney. Please step back or leave the room for a moment whilst I finish up todays checks."

Anger rises in me. Everyone in this hospital at the moment seems to be on fucking edge, the air is thick with tension and it gives me a sensation like I'm being strangled. Winking at Savannah I leave the room, walking to reception to grab a coffee.

The nurse on duty at the reception desk takes one look at me and speaks with an apologetic tone, "Sorry Mr Mackenney, we are all out of coffee."

I grab my hair in a fist. "Fuck," I mutter under my breath, but she hears me.

"Excuse me Mr Mackenney, but that language is not welcome in here."

I look at her behind the glass of the nurse station, apologising, "I'm sorry, but I need a coffee so bad. The tension in this hospital is overwhelming."

"Yes, Mr Mackenney, things have not been right since Doctor Rivnay's heart attack, but I'm sure things will be back on track soon."

"I'm sorry what? Heart attack?"

"Yes, Mr Mackenney. Doctor Rivnay had a mild heart attack a few weeks ago."

I don't reply, instead my hands curl into fists as I race back to Savannah's room to confront him. There isn't really any reason for me to be angry at him, but I don't think he's really in the best medical condition to be looking after Savannah.

Entering the room though, he isn't there.

"Baby, did you know Doctor Rivnay had a heart attack a few weeks ago?"

"No!"

"Well, apparently he did, and I'm not sure I want him looking after you."

She pats the bed next to her and crossing the room I sit next to her again.

"It's fine Hunter. He's a good doctor. He's probably just a bit tired."

"I know baby. But I just want everything to be ok, for you and our little boy."

"Me to, Hunter. He actually just said that I might be having him sooner rather than later."

"Why is that baby?" I ask, brushing a stray hair from her cheek.

"My blood pressure is not stabilising and delivering him early is the best treatment for both of us."

"I just want you both safe and well."

"Me too, and I want out of this hell hole."

"I know Savannah, I know," I say, taking in a deep breath.

Leaning forward I kiss her lips, deeply and longingly, biting her bottom lip softly, causing a sweet whimper to escape her lips when she opens her mouth to kiss me deeper.

I give her my all with this kiss, knowing I can't come in for a couple of days and will miss her like hell.

Breathless I pull back. "Baby, I have to go, and I can't come in for a couple days. There's too much to do at home."

"Ok, baby. I'll miss you."

"Oh Savannah, I'll miss you to. I love you baby, so fucking much."

"I love you to Hunter Isaak Mackenney."

She winks at me, when she says Mackenney. I love hearing my full name roll of her tongue.

Not many people know my middle name, not even Addison and if she knows the secret of our family I think knowing my middle name would break her heart.

"Oh Savannah, I love hearing you say my full name."

"I'm excited to soon be Savannah Esme Mackenney," she says gleefully.

"Me to baby. I'm so glad you kept your middle name. I'm sure your Mum would be happy to see you moving on."

"She would have adored you Hunter."

"I know baby, I would have loved to meet her. Anyway I gotta get going."

Kissing her forehead I stand up. "Get some rest baby, I'll see you in a couple of days."

"Bye, Hunter. I love you!" she calls out to me, as I'm leaving.

Poking my head around the door for a moment, I tell her with a wink, "I love you to, Savannah Esme Mackenney."

Watching the sweet smile that spreads across her face makes my heart swell.

I can't wait until the day she will officially be Mrs Savannah Esme Mackenney, my wife and partner in everything. That's all I've ever wanted, a family of my own and a partner to live the life I love with me. There's no doubts in my mind that Savannah is the perfect one, the one I'm meant to be wlth.

Savannah Esme Galison is my world and soon my world will be filled with even more love, with the birth of my son.

He will make my life complete.

(49) Samantha

Even though Quentin's sweet gesture of the card and carnation had me excited, I didn't turn up to his house that night. It all seemed overwhelming, and I'm petrified that he wants more from me than I can give him, not knowing my past insecurities.

Avoiding him at work is a challenge. He looks over at my desk from the other side of the room, anger on his face, but also it looks as though he's heartbroken. It doesn't make sense as to why he'd be heartbroken over me not turning up. He doesn't feel the same way as I do; I'm sure of that, if nothing else. But as the weeks go on I feel terrible and I know I have to make it up to him.

Strolling up to his desk, my heart is pounding in my chest. I try desperately to compose myself, so I'm not a bumbling idiot.

Just say you're sorry Sam, you still like him, admit it, tell him.

Standing next to his desk, he doesn't even look up at me when he spits words out in anger, "What do you want Sam?"
"Um...to um...say I'm sorry."
He looks up at me, upset evident in his dark eyes. "Sorry? That's it," he replies, his words sounding rhetorical.

Come on Sam, be brave, use words, don't be a little girl now.

"Im really sorry Quentin, for not showing up to your house."
"Yeah, well I'm sorry I asked," he spits at me again, my heart breaking a little, tears stinging the corner of my eyes.
"I was scared Quentin."
He stands up then, his body so close to mine I could explode on the spot.

His gaze locks onto mine. "Scared? Of what? Me?" he asks with a softer tone than before.

"Yes, I was scared you wanted something I can't give you..." I pause, letting my words sink in, watching his eyes as my words hit him.

He runs a hand through his unruly hair. "Sam, I like you a lot. And I'm sorry if I was too forward...but I..." He stops mid sentence, still with his gaze on mine. His eyes appear to darken more, with lust maybe, and before I can even think of a word to say he smashes his lips on mine.

This kiss is more demanding than the ones at the pub. It's fierce, deep and consuming. He bites my lip and runs his tongue along my lip making me whimper at the contact, but also at the sheer pleasure of a kiss that has desire running through my body.

No one has ever kissed me like this, and I'm absolutely consumed by it, forgetting for a moment where we are, as I let him in more. Breathless he pulls back.

"Fuck I'm sorry Sam....I..."

Be brave Sam, make him want you.

"Quentin, that was some kiss."

Colour rises in his cheeks. "I'm sorry. I just really like you, but you have to know my past is a little darker than you think."

"Um...ok," I say, sucking in a deep breath and turning my eyes to the floor.

"Sam, please, say something else."

"I can't."

With a finger under my chin, he lifts my face to look into his eyes again. The lust is still evident, but there's something else.

"Tonight? Can you come over tonight?"

"Yes," I reply exhaling the breath I'd been holding in.

Before I turn to walk away he presses a kiss to my forehead and sits back down at his desk.

My heart is pounding, and I feel as though everyone in the police station is staring at us and had witnessed our hot kiss. My lips are still tingling from his kiss and my whole body is on fire with longing.

I can't help but wonder what he'd meant by his past being darker than I think. The words both scare and excite me. This time I'm going to squash my fear and give into how Quentin Mackenney makes me feel.

The feeling in my lower body is something I've never experienced before and I'm not sure what to make of it, only knowing it feels damn exciting and I'm ready to explore it with Quentin.

(50) Quentin

As crazy as it is for me I'm again feeling nervous at the prospect of seeing Sam. Kissing her at work was a little reckless, even for me, but the kiss had ignited something deeper for her.

It wasn't the usual kiss I'd share with anyone that wasn't Addison but it definitely made desire for her rise in me.

It's wrong to want to strip her of her innocence but I feel like I'm again craving that control from darker sides of life.

Everything that had happened with Savannah and finally being with Addison felt like a complete crazy whirlwind.

Holding my finger against the trigger of the gun when facing Dante, had brought the rush for control back. The darker desires I'd exhibited when in the city, from trying to block out not being able to be with Addison were threatening to surface again.

Having that power over inflicting pain and pleasure, having someone completely at my mercy had come to mind many times again since that day I had the power to end Dante's life.

I thought it was maybe because even though I had that power, holding the gun in my hands I couldn't exactly exert that control like I could in other parts of my life.

I'd never wanted that control with Addison, being with her was more emotional, giving her my heart instead of just fucking her.

Telling her it was the best sex of my life was true, but it was only because it was more than just sex to me. Her rejection crushed me, but I couldn't completely face letting her go and my stupid suggestion of being fuck buddies would have damn near ended me.

No way in hell could I be with her again physically and not fall apart emotionally.

A soft knock on the door startles me, even though I know it's going to be Sam. Tiberius races up to the door, behaving like a dog when he sits down on his butt, awaiting for the door to be opened.

Wiping my hands on my jeans, I walk to the door, swallowing hard when opening it I find Sam, wearing a floaty black mini skirt and strappy pink singlet that dips low at her bust. I can't help but stare and gape at her outfit choice. She's definitely innocent, but some of little things she does, whether conscious or not, make me think otherwise.

I don't want to take advantage of her at all, I like her, but she makes it damn difficult not to think of the most wicked, darker desires I've been accustomed to in my past.

She scuffs her feet on the doorstep, not able to meet my gaze when she speaks, "Hi Quentin."

"Hi Sam. You look gorgeous. Come in, dinner is nearly ready."

A sweet blush rises up her cheeks when she steps inside closing the door behind her and following me to the kitchen. Her trepidation at being in my house is evident when she takes in the surroundings. Tiberius is walking around her legs, trying to get her attention.

"You have a cat. He's cute."

"Yeah he is. A cheeky bugger though," I say picking him up and kissing his head, before holding him closer to her, "Tiberius, meet Samantha."

She ruffles the fur on this head, and his purr starts up like a tractor. A sweet smile spreads across her lips.

"He must like you. He hardly ever purrs," I tell her with a smile.

Putting him down on the floor I cross the kitchen to the sink to wash my hands, and to finish dinner. The silence in the room is killing me.

Pouring the egg and cheese mixture into the pan with the pasta and bacon I have to break the silence. "I hope you like Carbonara."

"Um, yes I do. It smells delicious."

"Thanks. I hope it tastes good," I say, giving it a final stir before piling it into two bowls. Carrying them over to the dining table I nod for her to follow and sit with me at the table.

She sits down, inhaling the pasta in her bowl, her eyes gazing at me when I sit across from her.

Picking up my fork, I twirl some spaghetti on it, before I speak, "I'm really glad you came tonight Sam."

"Me to," She says meekly, taking her fork out of her mouth after her first bite.

"Taste good?"

"Yes, it's delicious," She says innocently.

We eat in silence and my mind is wondering about tasting her, because watching her eat, watching her lick her lips in delight is driving me crazy.

Once her plate is empty, I speak, my voice laced with the lust I'm feeling, "Sorry but I don't have dessert. I was hoping to have..." I stop before the words can roll off my tongue.

Don't go there Quentin, you want those dark desires with her, you can't do that to her Quentin, look at how innocent she looks biting her lip.

"That's ok. I don't feel like dessert."

I stand up from the table grabbing our bowls to take to the kitchen. Dropping them in the sink, with my back turned I press my palms into the bench trying to not think about what I really want for dessert.

But my composure is broken when I hear her footsteps and voice behind me.

"Um about what you said the other day I um...I want to know what you meant."

Sighing I step closer to her on the other side of the island bench. She's biting her lip again.

"No, Sam. You don't want to know."

"Yes, I do Quentin. I like you, a lot."

"And I like you to Sam, which is why I can't tell you what I meant just yet."

"But you'll tell me?"

"Well, it would be easier to show you."

Her eyes are locked on mine now, sweet innocent lust evident in them. And when she speaks my desire for her peaks, "Then show me Quentin."

"Fuck Sam. Do you have any idea what you just asked me?"

"Um...yes..,no," She says biting hard on her lip, before licking them.

Without thinking I grab her tiny waist, forcing her body against mine, and forcefully smash my lips to hers. She whimpers softly when I bite her lower lip, pulling it back slightly in my teeth. I've needed this kiss, a fierce demanding you're mine kiss for too long. I lick her lips with my tongue, my lips still locked on hers.

I can feel her smile when she opens her mouth to let me in to lace my tongue with hers.

She moans against my mouth and my desire increases, my hardness pressing against her belly. Breathless she pulls back and I expect her to run straight out the door but instead she coos softly, "Um that was...um hot."

A blush rises up her cheeks and before I can think she returns the kiss, pushing her hips against mine.

Wrapping her arms around my neck and running her hands through my hair she kisses me back like I'd just kissed her, biting my lip and licking across my lips.

But I can't let her have all the control, so thrusting my tongue into her mouth I tease her.

Grabbing her butt, I squeeze hard and she lets out a delicious whimper when she breaks the kiss.

She squeals in delight when I grab her by the waist, hoisting her up to sit on the edge of the island bench. With my palms resting on both sides of her, I lock my gaze on hers, my face almost touching hers and whisper, "If you ever kiss me like that again Sam I won't be able to control myself."

She bites her lip and asks, "Why?"

"Because Sam...I can't tell you yet."

Whether conscious or not she moves on the bench, opening her legs a little wider causing the mini skirt to slide up her thighs. It's so wrong, but the look in her eyes makes me want her desperately.

I slide a hand up her thigh, loving the way her skin heats at my touch and her breathing becomes rapid.

Reaching the lace of her underwear, I run a finger across her body, feeling that the lace is soaked through with want. "Has anyone ever touched you here Sam?" I taunt, my lips so close to kissing her mouth.

Shockingly she says breathlessly, "Yes, but I...I haven't..."

"Oh fuck Sam, don't tell me you've never come before."

Shaking her head she bites her lip and I ask her, "Do you want me to make you come Sam?"

This time she nods and says raspily, "Yes Quentin."

The way she so innocently says my name makes me want her so much more.

"Not here," I tell her, grabbing her by the waist again and throwing her over my shoulder to carry her to my bedroom.

Resisting the urge to slap her butt and throw her down on my bed is hard, made even more difficult by the fact that she doesn't protest.

Gently I place her down on the bed, stretching over her to kiss her hard. Pulling back I ask her, "Are you ready Sam?"

She nods and I demand, "Tell me Sam."

"Yes."

Watching her eyes, I slip a hand underneath her mini skirt, hooking a finger into the elastic of her knickers and yanking them down her legs.

She gasps, clapping a hand to her mouth in shock when I run a finger across her skin, teasing her bud at first. Instantly her body responds, her desire increasing when I plunge my finger inside her.

"Do you like that Sam?"

"Mmmm..."

"Tell me Sam...tell me how it feels," I command.

"Good Quentin...oh."

God I want to make her feel better than good.

"Just good?" I murmur, taking my finger out of her body and licking her juice from it whilst I look down at her.

She licked her own lips, and it drives me crazy. I slam my lips against hers, biting her lips again, and thrusting my tongue between her lips so she can taste herself on my tongue.

Breaking the kiss, a little breathless I pull back, grabbing her mound in my palm.

"So tell me Sam, has anyone ever kissed you anywhere other than your lips?"

She shakes her head, and her cheeks flush.

She's so innocent but I can tell she knows what I mean and fuck do I want to ravage her until she comes.

Grabbing her arms, I put them behind her head, her hands together.

"Do not move your arms," I command her.

Bending down I start kissing up her legs to her thighs. Her skin heats at the sensation and my own body is screaming for release, but this is all about her. All about making her come.

Reaching her sex I lick slowly from the bottom to the top, biting her sensitive bud for a moment, before I plunge my tongue between her folds, tasting her sweet nectar.

Her hips buck against my face, her pleasure increasing.

"Oh Quentin...oh...fuck...oh!" she trills when I lick over her clit again.

"Come for me Sam!" I demand, licking her furiously.

Her breathing becomes laboured, her hips slow and her release over my face is hard and sweet.

I lay down beside her, grabbing her hands down and lacing her fingers with mine.

"That...was...so...aaa...amazing," She purrs, a little breathless.

"You taste so delicious Sam," I murmur back.

So delicious, I want to taste her again, but I can't do that to her yet.

She leans over to kiss me, a soft kiss in thanks. But kissing her like that will never be enough, and I curse myself for letting my darker self take over.

Pulling back I brush the hair away from her cheeks. "I'm sorry Sam. I shouldn't have gone there."

"Why? I..I loved it."

"I know that, but now I want so much more from you and I can't ask you for what I really need."

She sits up on the bed, wrapping her arms around herself, like she's seeking comfort.

"I...I can't do that...I...I'm a..."

She doesn't need to say the words for me to know what she means, and the dark desire is there, just like it had been the first time I'd stumbled into the nightclub in the city, when my own innocence had been stripped away and I'd first experienced pain and pleasure all rolled into one fucked up lust filled night.

"I know Sam and I'm sorry...please don't ask me again about what I want to do to you."

"Um...ok..I..." She bites her lip and I have to stop myself from grabbing her and kissing her senseless.

Instead I speak softly, "Come here."

I pull her close to me in a hug, lying close together on my bed.

"There is so much I want to do to you Sam, but I promise I won't go there until you're ready."

"Can I still kiss you?" She asks so innocently it makes my heart skip a beat.

"Of course," I reply kissing her cheek.

She presses her lips to mine, softly and sweetly. I let her kiss me slowly, letting her tame the desire to control her and take all of her.

Breaking away she speaks, her eyes locked on mine, "I like you Quentin...and thank you for making me come."

I laugh softly, at hearing her say, *come* like it's the most illicit word known to man.

"It was my pleasure Sam..and I like you too."

She sighs, nuzzling against my neck. I whisper in her ear, "I don't plan on it being the only time I make you come."

She giggles, and pulls away, looking straight at me when her face flushes.

"Hmm," She muses softly.

Standing up from the bed, I pick up her lacy knickers. Handing them to her she smiles, standing up and stepping into them before sliding them up her legs.

I have to bite my own lip to curb the desire to want to take them off and taste her again.

"I should probably get home. Thanks for the most amazing night."

"You're welcome gorgeous," I say, taking her hand to walk her out.

At the door she stretches up to press a soft kiss to my lips. I cup her cheeks in my palms, deepening the kiss goodbye, letting my lips linger on hers for a moment, before I pull back and open the door.

"Goodnight, Sam. See you at work on Monday."

"Goodnight, Quentin," She calls back walking away and blowing me a kiss.

Shutting the door behind me, I run my hands through my hair.

I have seriously fucked up.

I don't want to go back to that dark place, the place where I took what I wanted and never gave a shit about how much I hurt anyone. But there's something about Samantha that makes that desire come crashing into my mind and fighting it when she so innocently asks me to show her what I want to do her is damn hard and it's surely going to be my undoing.

God I want her, so fucking bad.

Right now only one other person could tame the darkness and I can't have her again, can't make sweet love to her to calm myself down.
This darkness is all her fault. I never would have gone down the forbidden path if only she loved me back.

(51) Savannah

Being in the hospital for weeks has been hell. The only thing that made it bearable was when Hunter came in, showering me with his sweet affection and doting on me.

Everyday he shows me how much he loves me, and I honestly fall more in love with him everyday as well. I've never felt happier and the impending arrival of our son is filling me with even more love.

Thinking back to our first night together, after Hunter proposed I can't help but smile widely, knowing that the love between us, in finally being together conceived our son. My heart pounds just thinking about it, and cramps surge through my stomach. Afraid it's too early I slam a fist against the call button next to the bed.

Moments later Addison comes rushing into the room. I take a deep breath, waiting for her to speak.

"Savannah, whats wrong?" she asks, her eyes scanning the heart monitor.

"I'm having cramps."

"How strong are they?"

"Killer!" I reply, practically screaming the word and breathing hard when a particularly strong cramp surges through me. I feel panic rising in my chest, because it's the same feeling as my miscarriage and I'm scared.

"Savannah, you need to slow your breathing. I think you may be in labour."

"What? No! I can't be! It's too early!" I wail, the panic filling me.

"No, Savannah. You'll be fine. You're thirty-six weeks, so a little early but fine."

"Are you sure? I don't want to lose him."

"To be honest, delivering early with your Preeclampsia is not actually a bad thing."

I'm a little shocked, but remember Doctor Rivnay telling me a few weeks earlier that I was probably going to have him early, so I try to breath deeply to calm myself.

"I'm just going to check your cervix to see if you're dilating. Is that ok?"

I nod, and she lifts the sheet back and my nightgown up. I feel a little self conscious that I'm not wearing underwear, but I'd run out of clean ones and forgotten to ask Hunter to bring me some.

Addison doesn't notice, looking me over and checking my cervix with her gloved finger.

"I think you're about four centimetres, so a little way to go. And it appears that your waters haven't broken yet."

"Oh, so should I contact Hunter?"

"Thats up to you. I'll let Doctor Rivnay know your progress as he's your doctor."

"Um ok, thanks Addison. Is he not here now?"

"No, he'll be in later, so he'll probably be on duty when you deliver."

She leaves the room, and I grab my phone from the nightstand beside me to text Hunter.

Savannah: hey handsome. having cramps. our son might be coming soon
Hunter: hey beautiful. Thats good yeah?
Savannah: yeah but he's early and i'm scared. i need you
Hunter: it will be fine. I'll be there asap
Savannah: don't rush. my water hasn't broken yet

Waiting for his reply, I feel a gush of liquid and curse out loud, pressing the call button again.

Hunter: ok baby. i'll be there soon
Savannah: um...I think they just broke
Hunter: fuck baby...Ill leave in 10...love you xx
Savannah: love you too Hunter xx

Addison comes rushing back in.

"My water just broke," I acknowledge, looking down to the soaked bed.

"Oh," she starts, "I'll get things sorted for delivery. Hows the contractions?"

"Um...ok...but some pain relief might be good."

"I'll get the gas and air sorted. Did you contact Hunter?" she asks, pain in her voice.

"Yes, he'll be here soon." I gasp, a strong contraction hitting me.

"You ok?" Addison asks.

"Yeah, good, but the contractions are hitting hard now."

"You'll be meeting your little boy soon."

She leaves the room again, coming back with a wheelchair. She unhooks the monitors attached to my arms and helps me into the wheelchair before taking me to a rather large room near the emergency department that has a large bed with stirrups at the end.

The same monitors from the other room are in this one and without speaking Addison hooks me up to them. I sigh seeing my son's heartbeat on the monitor screen. It's truly exciting that he'll soon be in my arms.

"Get some rest if you can. I don't believe your labour will be long."

I close my eyes, concentrating on my breathing, in and out. I'm sure the next time I open them I will be about to give birth and my heart surges with love.

❧

"Savannah, baby, wake up. I'm here, baby," a familiar voice breaks into my dream.

My eyes shoot open, the moment those words hit my mind. Hunter has arrived, and seeing him in the room a smile spreads across my face.

"Hey, you're here."

"Yeah, baby, I'm here. How are you doing?" he asks, sitting on the edge of the bed, taking my hand in his.

"Ok, the pain's not too bad. I'm sure Addison will be in to check me again soon."

"Sorry I took so long to get here. The ute got a flat on the way." He yawns.

"I'm glad you're here."

"Awww, baby, me too," he coos, pressing a kiss to my forehead.

"Hunter?"

"Yeah, baby?"

"I can't believe we're going to meet our son soon."

"I know, I bet he's going to be as gorgeous as his mother."

My heart swells with love.

What did I do to deserve this amazing man? To feel such love and happiness?

"I think he'll be as handsome as his father."
Hunter laughs softly, bending down to kiss my lips so sweetly and lovingly I think my heart is going to burst.
"I love it when you call me handsome, Savannah."
I laugh then, poking his chest in jest. "I love you, Hunter."
"I love you, Savannah," he replies.
A strong contraction grips me and I squeeze Hunter's hand in mine.
"Ok baby?" he asks.
"Yes, but that was really painful."
He reaches beside the bed and presses the call button.

Minutes later Addison comes into the room. She doesn't even acknowledge Hunter and I'm a little upset at her insolence, but I don't really have time to think much of it, as another contraction grips me.
She doesn't even say anything until after she checks my cervix again.
"Well, you're at eight centimetres now Savannah. You're a serious trooper to get this far without pain relief."
I've been through a lot of pain before. This pain is nothing compared to that, and the fact it means I'm closer to meeting my son makes it bearable.
Still I ask, "Can I have some pain relief?"
"Well, it's a little late for an epidural, but if you..."
I cut her off, "Thats ok. I'll get through it."
"Ok, I'll come back soon to check on you. Press the call button if anything changes."
And with that she leaves the room.

∂⊸

Hunter has stayed in the room, sitting in the chair by the bed. We talked about getting home and showing our son his nursery and how much Blitz is going to love his little brother. I'm growing anxious with waiting to meet him.
"Hunter, um...I...think I need to push," I speculate.

"Wait baby, hang on. Just breathe," he reassures me, again pressing the call button.

I'm hoping Doctor Rivnay would be on duty by now, but instead Addison comes into the room. And I scream out, "I need to push!"

"Ok," she says, checking my cervix again, "Yes you're fully dilated. It's time to meet your son."

"Oh shit, it hurts!" I wail, hot tears streaking my cheeks.

Her eyes dart to Hunter and then back to me. Taking a deep breath in, like she's trying to suck up her feelings she says, "Ok Savannah, take a deep breath and with the next contraction I want you to push hard down into your bottom."

"Ok...I...can..do..that, " I say inhaling in and out, looking at Hunter and squeezing his hand tightly.

A strong contraction hits and all I can hear is Addison's voice, "Push, Savannah, push."

Pushing down hard I gasp, the burning sensation of his head crowning hitting me like a knife.

"Do you want to see his head?" she asks, not directly to me but with her eyes gazing at Hunter. He looks down at to the edge of the bed, smiling when he says, "Baby, I can see his head!"

"Ok Savannah, breath, and just a few more pushes and he'll be here."

"Oh fuck it hurts!" I cry out, the next contraction overcoming me.

"Good, Savannah, just one push and you'll be a mum."

My heart is pounding, sweat dripping down my forehead.

"Push hard Savannah," she insists.

A smile spreads across her face and Hunter's.

"Congrats he's gorgeous!" she coos, cradling him in her arms.

My heart instantly swells with love like I've never felt before. I even feel love for Addison in that moment, when she turns to look at Hunter, grabbing the scissors and clamp.

"Would you like to cut the cord Hunter?" she asks.

He smiles, taking the scissors and cutting through the umbilical cord with ease.

Addison takes our son away to wipe him down and check him. He's early so a few more tests have be completed by the nurses who came into the room.

Hunter looks down at me, again taking my hand in his.

"You did so good baby."

Our son is brought back over, and placed against my chest for skin to skin contact. Hunter kisses my forehead, and the forehead of our son.

"I love you Hunter."

"I love you too Savannah, and I love my son too."

Hearing him say, 'my son' makes my heart pound and the most perfect name comes into my head.

"How about River?" I suggest.

"Thats perfect baby!" Hunter beams, "River Alexander Mackenney."

Again my heart swells, it's the perfect name for our son. "Oh Hunter seriously your grandfather's name?"

"Yeah it's perfect for him," he proclaims, kissing River's forehead again, and touching his perfect little fist.

I can't help but glance at Addison. She hasn't said anything, but tears are evident on her cheeks. I start to say something to her, but she rushes out of the room, the tears taking over.

A couple of nurses come in, rushing around us to organise things because of River's arrival early arrival. They fuss around me as well, to help with delivering the placenta and ensuring I don't lose too much blood.

Hunter kisses my forehead again. "I'm going to go and speak to Addison about what we talked about, ok baby?"

"Ok Hunter," I reply, as he walks out of the room.

I look down at my son against my chest. He's absolutely perfect.

(52) Addison

The emotions from just helping Savannah give birth to the most gorgeous baby I've ever seen hit hard, the tears breaking through the moment I hand him to Savannah for skin to skin contact.

She looks at me smiling and I can't take it. Rushing out of the room, I race to my office, slamming the door behind me. I try to focus on my own breathing, to calm the pounding of my heart and stop the tears from falling.

Sitting in my chair, my head in my hands, I decide to just let the tears fall.

Barely a few minutes have gone by when someone knocks on my door. There's no way I want to speak to anyone right now. I want to just revel in my own self pity, so spit loudly, "Go away!"

The person knocking doesn't listen, and when he enters the room it makes sense. Even though I don't want to speak to, or see anyone when he enters the room with the biggest grin on his face I can't help but smile.

Sucking it up I speak, "Congratulations, he's gorgeous Hunter!"

"Thank you Addison," he says, walking closer to my desk.

Still I have tears in my eyes and find myself sobbing again, my words muffled, "Have you chosen a name?"

"Yeah, we have. It's River Alexander Mackenney."

The tears that are again threatening break through. "Oh Hunter! Your grandfathers' name."

"Yeah, but Addison please tell me you're ok? Something's up with you."

He sits on the chair in front of the desk before he speaks again, "Please, talk to me as a friend Addison." He reaches a hand forward and touches mine with the back of his. It's a sweet comforting gesture.

"Well, I um...thought I was um...feeling something for Zane, but then his wife turned up and now your baby is here...I don't know...I'm just confused."

"Thats understandable...but you need some time out. Things have definitely been crazy since you came back to Ridgehope," he says as though he's the wisest person ever.

I know I have to open up to Hunter. It's the only way I'm ever going to move on.

"Yeah, you're right...but um Hunter can I tell you why I really rejected your proposal?"

"You don't have to Addison. It's in the past."

Shaking my head, I declare, "No I want to."

He doesn't reply, so I take a deep breath before I speak, "I can't get pregnant."

He looks at me with so much pain in his dark blue eyes my heart lurches in my chest when I continue, "Well not can't but it's highly unlikely."

"What Addi? I'm so sorry, I just can't believe it."

"Yeah, and I wanted my love for you to be enough but I knew how much you wanted a family."

"And then Savannah came into your life and she got pregnant."

"Oh Addi, I'm sorry," he soothes with a sweet tone in his voice.

"I just got jealous and I've fucked everything up!"

"You haven't Addison."

"I'm sorry Hunter, for everything."

"You don't have to say sorry for anything Addison."

"Yes, I do, I'm still in love with you Hunter."

He sighs. "You can't help who you fall in love with Addi," he says, taking a deep breath before he continues, "You'll find your someone."

"I hoped that was you," I remark.

"I've never been the right guy for you Addison."

"I know," I start, finding it freeing to admit it to myself, "but it doesn't mean I don't love you."

He doesn't respond for a minute, and he's looking at me like he doesn't know what to say.

"Addison, can I ask you something? You can say no."

"Yeah, sure Hunter," I reply, a little trepidatious.

"Will you be godmother to River?"

A smile spreads across my face. I'm truly touched.

"I'd love to!" I exclaim.

Hunter's grin at my response is delightful.

"Will you come back to meet him officially?"

"Sure," I say standing up as he does to follow him back to the delivery room.

River isn't my son, and isn't my baby with Hunter, but he's Hunter's son and being a part of his life will be more than amazing. No doubt it will be hard, but even though I can never be with Hunter no matter how much I love him, I never want to not have in my life and I'm going to shower his gorgeous son River with all the love I feel for his father. It's the least I can do.

(53) Hunter

Witnessing the birth of your child really is nothing short of a miracle. Little River is the most precious gift, a true miracle as his arrival into the world at thirty-six weeks is a little early, but I have no doubts he's going to be a damn fighter.

Returning back to the room with Addison I smile watching Savannah holding our son against her chest. The love I feel for her is multiplied a hundred times after she'd given birth to our son, with no pain relief.

She's so strong, a fighter in her own right. She's been through so much horrible pain, that she grinned and bared the pain of giving birth, happy to give into it as she knew the pain, however unbearable was going to bring us so much joy.

My world feels so much bigger, and so does my heart.

Addison follows me tentatively into the room, stopping at the foot of the bed.

"Do you want to hold him?" I ask her, smiling.

"Oh Hunter, I don't know if I can."

I can see her heart is breaking, but I also know Addison and it's clear she wants to hold River in her arms. Bending down to Savannah I kiss her lips softly.

"You did so good baby, he's perfect."

Taking him in my own embrace, lifting him against my chest and patting his soft bare bottom, I rock him for a moment, sniffing his head and inhaling the sweet baby smell.

It feels so surreal to have him my arms. Addison is actually smiling, looking at me holding him, and it both makes my heart swell with love and break into pieces at the same time.

Gently I hand him to her. She cradles him, grabbing his little fist in her palms. He wraps it around her finger and I can't help but smile. There's so much love in the room, so much love focused on the most perfect little boy who is no doubt going to be spoilt rotten.

Addison crosses the room, placing River in the plastic crib next to Savannah. Savannah smiles at her. "Thanks for ensuring he arrived safely," She says, touching Addison's arm.

"I was just doing my job Savannah."
Savannah just smiles and I reply, "We truly appreciate it Addison."
We're all silent a moment, soaking in the love in the room. I have to break the silence. "So baby, I guess it's only wedding planning now huh"
Savannah laughs. "Let me get used to being a Mum first."
"Yeah I know baby. I can't believe I'm a dad."
Addison is about to leave the room, hearing my comment but she turns back and says softly as she touches my arm, "You'll be the best Dad Hunter."
Her sweet words make my heart pound. "Thanks Addi, that means a lot."
She laughs sweetly. "What's with you calling me Addi again?"
Looking across at Savannah, she nods at me and smiles, urging me to tell Addison what we'd talked about when discussing asking her about being a godmother to River.
"I just want us to be friends again."
"I'd like that Hunt," She says happily, using my nickname too.
I pull her to me in a friendly hug, noticing that even though she wraps her arms around me to hug me back, she doesn't melt against me like she used to.
It seems as though she's another step closer to moving on and I'm truly glad.
We are not meant to be together, I know that now. I'm not sure as to why, but I know it's the case.
Pulling away from hugging her I laugh, smiling as I look at her and across to Savannah before I speak, "It's funny how things turn out for the best."
"Yeah they do," Addison replies, before she excuses herself.
Again I kiss Savannah softly.
"Thank you baby," I muse, sitting on the edge of the bed next to her.
"For what?" She queries.
"Loving me. And for giving me my son."
"You're welcome Hunter," she starts with a sweet giggle, "and thank you for being you."
A full grin spreads across my cheeks at her words, a blush rising up my face.
"I love you Savannah, more than I can ever begin to tell you."
Her response is not one of words. Sitting up she wraps her arms around my neck, entangling her fingers in my hair, pressing her lips to mine in a demanding kiss, showing me how she loves me as desperately as I love her.

Making her my wife is now the only thing that is going to make my life better and I can't wait for the day when we make the declaration of *'I do'* because I do with all my heart.

(54) Savannah

Leaving River in the hospital to head home after a few days is torture. His precious body is still too weak to not be in the hospital after his early arrival. Saying goodbye he grabbed my finger in his tiny fist and it both made my heart swell and break at the same time.

Hunter comes up behind me, wrapping his arms around my waist, and whispering in my ear, "Baby, we'll be able to take him home soon."

I turn in his arms, pressing my head against his chest, concentrating on his heartbeat. Looking up at him I kiss him softly.

"I know Hunter, but seeing him like this, in here and the thought of leaving him here breaks my heart."

"Mine too baby, but he needs to gain some strength before we can take him home."

"Yeah I know," is all I can manage to say as tears are beginning to sting my eyes. Taking a step back from Hunter, I press a soft kiss to River's little hand and start towards the door.

Hunter calls after me, "Savannah, baby, wait!"

He runs to me, grabbing my hand, holding it in his and wiping away the tears on my cheek with his other hand. "He's going to be fine Savannah. Addison will make sure of it."

"I'm just scared for him Hunter. He's going to be all alone in here."

He pulls me into a hug again, softly speaking sweet words, "Oh baby, he's not alone. Addison and all the nurses will be by his side around the clock."

He kisses my hair lightly and I let my body relax and melt into his chest.

We stand there for a minute or so before Hunter speaks, "Are you ready to go home baby?"

"I guess so. I just wish we could be taking River home with us today."

"Me too baby," he says encouragingly as he grabs my hand in his and leads me out of the hospital.

As we walk out the doors he says with the same encouraging tone, "Hopefully next time we walk out these doors, we'll have our precious baby boy in our arms."

I smile at him, sliding into the passenger seat of the ute.
"Um Hunter," I start, biting my lip a thought comes to mind, "How are we actually going to take him home? We can't put the car seat in here."
He laughs reversing out of the hospital car park.
"Yes, baby, you're right."
"So what are we going to do?" I ask, feeling stupid.
"Baby, I have another car you know. I just haven't driven it for a while."
"What? Does it even run?"
"Of course baby. It's not an old piece of junk. It was Mum's actually.
"Oh ok," I reply, not really knowing what else to say.
Hunter clearly senses my unease, resting a hand on my thigh and squeezing it when he says, "If it makes you feel better baby, I'll check it out and make sure it's running perfectly the minute we get home."
"Thank you Hunter. I would love that and I love you."
"No worries, baby and I love you too."

We pull up to the farm not long after and after I've jumped out to close the gate, Hunter drives up to shed opposite the farmhouse. He gets out of the ute and slides the shed door across to reveal a fairly new white Toyota Corolla. Walking around to the drivers side, he opens the door and slides into the seat, turning the key in the ignition. It makes an odd clicking sound, like the engine can't start.
"The batteries flat," Hunter announces, jumping out and crossing to the other side of the shed to grab the jumper leads. I watch as he connects the leads to the battery terminals after he's started the ute back up. He lets the ute run for a moment before he again turns the ignition key to start the Corolla. The engine rumbles on and I let out a breath I didn't realise I was holding.
Hunter disconnects the jumper leads, and lets the Corolla engine idle a bit to charge the battery.

After turning the engine off, he pulls the key from the ignition and holds the key up to me.

"All yours now baby," he teases.

"Thank you," I say sweetly.

"We better get that car seat in the back," he says when we walk towards the farmhouse, "I've heard they are near impossible."

"Yeah me too," I reply with a laugh, stepping up on the verandah to be greeted by an excited Blitz.

"Hey, buddy," I coo at him, patting his head. He sniffs me hard, sensing that something is different. He'd been so attentive and loving towards me whilst I was pregnant that it made me love him so much more.

Hunter and his dog are both gorgeous. It would be almost impossible to not have fallen in love with them both.

Bending down to Blitz I speak softly, "He'll be home soon, buddy."

He barks in response and I wrap my arms around his furry body. Only bringing our son home will make things complete now, as everything else is more than perfect.

ॐ

A month later

Much to my annoyance we'd walked out of the hospital a number of times without our little boy, but a month has gone by and he's as strong as he could be. Hunter had successfully installed the car seat and the car had not skipped a beat since he'd fired it up a month ago. I'd loved having a car back, the freedom it gave me when Hunter wasn't home was great.

With Hunter out in the paddocks for the day, I decide it's time to get out on my own. I drive into town and park outside the supermarket.

Sighing I think back to that horrible day when Dante had found me. I can still hear his voice in my head, and the pain stabs my body just at the thought of what he did to me that day.

But now nearly a year down the line, he's gone, hopefully a lot further down than six feet in the fiery pits of hell.

Taking deep breaths in and out, I turn the ignition off, grab the key out and I open the car door and cross the footpath to walk into the supermarket.

Further thoughts flash in my mind once I get inside the supermarket.

The checkout girl smiles at me when she speaks, "Hi Miss."

"Hi Annie," I say tentatively, focusing on her name badge.

When I grab a basket she leaves the side of her register and comes over to me. I feel a little scared, but she seems friendly enough, just as she was on that horrible day.

Lightly she touches my arm, the recollection of who I am hitting her.

"I'm sorry I didn't do anything that day," she says apologetically.

Smiling at her, I reply, "You weren't to know. It wasn't your fault."

"Thanks," she says, "I just feel so bad, after I found about what happened from my Dad."

"Your Dad?" I query.

"Yeah, the Sergeant."

"Oh ok, makes sense now."

"Yeah, can I help you find anything?"

"I'll be fine thanks Annie. And my name is Savannah," I tell her.

"Nice to meet you Savannah," she replies sweetly.

"You too," I reply with a laugh.

She turns to go back to the register, and suddenly lets out an excited giggle, before she turns back to me for a moment. "Is it true you're marrying Hunter Mackenney?" she asks, a wide grin on her face.

"Yeah I am."

"You're so lucky. He's gorgeous," she squeals.

"You've got that right," I reply, again laughing, heading down the small aisles to grab the groceries I need.

Stepping up to the register, Annie can't meet my eyes.

"Are you thinking about Hunter?" I ask.

"Yeah, kinda silly for me to have a crush on him, I know."

"No, it's not. I get it completely."

She starts scanning my groceries.

"I guess I can't fantasise about kissing him now. I bet he's an awesome kisser," she says so innocently.

"Oh, Annie. You have no idea."
I feel a little sorry for her. She can't be any older than eighteen and has obviously been crushing on Hunter for a while. I can't blame her for feeling something for my gorgeous fiancee. It's kinda sweet.
"I'm sure there's some nice boys your age," I suggest.
"Yeah, there is one boy I kinda think is ok," she says, blushing.
"I'm sure he's great if you like him."
She smiles widely and I know Hunter is no longer on her mind.
"That will be twenty-five dollars. Cash or card?" she asks, back to business.
"Cash," I say, handing her two notes from my purse and grabbing my bags of groceries.

❧

Walking out of the hospital this time, a month later with River is the most amazing feeling. I feel absolutely giddy with excitement and love. Hunter helps me strap River into the carseat, before we both get into car.
I smile at Hunter as he drives us home and I decide to tease him with the information I'd found out at the supermarket.
"Hey baby, you know Annie from the supermarket?"
'Yeah, Sarge's daughter."
"She has a mega crush on you!"I jeer at him.
"Oh come on baby, seriously?"
"Its true Hunter. She told me the other day when I was in the supermarket."
Laughing he says, "Well I'd never go there, one for obvious reasons she's like eighteen and plus I only have eyes for one woman."
He grabs my hand, pressing a kiss to it.
"She said I was so lucky to be marrying you."
A full dimpled smile spreads across his face. "I'm the lucky one baby."
We pull up to the farm gate, and Hunter jumps out to unlatch the gate. I look back towards the back seat at River. He's just so precious.
Pulling up to the house I'm out of the car almost immediately, and fumble to get River out of the carseat.

Cradling him in my arms I step up onto the verandah. Blitz lets out an excited bark in greeting. I sense when Hunter steps up behind me. We both bend down to Blitz's level and I say to him, "Blitz meet your baby brother, River."
He licks River's cheek, a big sloppy dog kiss that makes River screw up his little face in disgust.
Standing up I look at Hunter, and smile back at him, seeing the full dimpled smile on his face.
Everything is perfect, and will only be made more than perfect when I become Mrs Savannah Mackenney. I have no doubts that Hunter is going to be the perfect husband.

(55) Zane

The last few months just seemed to pass by in a blur. I've not spoken to Addison since waking up after my heart attack and confessing I'm in love with her.
I've seen her at work, but she'd constantly given me the cold shoulder, refusing to look at me, let alone work with me. And it hurts like hell.
The hurt is made even more difficult as I have had no chance to even think about trying to approach Addison when Amy has decided she wants to play happy family.
I'd much rather see her on her arse in the red dirt than let her into my house like I did a few months earlier, but despite her initial reaction when I'd fallen victim to my self inflicted illness this time she seemed to genuinely care and wanted to stick around. Getting to know my son is a bonus, but even his cuteness can't quell the emptiness I'm feeling.
My whole body is aching for Addison, my heart aching the most. I just can't believe that after all these months, and the kisses we've shared that she could feel nothing for me.
There's been something between us from the first day I'd walked into Ridgehope hospital, but I'd never thought the connection between us would be so volatile. Her constant rejection of me has driven me crazy with want, which hasn't helped, but every time she kisses me and lets her guard down the connection between us has grown stronger. There's no way, other than being with her completely that's going to get her to open up to loving me as much I love her.
Amy is driving me a bad kind of crazy though, being fussy and needy, telling me take my insulin and cooking meals that taste like cardboard, as well as trying to sleep with me, in both the literal and sexual sense.
I really just want her to rack off, as I know now that the moment she walked out on me after I first ended up in the hospital I'd no longer loved her.
She's still attractive, but now comparing her to Addison I can't say I find Amy beautiful anymore.
She's sitting on the couch, watching kids cartoons with Zach giggling beside her.

I hand her one of the coffees I'm holding and she smiles, biting one corner of her lip.

"Zane, we need to talk."

"I've got nothing to say to you Amy."

"Don't be like that Zane. I'm trying to make an effort."

I sit on the couch next to her, clutching my coffee cup and sipping it slowly.

"You've been so distant since you got out of the hospital."

"I was happy Amy. I didn't tell you come here."

"Happy, really Zane?"

"Yes, I was!" I stammer getting up from the couch. The truth is I'm not happy and it has nothing to do with Amy, but Addison.

I start to walk back to the kitchen, wanting to escape from the conversation.

The divorce papers are still on the island bench where I'd first left them and I've not touched them or looked at them since the day I'd opened them.

Amy has entered the kitchen, dropping her empty coffee cup in the sink with mine.

The silence is deafening and I'm contemplating heading out for a run to escape and running to Addison's door.

But Amy grabs my arm, a look on her face that is unrecognisable.

"Don't you love me anymore Zane?" she stutters, unsure, as though she's truly worried about my answer. I'm a little shocked that she's actually showing genuine feelings, but it's too little too late.

"No, I don't."

"But Zane...I..." she stutters again.

"No, Amy! I think I've not been in love with you since you left me," I declare, feeling like a weight has lifted off my shoulders and my heart.

Amy finds her voice then, as my words hit her, and she asks, "And that woman you were kissing, are you in love with her?"

I ponder her question a moment, watching her thinking about what I'm going to say. But I'm only torturing her, the answer could have rolled off my tongue the second she shut her mouth.

"Yes, I am," I declare, my heart pounding as thoughts of Addison come to mind.

Amy is angry at me. She balls her hands into fists, as though she's fighting the urge to slap me.

"Seriously Zane! Why'd I waste my fucking time?" she bellows, her words causing spit to fly in my direction.

Wiping a hand across my face, I spit back at her, "I don't know Amy."

Turning away from her I grab the divorce papers, flipping straight to the last page where I have to sign.

Yanking the drawer of the island bench open forcefully I search through the paper and other random junk for a pen. Finding a black pen, I scribble my signature above my name, before flipping the pages back. Scrunching them a little in my hand I shove them against her chest.

"Here take them! And fuck off out of my life!" I bellow at her raising my voice so much Zach cries.

I feel a pang of guilt, a sense of loss that I've just found out about him and now I'm going to lose him, but if the only way I can see him is to have Amy around then I'll have to live with not seeing him, no matter how much it will hurt.

Amy is clutching the divorce papers against her chest, her arms folded across them like they are precious. Tears are stinging her eyes.

"But I...Zane I..." she protests, through sobs, acting as though she's trying to get me to care when my care factor is zero, absolute zero. She didn't care about me when I'd needed her, and chose to walk out of my life.

"I don't want you here Amy! So just fucking leave!" I demand loudly, anger rising even more when she starts to cry, turning away from me.

My feet are frozen to the floor, and I turn my head watching her as she walks down the hallway to collect her luggage from the guest bedroom.

Before she returns I cross the room to Zach, kneeling beside the couch and hugging him. I whisper to him, "Bye son. I'm sorry."

He coos, baby talks back at me.

Amy enters the room, still visibly crying, wheeling the suitcase behind her. Standing up I step back from the couch, and she scoops Zach up, holding him against her hip.

Without saying a word she walks slowly to the front door, letting go of the suitcase a moment to open the door. Zach waves with his tiny hand at me, taking a piece of my broken heart with him when they both walk out the door and it slams shut behind them.

Caz May

Before I'd found out about Zach I'd never thought about having kids, and after what Addison had told me about her history I'd started to resign myself to the fact that as long as I loved her, I'd not be a father. But I am and watching my ex-wife walk out the door with my son breaks my heart into pieces.

Pieces that I want Addison to mend, even though she can't. I'm not a religious person, but I'm about to start praying for a miracle because now more than ever I want to be a father and want Addison by my side in that journey.

Miracles happen everyday in a hospital, so I desperately hope for my hearts sake that I get my very own miracle.

(56) Addison

It has been insanely difficult to avoid Zane for the past few months since his heart attack and the untimely entrance of his wife. I'd come so close to confessing my feelings for him, but in some ways I'm glad I haven't said anything as he's clearly going back to his wife and nothing is ever going to happen between us again.

My heart is breaking, and it's stupid. I'm not in love with him, and despite his admission of being in love with me I'm not sure I can ever believe him.

He'd not defended me, not said a word to his wife about who I am, after all the kisses we've shared in the past months.

Admittedly, even though I've started to let go, I still love Hunter. There's no way I'll ever not love him. Something has changed though, it's almost a different kind of love between us, and I don't feel attracted to him in the same way I had before.

Now sitting across from Savannah at the kitchen table of their farmhouse, I watch her looking at Hunter and Quentin talking in the lounge room.

The love evident in her eyes is endearing. Hunter catches her staring, and smiles sweetly at her, his eyes evident of the love he has for her. It could be a case of one big happy family, if I was with Quentin, but I can't make myself feel that way about him, no matter how much it makes sense.

He's even started to move on with Samantha. It makes me feel like I'm going to be alone forever.

River is crawling across the kitchen floor. Scooping him up, I place him on my knee, and proceed to play peek-a-boo with him. He smiles wide, giggling, showing his cute baby dimples and his absolute likeness to his gorgeous father.

Savannah smiles before breaking the silence, "You're so good with him Addison."

"Thanks. I love him to bits," I reply.

"I know, but are you sure you're ok, you know being his godmother and all?" she asks, a look of sweet concern on her face.

"Yeah I am, and Savannah I'm sorry I still love Hunter too."

She laughs a little. "Don't be. I trust you both."

"I don't get you." I stated.

"I know he loves you too but just not romantically."

"Yeah, I know how much he loves you."

"I'm sorry I took him away from you," she apologises sweetly.

"You didn't Savannah. I did that myself. Plus he fell in love with you and I can't blame either of you for that."

She again smiles at me, nodding towards the lounge room. "What about Quentin? He seems to still have it bad for you. I've seen how he looks at you."

"I've tried to see him that way, and I just can't feel anything for him."

"And Zane?"

"I don't know...I like...I miss kissing him and he is pretty good looking but..." I stop, not sure what else I want to say. I can feel tears stinging my eyes and my heart is pounding thinking about everything I've already shared with Zane.

My heart is also a little overwhelmed at the genuine affection Savannah is showing me too. She's a true sweetheart and I completely understand why Hunter has fallen in love with her.

Her words to me then are so kind, "Just go with it Addison, you need to open up to him. You never know."

"Yeah I know. Thanks for everything Savannah, you're so sweet."

She blushes, and excitedly says, "So I was thinking about ruby red for the bridesmaid dresses?"

"That sounds wonderful." I smile back.

Putting River down on the floor again, I stand up. "I should get going, I have an early shift at the hospital tomorrow."

Savannah stands up, pulling me into a friendly hug. I don't deserve her friendship, but it feels damn good to have someone show they care about me.

"Just think about what Ive said about Zane, yeah?"

"I will," I muse, turning and waving back as I leave.

And think about it I am. Every kiss I've shared with Zane is embedded in my mind on replay and the time I came undone on the desk made my body ache for him. If only I'd not missed my chance to tell him how I feel.

(57) Zane

Since Amy had walked out the door mere hours ago, I'd not left the couch.
For once though I'd not turned to my old friends whiskey and vodka but instead I'm downing another coffee. Caffeine is my favourite drug and it doesn't really have the effect on me of keeping me awake as I consume it like water most days.
Now, I kinda want to sleep though, to escape from the situation I've put myself in. My phone is sitting on the table, taunting me to pick it up and text Addison, but she'd made it clear she doesn't want to see me and it hurts like hell.
I've pushed Amy away because I don't love her but I love Addison and all I've done is confess how I feel.
I've been kicking myself for months that I hadn't said something about who Addison was when Amy burst into my hospital room. Watching Addison walk away from me shattered my heart and it's still in pieces now. Only she could put it back together and I don't want to be the one to make that happen.
I love her, but this time I'm not going to do damn thing about it. She will have to show me that she loves me too.

ॐ

At some point despite the copious amount of coffee I've drunk I must have dozed off, as I'm startled awake by a sudden pounding sound.
At first thinking it's in my head I stand up and stretch, rubbing my temples. But it continues, and sounds more like Morse code.
Realising it's the door, I stumble sleepily to open it and when I see her standing on my doorstep in track pants and a t-shirt that clings to her body, her face deliciously flushed, my heart skips a beat before it pounds a hundred miles an hour.
I feel completely tongue tied, and have to fight with my brain to cooperate to get the words out, "Addison, what are you doing here?"
"I'm sorry Zane."
"For what?"

"Everything...I..." she stutters, pausing to push her hands against my chest; feeling my racing heart.

She pushes me inside, kicking the door shut behind her with a foot. Stopping a moment she looks up at me, smiling and biting her lip.

We need to talk, but the tension between us is like fireworks.

Before I can even think of a word to say she's wrapped her arms around my neck and is pulling my lips to hers in a fierce kiss, taking my breath and all thoughts of talking away. Her tongue grazes my lips, begging for entrance, that I can't help but give her. This kiss is everything, raw, passionate and consuming.

Her tongue laces with mine, and she moans, driving me crazy.

Breathless she pulls away from the kiss, about to speak, but I put a finger up to her mouth for a moment before wrapping my arms around her waist, pressing my arms into her back, and squeezing her butt, urging her to jump up and wrap her legs around me.

I hold her close to my chest, again kissing her hard whilst we stumble to the bedroom, our lips not parting until I drop her against the bed.

Crawling back further onto it her eyes are locked on me, filled with want.

Stretching over her I kiss her furiously, licking her lips, revelling in the sweet taste of her mouth. The fact that she isn't resisting or rejecting me is making the desire increase in my shorts.

Pulling away breathless my eyes can't look anywhere but into hers when she sits up and lifts her t-shirt over her head, exposing her naked breasts.

I can't help but wonder if she has any knickers on underneath her black track pants.

"Oh Addison, you're so fucking beautiful," I muse before bending over her to kiss her neck, towards her collarbone and down towards her breasts that have risen to attention. Taking one in my mouth I tease her more, licking around the sensitive bud, before biting it.

Her hips buck up to meet mine, and she lets out a delicious moan when she feels my erection against her body.

Stopping I look down at her. There's no doubt I want her, all of her but I have to be sure. "Are you sure you want this? Us?"

"Yes, Zane, I want you," she admits, grabbing at the hem of my t-shirt to lift it over my head. Sighing she runs her hands up and down my chest, causing a shiver to run through me. Her hands actually touching my bare skin is almost enough to send me over the edge but I need all of her. She stops her teasing at the elastic of my shorts, running a finger across my hips teasingly.

"Oh Addison, please," I beg.

Giggling she yanks my shorts and undies down to my knees, her mouth falling open when her eyes take in my nakedness. She grabs my dick in her grasp and I moan, "Don't you dare tease me now, Addison."

Taking her cheeks in my hands, I smash another kiss to her lips, running my hands down her sides and across the sensitive skin of her hips, before wrenching her track pants down her legs. Just as I'd thought she has gone full commando and now is completely naked sprawled across my bed.

She's never looked more beautiful than she does now and I want her so fucking bad.

Reaching down between her legs, I tease her with a finger. She's gloriously wet, and her hips rise to the attention I'm giving her.

I know how to make her come from simply touching her and I've thought about tasting her for months.

"Tell me Addison, tell me what you want," I taunt her, taking my finger out and licking it clean.

She doesn't speak, instead grabs my head between her palms and pushes my head down between her legs.

Her actions are driving me wild and her obvious want makes me desperately want to do what she desires.

Firstly I place soft kisses over her clit, teasing her, licking it and savouring the way her hips lift towards my face. Her taste is like honey that I'll never be able to get enough of.

"Zane, please, more," she pleads.

I plunge my tongue deeper into her folds, lapping up everything she's giving me and loving every second of having her finally giving into me.

With a final lick over her clit, she comes hard over my face, screaming out my name. Hearing her say my name in the throws of pleasure is nothing short of amazing.

I again stretch over her body, kissing her zealously and lacing my tongue with hers, so she can taste herself on me. She starts moaning deeply, feeling my body pressed against hers.

Shifting my hips slightly I slide inside her, thrusting deep when her hips rise to meet mine. Slowly I start to thrust in and out, harder when she wraps her legs around my butt and drives me further inside her, filling her completely, our bodies fitting together perfectly.

As the pleasure increases I brush a hand across her cheek, kissing her longingly, moving my body in sync with hers. She breaks the kiss, thrusting her hips hard against mine, her body starting to twitch, getting closer to coming again.

"Oh Zane, fuck, I'm gonna come," she screams out, biting down on her lips when she comes again.

Feeling her explode around me is all it takes for one last thrust into her to send me over the edge, and letting go releasing into her body I cry out, "Oh fuck Addison, I love you!"

Rolling off and laying next to her she can't meet my gaze.

"I'm sorry Zane. I have to go. I'm sorry," she suddenly apologises standing up and picking up her clothes from the floor. She pulls them back on without even looking at me.

"Addison, please stay."

"No, I can't Zane. I'm sorry, I um...I," she mumbles, racing out the door before I can even think about following her.

I hear the door slam behind her and I curse out loud. Being with her was unbelievable, but again she ran from me and I'm beyond confused.

 It feels as though I've more than fucked up, letting my desire for her cloud my better judgement, given our track record. But I also know that I'm not sorry for finally being with her. It was clearly just as amazing for her as it was for me. And I'll be damned if I'm not going to do everything I can to be with her again, and make her see that she can love me too.

Tugging my shorts back on, I run outside, bracing myself as the cool night air hits me hard in the face. Part of me wants to run to her door and take her again, make her scream my name in pleasure again, but I also know I need to give her space too.

Doctor Attraction

So much to the protest of my feet I run in the opposite direction, smiling as my feet hit the ground in rhythm, like the in and out thrust of being one with Addison.

I'd hoped running would calm me down, but nothing is going to get the image of making love to Addison out of my mind.

I'm a lost cause, hopelessly in love with someone who doesn't love me back.

(58) *Addison*

Broken. That's how I feel as I start to drive out of Ridgehope, three hours away to Jett's farm. Tears stain my cheeks, firstly appearing when I drive past Hunters farm and his stupid crazy dog is jumping around, with River crawling behind him, grabbing his tail.

The sweetness tugs at my heart, breaking it more when I think about the life I could have had with Hunter if I didn't fuck it up years ago.

And now my heart is so conflicted, torn between the love that has always been there for Hunter and the tug of love I'm feeling for Zane.

My head is all for moving on with Zane, just as I'd done a few days earlier when we slept together. The way he'd taken his time with me, slowly driving me over the edge of climax twice shows he genuinely cares about me, but yelling out that he loves me when he reached his climax felt like a stab to my heart.

My head won't let me go there, like it knows my heart doesn't really feel the same way as my body.

And I feel terrible for rushing out of his house, after we'd finally been together, even more so than when I'd slept with Quentin.

God I'm such a hussy, you can't keep going around fucking everyone who cares about you, Addison.

My conscious is more than right, but sex is easier than love, pleasure is better than pain and I'm petrified that if I give my heart to Zane my whole world will come crashing down and I'll be in overwhelming pain, so instead I give into him in times when I know that all I'm going to feel is overwhelming pleasure.

Getting closer to Jett's house, in an attempt to block out my thoughts I crank the stereo up, only to find a song blaring out that makes me burst into tears, because every word of *'Beautifully Unfinished'* reminds me of Zane and the monumental fuck up I'd made by turning up on his doorstep, throwing myself into his arms and falling into his bed.

***

Pulling up to Jett's farmhouse, I cut the engine of my car, wiping a sleeve over my eyes so he won't be able to see that I've been crying. But knowing my older brother he'll know as soon as he looks at me that I'm upset.

Stepping out of the car, I unlatch the boot and lug out my large suitcase. I've only taken a month off, but brought enough clothes to last a lot longer. I felt terrible leaving the hospital in the lurch at the tail end of winter, but speaking to Herbert I'd said I needed a break to know if I wanted to stay in medicine.

That isn't really my reason for needing a break and I think Herbert knows that. This break is hopefully going to help me sort out my feelings for Zane; and Hunter.

Dragging the suitcase across the dirt, I take deep breaths to calm myself and to quell the heavy feeling in my heart.

Knocking hard on the door, I wait for Jett to open it and smile wide when he answers, half dressed in track pants and bare chested.

"Hey Jett, don't you dress up for company?"

"Hey Addi, and you're not company, you're family," he says winking and laughing when he opens the door, grabbing my suitcase as I follow him inside.

He doesn't speak as he wheels my suitcase down a narrow hallway to a small bedroom.

"Thanks Jett. I'm really glad I could come stay with you for a while."

"No worries Addi. I know its not much, but..."

"Its fine Jett," I say, reaching out to hug him.

I've missed my brother so much. He's always been protective, but lately he's seemed different.

Pulling back from the hug he asks, "Coffee or alcohol?"

"Alcohol might block out the pain, but coffee will take the chill away."

"Yeah, sorry about how cold it is. There's extra blankets in the wardrobe if you need them later."

"So, coffee sounds great," I tell him, following him to the kitchen and sitting down at the dining table whilst he starts to prepare coffee's for us.

Sitting across from me a couple minutes later, he hands my coffee to me and I take a slow sip.

"So Addi, whilst I'm more than happy to have you visit, you need to spill. Whats up with you?"

"I don't know where to start Jett," I confess, gulping down more coffee.

"From the beginning Addi, like maybe what happened with Hunter?"

"You know he rejected me, and he's with Savannah now."

"Yeah and they had a son?"

"Yep, he's gorgeous too but I don't know Jett, I don't think Hunter was ever the right guy for me."

"God Addison, I've been waiting years for you to say that. Do you know anything about the Mackenney's past?"

"No, what are you talking about?" I ask, incredulously.

"Look Addi, I don't know much either but I think it has something to do with Grandfather."

My mouth falls open in shock, and I blurt out confused words, "What? Did the Mackenney's do something to get him sent to jail?"

"I don't know Addi, but let's not talk about that. I want to hear more about Zane."

"Well, um...thats kinda why I'm here."

"Addison May Yorke, you didn't did you?"

I can feel heat rising in my cheeks. "Um...I might have."

"Oh you dirty girl," he jeers at me with a chuckling laugh.

"But I ran out after you know."

"What? Why? Wasn't it good?"

"It was amazing...but he yelled out I love you when he you know," I say embarrassed.

"Oh god Addison, that is hilarious, but so sad at the same time."

"I know and now I'm just really confused."

"Because you're still in love with Hunter?"

"Yeah and I know it's stupid of me, but I just can't let go."

"Do you feel anything for Zane at all?"

"To be honest I have no idea. We definitely have a physical connection and sometimes I feel like I'm falling for him, but I'm so scared that loving him isn't going to be enough."

My protective older brother looks concerned and reaches over to touch my knee in comfort. "I don't understand what you've got to be scared about?"

"I can't be his everything."

"Why Addi?"

"Jett, I...can't tell you."

"Addison, you can tell me anything. I'm your big brother and I'll love you no matter what."

Taking a deep breath, I sigh. "I can't get pregnant."

"Oh Addison, I'm so sorry sis...but how do you know that?" he asks, genuine concern on his face.

"Because when I was nineteen I had a miscarriage that damaged my body."

He stands up suddenly, obviously angry, as he slams his hands against the table. I curse myself for telling him, this reaction the very reason I've not told him before.

"When you were nineteen?" he states, not really as a question, "so meaning that you got pregnant to Hunter fucking Mackenney?" He's yelling, not meeting my eyes.

"Yes," I whimper.

He turns back to look at me. "Well Addi, I'm sorry about the issues it has caused you but I'm not sorry you had the miscarriage because..."

Tears are staining my cheeks. "Addi I'm sorry I didn't mean to make you cry, but honestly if you'd had Hunters baby...God I can't even bear to think about it."

"Jett, please tell me," I say through sobs.

"I can't Addison, not yet anyway....Not when you still have any feelings for Hunter."

"Fine. I'm going to bed. I'll speak to you tomorrow," I spit at him slamming my empty coffee cup on the table when I stand up and storm down the hallway towards the guest room.

It's clear that Jett knows something about our Grandfather going to jail and it appears it has something to do with the Mackenney's. I'm throughly confused and want to know the answer. It would probably help me let go of Hunter completely, but in all honestly I don't need to know to let go of Hunter.

Confiding in my brother about what had happened with Zane, has made me miss him and climbing into the soft sheets of the guest bed I think back to being with Zane, all the hot kisses we'd shared, how he touched me and made me come undone so easily.

I can still feel his lips on mine, like they are bruised from his intense kisses and I can still feel where he touched my skin with his fingers.

Just thinking about how remarkable we were together has left my body aching to be with him again. My body most certainly wants him. I just have to convince my heart.

❧

I'd been staying with Jett for about three weeks, when I see his picture flashing on my phone screen. My heart lurches in my chest, thinking something has happened to River, so I slide my finger over the screen to accept the call.

"Hi Hunter, is everything ok?" I ask, trying to remain calm, even though my heart is pounding.

"Hi Addison, and yes everything is fine."

"So why are you calling me?"

"I need to ask you something. And you can say no."

"Um yeah ok, what is it?" I ask, thinking back to the last time Hunter had said a very similar thing to me.

"Savannah and I would like you to be our maid of honour."

I choke on my reply, "Sorry um what?"

"You heard me Addison."

"Um...so...um when are you getting married again?"

"Well, that's the thing, we've actually decided on a week from today, but Savannah didn't want to ask you because you ran out when she asked you about the bridesmaids dresses."

God, I'm such a bitch, Savannah just wanted a friend and I up and ran out of their house, I guess I have to accept now.

"Oh Hunter I'm so sorry. I didn't mean to upset her."

"Its ok, so will you?"

"Yes, Hunter I will," I respond, feeling like I'm accepting his proposal instead of accepting to be a part of his wedding to someone else.

"So can you come over tomorrow maybe, to try on a dress?"

"Um...not tomorrow. I'm actually at Jett's."

"Oh right, when will you be home?"

"I was planning on coming back next week, but I'll head back in a day or so."

"Ok great, Savannah will be so happy."

"I'm glad, and Hunter?"

"Yeah Addi?"

"Would it be ok with you if I invite Jett to come?"

He sighs into the phone, and then replies, "I guess so Addi."

"Great. I'll text you Hunt," I reply, a little too eagerly.

"Bye Addi, drive safe."

I don't get to say goodbye, hearing the click of the phone call ending in my ear.
How in the hell am I going to stand up the front of the aisle and watch the love of my life marry someone else, and be happy about it?
As usual, I've put my fucking foot in it and now I have to suck it up and make myself move on.
Hunter Mackenney was never meant to mine, at least that's how it seems in hindsight.

Fuck, I'm going to be someones Maid of honour, even though I probably don't deserve to be.
I wonder if I'll ever be a bride.

(59) Jett

Everyone knows how much I love my little sister, always her fierce protector and forever worried about her wellbeing.

Having her call me a few weeks earlier telling me she needed to get out of Ridgehope as she'd done something bad I instantly felt worried for her and of course told her she could come to my farm immediately.

Her confession of sleeping with Zane, despite it not really being the bad I was thinking and even though I joked about it with her, it had really irked me.

I wanted to punch the idiots lights out for doing the dirty with my sister; as well as punching Hunter Mackenney's lights out as well for knocking her up when we were younger.

I still can't believe I'd ever been best friends with him.

Everyone thinks he's so sweet and loves him, but I know his bad side and he'd hurt my sister—multiple times—so inevitably I hate him.

The universe though always has a fucked up way of messing with our lives, and after Addison begged me to be her plus one I'm now sitting in a white wooden folding chair at Hunter's wedding.

He can't even look at me, but has a smug smile on his face that I want to wipe away with a fist to his face. It's not that I want Addison to be marrying him, she doesn't know the history between our families and I don't want to be the one to tell her either, because technically it isn't my story to tell, but I don't want Hunter to be happy either.

Still, I'm here and have to suck it up, put any vindictiveness I have against the Mackenney's aside for my sister.

She still cares about Hunter—a hell of a lot more than she should—but she does.

Some sappy music starts, and the small crowd of people turn to the end of the aisle. My sister is there, slowing walking towards the arch at the front in a ruby red dress.

She has a smile on her face that I can tell is fake. There's no way she's happy being a part of his wedding, but she's sucking it up.

Her eyes scan the crowd for me, and I give her a little wave when her eyes lock on me.

Once at the front, I watch her as she looks at Hunter and he mouths, *'Thank you'* to her and smiles at her sickly sweet.

Next to come down the aisle is Hunter's son. The kid is damn cute, and I feel a pang of longing to have kids of my own.

Nearing thirty-five I desperately want to settle down, but have devoted my time to farm life and pretty much have a non existent social life.

My down time consists of downing a few beers whilst binge watching crappy shows on Netflix. There isn't exactly any eligible women so far away from town anyway, so I've started to resign myself to the forever single bachelors club, which also means the forever not a father club.

Shaking myself back to reality, I scan the crowd a bit again, looking for Zane. Addison has told me what he looks like, and it isn't hard to tell who he is either as his eyes are clearly focused on Addison at the front of the aisle—even when the music changes and everyone stands up for the bride—who I have to admit is definitely beautiful. I can see why Hunter had fallen for her and I don't even know her.

Once she reaches the front, Hunter scoops up their son in his arms and he kisses her cheek. He holds him against his hip, as they exchange vows that both tug at my bachelor heart and make me want to vomit at the same time.

It's a quick ceremony, over before I know it.

The world stops a moment, when the celebrant announces them as, *'Mr and Mrs Hunter and Savannah Mackenney'* and with their son between them, holding a hand each they begin to walk down the aisle.

I hug Savannah first in congratulations, and she's a little taken aback until I hug Hunter as well.

"Congratulations Hunter, for today and this cutie," I remark looking down at the kid clutching his father's hand.

Savannah looks across at her now husband when he replies to me, "Thanks Jett, I'm glad you came."

That makes one of us.

"I'm here for Addison, not you, but yeah."
He doesn't reply, and Savannah scowls as they continue to walk down the aisle.
I wait until they get to the end of the aisle and look to Addison who's now
following them down the aisle holding Quentin Mackenney's hand in hers.
She hasn't mentioned anything about their relationship at any point, but they
appear to be comfortable with each other, sharing a giggle about something he
whispers in her ear. When they pass me, I reach out and grab her hand, asking
with a whisper, "You okay sis?"
"Yeah, Jett, I'll see you at the reception in town later, yeah?"
"Ok Addi," I reply sighing, nodding at Quentin who gives me a slightly sly smile,
that makes my insides knot with what it insinuates.

*God, I seriously hate the Mackenney brothers. I hope Quentin is not buying for
my sister now.*

⁊❧

Arriving at the only restaurant in the town of Ridgehope half an hour later for
the reception, I gratefully accept the champagne that's handed to me;
practically downing it in one gulp.
It hits my head hard, and I decide that drinking excessively probably isn't going
to be a great idea. If I drink too much, I'll probably lay into Hunter and quite
possibly Quentin, and even though I hate them both I don't want to be the bad
guy that ruins Hunter's wedding.
I don't think even Addison would forgive me if I ruin Hunter's special day.
I scan the decorated room, noting the wildflowers on the tables and looking for
my name on the place cards. I'm seated at a table with no one I know, which
actually makes me happy. I can only hope I won't have to engage in awkward
small talk with random strangers.
Taking my seat I grab my phone from my pocket, in an effort to waste some time
before the bridal party arrives. Something tells me I'm going to have to keep a
close eye on my sister tonight as her tendency to be a Cadbury isn't going to go

down well, with the fact that tonight she'll probably want to drink herself stupid to block out the pain that she's now officially lost Hunter. I for one am glad though, but I'm not going to tell her that.

All I want is for this day from hell to be over, so I can officially forget about the Mackenney brothers too.

(60) Addison

Being a bridesmaid in the wedding of someone you're in love with is cruel torture and I've been cursing myself for saying yes the entire day.

Standing under the arch in Hunter's garden when he exchanged sickly sweet vows with Savannah had made me want to wretch. He absolutely adores her, and it tore my heart to pieces listening to their word vomit.

The sick feeling in the pit of my stomach wasn't helped by the fact that Quentin was standing on the other side of the aisle with the oddest grin on his face when he looked at me.

If he thought he was going to get wedding sex he was going to be disappointed. I'm sure his sweet new girlfriend Samantha who was in a seat a few rows back from the front wouldn't want him being with me again. She was grinning like the damn Cheshire Cat and I wondered even though it's wrong if she's fucked Quentin yet. If she hadn't it would explain why he'd been making eyes at me the whole ceremony.

I could also feel another set of eyes on me, and could tell they were stripping me of my ruby red dress in his mind. He'd not made any attempt to contact me after we'd slept together a few weeks earlier, and I'm partly angry at him, but I've made no effort to contact him either so I can only really blame myself.

But I have my reasons playing in my head constantly, and I know he doesn't want to hear my excuse for running out on him after.

I should have stayed in bed with him, gone for round two, because I can't deny that fucking him was beyond amazing and I've never come so hard in my life.

Now, I have to continue sucking it up, walking into the restaurant for the reception holding Quentin's hand in mine.

He leans into my side and whispers in my ear, "Don't forget you're a Cadbury Addison."

"Funny, Quentin. But I plan on getting blind or I'm not going to get through another minute of this torture." I grunt when we sit down at the bridal table.

He grabs two champagnes, handing me one and clinking his glass against mine.

"To sweet torture," He muses.

"Yeah whatever," I snap back, downing the champagne like it's water.

The happy couple enters the room then, River tottering in between.

It's so sweet it makes the champagne rise up in my throat and I swallow hard to gulp it back down when Savannah sits next to me with River on her knee.

❧

The rest of the night passes by in a blur mostly, as I continue to down champagne and various other glasses of alcohol, barely stopping to ever let food into my mouth. Quentin is standing on the other side of the room, with an arm around Samantha whilst chatting to some people that I don't know.

The whole room is spinning slightly as I make my way over to him.

When I reach the group, no one appears to welcome me and Samantha steps back from Quentin like she's intimidated by me, which I think is rather hilarious.

Poking Quentin in the arm I jeer, "How about we you know?"

He looks cross when he replies, "Addison, you know I love you, but stop yeah, you're drunk."

"But I want you," I say, leaning closer to him in an attempt to kiss him.

"No, you don't Addison. Leave me alone yeah."

"Fine Quentin. Go back to your new girlfriend then," I taunt, pointing at Samantha when I walk away, spotting the delicious groom in the middle of the dance floor.

Sauntering up to him, completely ignoring Savannah dancing next to him with River I throw my arms around his neck, hollering, "Hunter I love you."

He pushes me away, and speaks with vengeance in his voice, "Come on Addison, let up! It's my wedding day!"

His angry tone rings in my ears, the alcohol making them hit harder and I have no response, about to try again when I feel comforting familiar arms wrap around me from behind.

Turning in the embrace I fall into Zane's arms, until he pulls me back and says, "You should probably listen to Hunter, hun."

Anger rises in me; I hate when he calls me hun. He hasn't for a while and I kinda wonder why but brush the thought aside when I see my brother crossing the room towards us.

No doubt he's going to berate me for my behaviour but he'd not had to watch the love of his life marry someone else, so he can't judge me.
Zane extends a hand to him. "Zane Rivnay. You must be Jett."
"Yeah I am." He scowls at Zane, not taking his outstretched hand.
I feel as though I'm about to pass out, so take Zane's hand as he's the closest person to me.
"Looks like I better take this one home," He says, looking directly at my brother, who looks like steam is going to come out of his ears.
Grabbing my hand from Zane's he spits, "No mate! I'm taking my sister home!"
Dragging me out he stops to see Hunter.
My drunk clouded mind thinks he's going to congratulate him again, instead he puffs his chest out in anger, his hands in fists and one raised at Hunter when he seethes loudly, "I never should have let her come to your fucking wedding! You fucking Mackenney's always fuck up our lives!"
Hunter is absolutely shocked, his mouth falling open at Jett's words and utter insolence.
Jett tugs on my arm, dragging my drunk arse out the door.
Looking back at Hunter I mouth, *'I'm sorry'* and he smiles slightly.
I've fucked up his wedding day, and he's probably sorry he'd even asked me to be a part of it.
It was hell for me—the whole entire day—but I would have done anything to make Hunter Mackenney happy, and now the only thing that will make him happy is for me to let go of him and let myself love somebody else.
But that's easier said than done.

(61) Zane

Unlocking your front door after an eventful day is rather lonely when you don't have a pet or a partner to debrief with.

After the events of Hunter's wedding I'd wanted to try and make amends with Addison, say I was sorry for blurting out I love you when my dick was buried inside her.

I'm not sorry of course but she doesn't need to know that.

What I hadn't counted on was one; her being insanely drunk and falling all over every guy in the damn room and two her over protective older brother who was so full of himself and stuck up he couldn't even shake my hand.

He demanded to take her home and I'm left to another night of loneliness, not that I want to be with her or could have been with her when she's so drunk.

Pulling off my suit jacket, I dump it on the floor before unbuckling my belt and undoing the zip of my pants to let them fall down my legs to the floor as well. Taking off my shirt seems too much effort, so instead I pull back the shabby unmade covers of my bed, sliding into it and closing my eyes as I clutch the pillow, pressing it against my cheek, my mind imagining I'm kissing Addison goodnight.

As I drift to sleep I plan in my head what I need to say when I talk to her and it will start by going to her house first thing to say, *'good morning'*.

இ

After waking up from a surprisingly good sleep, despite dreaming of being with Addison again I jump out of bed and tug on some black adidas track pants, tucking in my white dress shirt to them. I can't be bothered changing it and want to get to Addison's house as soon as possible.

I don't even worry about shoes, and curse when my feet hit the hot red dirt, that's stinking hot from the morning sun beating down on it.

At her door, jumping up and down on the spot to cool my feet on the concrete of her porch, I pound on the door with my fists.

When it opens, I'm not face to face with Addison, but her insolent older brother.

He looks my outfit up and down, scoffing at my dishevelled appearance.

"What do you want mate?" he snarls at me with gritted teeth, like he's a guard dog for his sister.

"I want to speak to Addison please," I insist, feeling like a kid begging a father instead of a grown man speaking to another man.

"She's asleep," he points out, "so can you just rack off, my sister needs some space."

There's no way I'm going to listen to him. I need to speak to Addison and tell her again how I feel and make her see that despite her resistance she feels something for me.

"Please mate, I just want to see her."

"Yeah, well I don't think she wants to see you," he suggests, a hint of wariness in his tone.

I'm not sure what she's told her brother about me, or how she feels about me, but telling him how I feel is the only way I'm going to get to see her; at least I'm hoping that's the case.

"I'm in love with her man, please just let me see her."

"Fine, wait here," he offers, ushering me inside.

He leaves the room, as I shut the door behind me.

Again the feeling of being a kid rises inside me, like I'm meeting the parents for the first time. I'm literally that nervous, but I'm definitely going to make her realise this time that she loves me.

Maybe not as much as I love her, but I know in my heart that she's in love with me. She wouldn't be so scared to admit it or give into me if she wasn't.

I literally can't wait for the day Addison tells me she loves me.

(62) Jett

The light is flooding into Addison's bedroom, but she hasn't stirred from her drunken slumber. Sitting on the chair by her bed, I reach out and shake her slightly.

"Addi, wake up," I coax.

She stirs, looking up at me, rubbing her eyes, smudging the mascara under her eyes more.

"Oh hey bro," she murmurs.

"Morning, Addi. Zane is here to see you."

Sitting bolt upright, she crosses her arms over her chest, worry on her face when she speaks, "Fuck, I did something bad last night, yeah?"

"Yeah, you only threw yourself at Quentin and confessed your love for the umpteenth time to Hunter after he'd married someone else," I jest at her.

"Fuck, he'll hate me. I won't be able to see River again."

"He won't hate you Addison."

"But I was an idiot," she protests.

"Yes, you were but Addi, do you honestly still love Hunter?"

"Yeah but I have to move on," she notes, uncrossing her arms and leaning closer to me.

"Did you say Zane is here?" she asks her eyes lighting up when she says his name.

"Yeah he is, just out in the lounge room."

"Did he say anything to you? You know about what I told you?"

Jokingly poking her in the ribs I tease her, "Yeah he did actually."

"What Jett? Tell me!" she demands.

"He's in love with you," I tell her smiling, before taking her hand in mine, "And I think you should give him a chance to explain everything."

"I know, but I'm..."

"Addi, please. Just talk to him," I plead standing up to walk out of her bedroom.

"Ok, I will," she says, standing up to hug me.

Pulling back, I kiss her forehead. "I'm gonna head off, but seriously Addison get out there and take a chance."

Without even looking back at me, or without another word she races out to the lounge room in her oversized t-shirt and knickers.

Walking out a minute later I smile seeing her hugging him close, as though she never wants to let him go.

It's going to take me awhile to warm up to him, but I can tell he's the right guy for her, if she'd only let him be.

I need to check out and head home to let her make the choice for herself, without her big brother telling her what's right or wrong.

(63) Zane

Hearing her bare feet on the floorboards, my heart starts pounding in my chest when I turn to watch her rush into the room.

She's only wearing a slightly too big navy t-shirt that grazes her belly button, showing a little skin between that and the white cotton boy leg knickers that hang low on her hips and hug her thighs. Her long blonde hair is tousled from sleep and falls about her shoulders, begging to be in my fists as I kiss her.

Gorgeous is an absolute understatement to how she looks, beautiful doesn't even cover it either.

Before I can even think, or worry about the obvious desire in my pants, she throws her arms around me, nudging into my neck. I can feel her breath on my skin, and hear the sniff of her inhaling the cologne I'd not washed off from the night before.

Her brother walks out, a gym bag slung over his shoulder. Looking across at him, still with Addison clinging to me like she doesn't want to let go, I smile at him and he gives me a friendly wink back.

Addison pulls away slightly, looking at her brother when he announces, "Addi, I'm off. I'll let you know when I get home."

Addison nods, as her brother exits the house and she steps back from me, looks me up and down, licking her lips in a deliciously teasing gesture.

I bite down on my lips, in an attempt to not lick my own lips back, taking in the luscious sight of her in front of me.

Her nipples are visible through the fabric of her t-shirt and I'm seriously fighting the urge to grab her tits in my hands.

She stretches up to graze her lips against mine, biting my lip softly.

Desperately I want to deepen the kiss, but we need to talk and to not just fall in bed like usual.

Pulling back, I gulp, trying to quell the desire to kiss her when I speak, "We need to talk first Addison."

"I know," she agrees, sauntering to the couch and lying down on her belly, propped up on her elbows.

I sit next to her, so close to her arms she could reach out and tease my package until I give in but instead she smiles, waiting for me to speak.

"So tell me what happened last night?" I question, even though I know exactly what happened. I need to hear it from her.

"I don't know," she starts, embarrassment rising in her cheeks as they turn crimson when she continues, "Jett told me I threw myself at Quentin and confessed my love to Hunter again."

"Yeah that pretty much sums it up." I laugh.

She looks down at the couch in shame, shaking her head slightly. "I can't believe I did that to both of them."

I lift her chin up with a finger, gazing directly down into her eyes when I inquire, "Do you really still love him Addison?"

She gives me a slight nod that feels like a stab to the heart, but her words have promise.

"Yes, but I'm..." she starts, biting her lip unsure if she should continue. There's something I've wanted her to say for months, but I don't want to get too excited.

"What Addison? Tell me please," I insist, hoping that she will finally say the words.

"I can't."

My heart again feels like it has been stabbed. She feels something for me, but can't tell me and it's infuriating.

"Don't give me that excuse Addison," I retort, sighing a moment and watching her expression that's eager to hear what I have to say because she clearly has nothing else to say.

"I'm in love with you Addison, I have been since the day I first kissed you in your office," I confess.

She looks at me confused.

"But you're married."

Holding up my left hand, I wiggle my bare ring finger at her.

"Not anymore. She left me again when she realised I'm in love with you."

The want rises in my pants again when she bites down on her lips again, a slight smile spreading across her face.

"Do you know how sexy that is?" I purr at her, looking into her eyes, and down to the want in my pants.

"Really?" she teases back.

"Yes, seriously Addison. You're such a damn tease."

And her next words are all I need for the longing for her to hit me full on.

"Kiss me Zane, please."

Leaning down towards her on the couch I press my lips softly to hers. She murmurs softly, the desire in my pants responding.

Pulling back she slides up the couch towards me, giggling when she sits on my lap, a leg either side of me. Her white cotton boy leg knickers are now positioned perfectly against my aching groin, and she wriggles slightly, grinding into me.

"Oh fuck, Addison," I murmur before smashing my lips to hers, not so gentle this time.

She bites my lip, pulling it back a little with her teeth, teasing and licking my lips in a kiss so demanding and desire filled I could come undone.

Tantalisingly I lick her lips to force her to give me entrance to lace my tongue with hers and when she moans in pleasure, even though my body is screaming I break the kiss, taking a moment to calm my breathing before I ask the question plaguing my mind, "Addison, are you sure?"

The look on her face is far from confused and evidently is a mix of lust and something far more.

I'm not sure if I'm ready for her answer.

(64) Addison

Zane is looking at me like he's searching my face for an answer that I'm not sure I have. The only thing I know is that being with him is what I need to move on from Hunter. My body is ready and my heart will inevitably follow.

Nodding I lock my gaze on Zane's before speaking with a lustful tone, "Yes I'm sure."

Zane lets out a deep laugh, that stirs something in my belly.

"You said that last time we were together and we both know how that turned out," he says laughing with the same deep tone.

"I'm just scared that's all."

"Of what Addison? Im not going to hurt you," he affirms, putting an arm around my shoulders.

"I'm scared I'm falling in love with you," I admit, feeling like a weight has been lifted from my body, finally admitting my feelings.

"And why is that a bad thing?" he asks, smiling wide.

"I've never loved anyone but Hunter and I'm scared that if I fall in love with someone else it will all be taken away from me," I reason, trying to tell him why I'm so afraid.

Again he smiles wide, pressing a soft kiss to my forehead, before he declares, "I promise if you let me love you, give yourself time to fall in love with me that no matter what I won't be going anywhere."

"But you will. I can't give you everything," I object.

"What do you mean?"

"I can't have kids Zane. You know that and I can't begrudge you a family."

He laughs again. "Addison I don't care! I already have a son but that's not the point."

"You don't talk about him?"

"Yeah, he was the little boy with Amy that day. He's living with her but anyway it's a long story that I'll tell you later."

"Um, ok," I say, not really sure of how to respond to his words.

"And seriously Addison that is not going to make me not love you."
A smile spreads across my face that I can't stop.
"Really?"
"Yes, if I have your heart I'll have everything."
Again I climb onto his lap, straddling him and pressing my lips fiercely to his, an all consuming kiss to show him I'm ready to open up to him and despite the fact we've already slept together, being together again is going to be as though it's the first time.
He pulls back from the kiss, brushing a few stray hairs from my face.
"So tell me which way your bedroom is again?"
"Why?" I jeer, standing up and turning away from him, my arse at face level.
He slaps it playfully when he stands up, wrapping his arms around my waist and nudging his crotch against my arse.
In my ear he whispers seductively, "So I can show you how much I love you."

(65) Zane

Freeing herself from my grasp Addison races down the hallway, her blonde hair billowing behind her and a delightful chortle of laughter escaping her lips.
She turns back to look at me, still frozen by the couch, utterly mesmerised by her. She stops by her bedroom door, that's just visible down the hallway and leans into the door jamb seductively when she teases, "Aren't you coming?"

Oh fuck she said coming, oh yes I'm coming, I'm going to...

I don't reply, instead force my feet to move, to saunter over to her. Her giggles when I grab her by the waist, tickling the sensitive skin of her stomach and hips sends desire straight to my pants.
Desperately I want to strip her of the barely there clothes she has on, but also this time I want to savour every second I have with her, like it's the first time and definitely not the last time we'll be together.

Giggling again, she smashes her lips to mine, wrapping her hands around my neck to pull me closer. I grab her arse, to crush her closer to my body that's rising in temperature when the kiss becomes desperate and needy.
She murmurs feeling my arousal against her stomach and breaking the kiss, breathless and panting she reaches for the hem of her t-shirt, lifting it over her head exposing her naked breasts at attention.
"Oh Addison, you're so fucking beautiful," I declare, taking one of her breasts in my mouth, slowly licking and teasing the sensitive bud.
Exquisite moans escape her lips, my lips licking between the crevice before taking the other delicious bud in my mouth, giving it the same sweet torture.
"Oh Zane, please...oh..." she gasps, my hand finding its way against the cotton of her boy leg knickers.
They are soaked through with want and it drives my desire for her higher.
Grazing the elastic at the top I revel in the way her hips buck at the simple touch

of my hands on her hips. Plunging a finger inside the knickers, I stop a moment, looking into her ocean blue eyes, before I tug them off her body.

She bites her lips, pleading, "Touch me Zane."

The tone in her voice is so full of lust, her eyes so full of want, I could never not do as she asks.

Seeing her in pleasure almost makes me release, so I tease her first, swirling my finger over her entrance and down her thighs. Her hips respond, urging me to touch her more and the moans that escape her lips are spurring me on.

Gliding my finger inside her, she moves her hips trying to take control as I find the spot inside her that will bring her to release.

Pulling my finger out for a moment I take hold of her by the hips, carrying her to the edge of the bed and asking her as she falls against it, "Do you want me to make you come Addison?"

"Yes, Zane, I want you to make me come," she replies, her tone raspy when she edges back on the bed, opening her legs wide.

Again I plunge my finger inside her, in and out, watching her pleasure increase, her climax building when I slide another finger in.

Still caressing her with my fingers I stretch over her hot body to kiss her deeply. She fumbles with my shirt as we kiss, ripping the buttons to get it off my body. It falls loose around me, but still I kiss her, teasing her mouth with my tongue, my fingers still teasing her folds.

Without warning she bites my lip as she kisses me, her glorious climax overtaking her body. Pulling away I toss my shirt aside, and discard my track pants and boxers to the floor. She gasps at my erection waiting for her.

"Can I make you come now?" she teases.

As much as I want her mouth on me, more than anything I need to be inside her again.

"I'd love that Addison, but right now I'd rather be inside you."

"Mmm..." she muses, pulling me down to her to kiss me.

As she pulls away she bites my ear softly before whispering in it, "Can I ride your cock hun?"

"Oh god hun, that sounds amazing," I taunt back, pulling her to the edge of the bed and sitting beside her.

She lets out her delightful giggle again, and she stands up a moment before straddling me, a leg over each of my thighs against the bed. My arms wrap around her back to hold her steady.

Crashing my lips to hers, I playfully run my tongue across her lips, kissing her as though I'll never get enough of her and her exquisite mouth.

She begins moaning against my mouth, grinding her core against my aching groin.

"Please, Addison, ride me now. I can't take…" I beg, my words cut off as she impales herself on my hardness.

Her mouth opens and closes in ecstasy as she slides up and down on me, taking control. Her hair sashays around her shoulders and her breasts rise and fall each time she lifts her hips from mine, just for a moment each time.

It's crazy to admit that I've never had a woman make love to me cowgirl style and I'm loving every second.

She stops a moment, slowing her up and down pace to kiss me deeply, pushing my body down on the bed, her breasts pressing against my chest.

Pulling back breathless, I speak with a raspy tone, "I love you Addison and I want you to come for me, hun."

Still lying back on the bed, she rocks her hips up and down, moaning as she begins trembling, her pleasure rising.

"Oh Zane….fuck…I'm…"

"Yes…Addison…oh yes!" I call out, my own end hitting me fast.

"I'm coming…Zane…fuck," she exclaims as I fill her with my own climax, feeling her clench around me and explode in a shattering climax.

Grabbing her by the hips I pull her against my side, scooting up onto the bed.

Entangling my legs with hers I pull her body closer to mine, kissing her passionately until we're both panting breathlessly.

"That was absolutely incredible Addison."

"I know," she muses, rolling over and pressing her arse against my groin.

"I wouldn't mind round two, but I think we both need to sleep first," I say into her ear.

"Mmm…yeah," she murmurs, closing her eyes.

Closing my own eyes, I sigh, loving holding her naked in my arms.

It seems like only mere moments have passed when I hear her sigh and she turns her head back to look at me. Even though my eyes are still closed I can feel her breath on my face when she mumbles softly, against my cheek, "I think I love you Zane."

I don't want to scare her, so I slowly open my eyes, smiling and pulling her closer to press a soft kiss to her lips.

"Did you hear me?" she asks.

"Yes, hun, and I'll be right here waiting until you know you love me."

She kisses me hard, longingly and deep. She'd only said, *'I think I love you'* but she's kissing me as though she's already fallen in love with me and I know that in time she will tell me.

After she breaks our kiss I slip away into sleep, dreaming of making love to her over and over and finally hearing her say she loves me as much I love her.

Hearing her say the words will make my heart burst with happiness.

Nothing will be better.

(66) *Zane*

A month or so has passed since Addison had finally given into me and nothing had been sweeter than having her in my arms, waking up beside her as the sun shone into my bedroom.

This morning is particularly sweet knowing we both have a rare Saturday off together.

She murmurs a little in her sleep, rolling over to face me beside her.

Pressing a kiss to her forehead, she again murmurs as she wakes up, her eyes struggling to focus on mine.

"Zane...kiss me," she mutters in her half asleep daze.

"Nah, hun, your morning breath is the worst," I jeer at her, laughing and poking her in the belly.

"Haha not funny hun," she jokes back, grabbing my cheeks in her palms and kissing me hard.

Pulling back, she says, "Mmm, you still taste like the whiskey we downed last night."

"Yeah you to hun, how's your head?" I ask, because she'd gulped down twice as much of the whiskey as I had.

"Fine actually," She says sitting up on the bed, not caring that the sheets fall in a pool at her waist and her nakedness is exposed.

My eyes drift towards her breasts; it honestly wouldn't matter how many times I see her naked, I'd still find her breathtaking.

She laughs sweetly. "Hun, my eyes are up here."

"Sorry hun," I say looking up at her, "you're just so fucking beautiful I can't help but stare."

"Zane, don't start," She jeers, poking me in the chest this time.

"It's true Addison," I say pushing her down on the bed and kissing down her neck, over her collarbone and down towards her breasts.

She lets out little moans when I kiss them softly.

"Mmm...Zane I...lll..."

Doctor Attraction

I stop teasing her, locking my eyes on hers, just hoping she's finally going to say the words I long to hear.

"Why'd you stop?"

"Um because you were about to say something important."

"Um...no I wasn't," she says biting her lip, anxiously.

"Oh well in that case, get up and get dressed."

"Why? It's like eight am and we haven't had a Saturday off together in well...like ever," she complains, pouting at me.

"I know," I say standing up and stretching, "but today is no ordinary Saturday."

"What?" She spits at me, a tone in her voice that's so innocent and annoyed.

"You have to get dressed to find out what I mean."

"Fine," she huffs, getting out of bed and wrapping the sheet around her body as she trudges out of the bedroom to the bathroom.

"You know I've seen you naked hun," I call out, watching her from the bedroom door. Dropping the sheet in the hallway she blows me a kiss.

Whilst she showers I make sure the item I need is safe in my jacket pocket. It had cost me far more than the one I'd brought Amy years ago, but for Addison I'd have spent far more on getting her one that's truly as amazing as she is.

Standing in the kitchen, I wait for her to be ready. My heart is pounding, my mind running over my plans and the words I want to say.

Breaking my thoughts she enters the kitchen. "Do I look ok?" She asks.

"Of course hun, you look stunning!"

Her outfit is a simple long sleeve skater style dress, with a galaxy print that clings to her body everywhere it should. Underneath she has paired it with semi sheer black tights and purple Doc Martens.

"Thanks hun, you look quite nice yourself."

"So are you ready for the best Saturday ever?"

"I guess, but I kinda would like to know where we are going?"

"Not a chance, hun," I tease, grabbing her hand to lead her out to the Mustang.

Opening the door for her, she slides in and I suggest, "Sit back and relax, put your feet up on the dash and enjoy the ride, hun."

Once in the drivers side, I smile at her, revving the engine.

"So I seem to remember awhile back that a gorgeous blonde showed me how to drive this car."

She bites her lip. "Hmmm, I wonder who that was," she teases when I reverse away from the front of my house.

Pushing my foot hard on the accelerator I swiftly change the gears as the engine purrs. I'm also trying to focus on the road and not look at Addison laying back against the seat with her feet on the dash.

Driving a little too fast it doesn't take long to arrive at the picnic ground on the outskirts of town.

Pulling up, I notice the confused look on her face when she takes in the surroundings.

"Zane, why are we here of all places?"

"For the best Saturday ever."

"Hun, going to a park is not exactly my idea of the best Saturday ever."

"Just wait," I say, sliding out of the car to help her out.

Pressing her body against the car, I tease, "So I also remember that same day the gorgeous blonde drove my car that she teased me and do you know what I wanted to do to her?"

"No, hun, I don't," She taunts, clearly enjoying my little game.

"This," I muse, smashing my lips hard against hers in a fierce consuming kiss, teasing her lips with my tongue, taking her mouth with mine like I'll never kiss her again.

Breathless she pulls back, muttering, "Zane, I...um...I.."

"Don't Hun, just follow me,"I say taking her hand in mine, lacing our fingers together.

Her eyes are still scanning our surroundings and light up when we stop between two large gumtrees in the middle of the picnic ground.

Scattered between the leaves I've hung battery operated fairy lights that thankfully are still on and between another two branches is a banner, that reads *'Marry me, Addison?'*

Her hands are over her face and she gasps, "Are you serious, Zane?"

Bending down in front of her on one knee, I take the ring out of my pocket opening the box presenting it to her when I speak, "Of course I'm serious hun, I've loved you from the moment I first saw you and even though you haven't told me you love me, I know you do. All I want Addison is for you to be my wife, so please hun, will you marry me?"

She doesn't hesitate, letting out a delightful squeal, "Yes Zane, of course I'll marry you."

Standing up I slip the three carat rose gold diamond ring on her finger, and smile when she holds it up to see it glitter in the morning sunlight. "Zane this must have cost a fortune."

"Yeah a little, but you deserve it hun. I love you."

She doesn't reply with words, instead embraces me hard, before kissing me, so sweetly and full of love I have no doubts that this time around I've made the right choice in asking her to be mine forever.

(Epilogue) Addison

Eight Months Later

It always amazes me how things have a way of turning out right. I'd stepped up to the door of the church many times before but now is different as my arm is linked with my father's.

The fact he'd actually made the effort and could leave Adelaide to be here in Ridgehope for my wedding is a big deal, since everything that happened to our family in the past and the fact his medical prognosis is far from ideal.

The most amazing part of standing outside the door of the church on this day, is that I'm finally a bride. It's my turn to be the one in the white dress, the one walking down the aisle to marry the amazing man waiting for me.

Dad pushes the wooden doors open and the music starts, the marvellous lyrics of *'The One by Kodaline'* begins playing.

"Are you ready dear?" my father asks.

"Yes, Dad, I'm ready."

Taking a deep breath I tentatively step forward, putting one foot in front of the other, thanking myself for wearing soft soled white ballet flats with my flowing gown.

I'm not about to marry who I thought I'd be marrying, but who I'm meant to be with. Looking around at my family and friends confirms this, as getting closer to the front I see Hunter. He has River against one hip, an arm around him and his other hand is clutching Savannah's hand with his.

They look beautiful together, and Savannah is even more radiant, pregnant again and about four months along. Her belly has swelled and in my opinion, not being her doctor again I'd not be surprised if she's having twins.

In the very front pew sits my mother, a wide smile plastered on her face, with tears in her eyes. She's leaning against Jett, who also can't help but smile.

Doctor Attraction

He winks at me and I focus on the front of the church, reaching the altar to meet the man waiting for me.

My father presses a kiss to my cheek, handing me over to my groom, and what a groom he is—in his navy suit, white shirt and electric blue tie.

He has a slight five o'clock shadow grazing his jaw and his eyes are full of love as he takes me in. He pretends not to notice how my dress drops low in the front, exposing my cleavage or how it hugs my hips, but stepping up to him, he takes my hand and licks his lips when we turn to the altar.

For the next few minutes, I try to focus on the words of the priest, eager to get to part of declaring my love for Zane. It has been nine months since he'd told me he'd be waiting until I knew I love him and I'd not yet said, *'I love you'* to him, even though I do love him.

The priest looks to Zane as he starts to speak the vows to repeat, after we'd said, *'I do'*.

Zane is looking right into my eyes as he repeats back the words, " I Zane Rivnay take you Addison May Yorke, to be my lawful wedded wife. I promise that I will love you, protect you and be by your side in sickness and in health, in good times and bad for as long as we both shall live."

If I had my way I would skip straight to kissing him, but instead I repeat back the words, "I Addison May Yorke take you Zane Rivnay, to be my lawful wedded husband. I promise that I will love you, protect you and be by your side in sickness and in health, in good times and bad for as long as we both shall live."

Smiling wide at me and then at Zane, the priest declares, "Now Addison has some special vows she'd like to share with her groom."

Zane's eyes light up and I can't help but smile when I start to speak, "Zane, firstly I wanted to say I'm sorry for everything I've put you through to make it here today. But today is our wedding day, and I wanted it to be perfect and I wanted it to be the first time that you hear me say the words."

You can almost hear our friends and family gasp when I finally utter the words, "I love you Zane."

"Oh Addison, I love you too," He says, grabbing me by the waist and hugging me, lifting my feet off the floor.

We continue the ceremony then, exchanging rings and promising to love each other forever, as a circle has no end.

My heart skips, nearing the end when the priest declares, "Now by the power vested in me by the Church, it is with great pleasure I declare you husband and wife. You may kiss the bride!"

Zane grabs me by the waist, dipping me low as he smashes a delicious teasing kiss to my lips. Our family and friends wolf whistle, cheering and clapping at our first kiss as husband and wife.

When we turn towards the church doors, ready for the recessional the priest declares, "I am pleased to present the newly married, Mr. and Mrs. Zane and Addison Rivnay!"

Leaning into Zane's side, we start to walk down the aisle and I whisper in his ear, "I'm pregnant."

Squeezing my hand tight, as we continue walking down the aisle he whispers back, "See I told you, 'Mrs Rivnay' that if you gave me your heart you'd have everything."

We begin hugging our family and friends and my heart swells with love.

My husband is right; I had let go of my past, my fears of not being enough and had let myself fall in love with him.

And I now I have everything I'd ever dreamed of.

And the most amazing part of the dream is that it's only just beginning.

Playlist

Below is the playlist of songs for this story and the associated chapter if applicable. They are not in order. The Spotify playlist link is at the bottom.

1. I want you-Savage Garden (Ch 6)
2. Loneliest-Incubus (Ch 24)
3. Hold on-Chord Overstreet (Ch 42)
4. Don't play games-Aron Wright (Ch 43)
5. Arms wide open-Creed (Ch 53)
6. Get out of my life woman-Lee Dorsey (Ch 55)
7. Beautifully Unfinished- Ella Henderson (Ch 58)
8. My last goodbye-Trading Yesterday (Ch 60)
9. If our love is wrong-Calum Scott (Ch 61)
10. Figured you out-Nickelback (Ch 57)
11. Yours-Ella Henderson (Ch 65)
12. The One-Kodaline (Epilogue)
13. Meant to be-Bebe Rexha feat. Florida Georgia Line (Ch 66)

Spotify Playlist

About the Author

Caz May is a librarian/teacher by trade, but was always destined to be an author from a young age. In her spare time, she can be found devouring books or writing her own stories with characters that may not be the typical romance heroes but are loveable just as much.

Caz is married to her own real-life bearded hero and has two fur babies.

She lives for Iced coffee, especially from Gloria Jeans or a Farmers Union but pretty much just loves food in general.

When she's not writing, or reading a book most likely she can probably be found asleep or binge-watching shows on Netflix and Stan. And probably also drooling over her character inspiration on Instagram as well.

Check out her Instagram or other socials to get in touch. She loves chatting with her readers whilst they're reading her books and after as well.

Instagram- @cazmayauthor

BookBub-Caz May https://www.bookbub.com/profile/caz-may

Goodreads-https://www.goodreads.com/cazmay

Facebook- @CazMayAuthor

Spotify- cazcat25

Website- https://cazcat25.wixsite.com/cazmay-author

Look out for Book Three of
The Mackenney Family Saga

(Quentin's story)

(Prologue) Quentin

Watching someone you've loved desperately for so long walk down the aisle of a church to marry someone else whilst your in the pews is like being in hell.

It's an uncanny feeling, being in a church and feeling like I'm in hell.

She walks in, her arm linked with her father's, wearing an off white gown that clings to her curves and extenuates her ample cleavage.

From her hips the fabric flows down to her feet and swishes around her legs as she walks. She's so elated the grin won't leave her face.

She doesn't even glance at me for a moment and my heart sinks.

She can't even acknowledge me with a nod after we'd slept together a year or so ago and she'd torn my heart out by rejecting me.

My stomach is in knots, as all the memories came crashing into my mind and all I really want to do is squeeze past whoever is next to me to race out the door of the church and run away like I'd done in the past, when I couldn't be with her.

But this time the pain is even more raw, more real, as this time she's actually marrying someone else.

She isn't in love with my older brother anymore, and she isn't in love with me, no matter how much I want her to be.

As she approaches the altar, I turn to look at my ex-girlfriend sitting a few rows back. Her eyes look sad, but her lips upturn in a scowl when she catches me looking at her. If we weren't in a church with most of the town around I think she'd have flipped me off.

I hadn't meant to break her heart, but no matter how much I'd wanted to I couldn't make myself fall in love with her, like she'd fallen for me.

My older brother was a little taken aback and worried about me when I'd told him we'd broken up. Telling him it was because I'm still in love with Addison is only half of the reason and now that Addison is marrying Zane, as difficult as it's going to be I need to tell my brother the real reason.

I need to move on from Addison and I need to stop thinking about how my past has fucked me up when it comes to love.

Doctor Attraction

It's time to let go of the darkness completely, and step one is telling Hunter that I'm not the innocent flirtatious little brother he thinks I am.

ॐ

As soon as I enter the pub for Addison's cocktail style wedding reception, I grab a champagne from the waitress walking around with a tray load of glasses of the pale yellow gold. Downing it one gulp I put it back on the tray before she even steps away. She gives me a smile, and queries, "Rough day Constable Mackenney?"

I squint at her name badge, intrigued as to how she knows me. "You could say that Mary."

Holding a up another glass to me, she says, "Have another, I won't tell anyone." And walking away she winks at me flirtatiously.

It's gonna be one long arse night, and there's no way champagne is going to cut it. Getting blind drunk probably isn't the best idea, but it's the only thing that's going to dull the ache in my heart.

Samantha walks in, showing a little more confidence than she would have a year ago. Her brown hair falls over her shoulders and her dress shows off her sweet body that's usually hidden under her boyish work uniform.

I still felt guilty now for breaking up with her, but her innocence damn near became my undoing. It not only brought the dark desires from my past crashing back, it made me crave them and with her.

Her sweet nature couldn't handle what I'd wanted from her but it didn't stop me from missing her though, as it had been nice to be with someone again.

Again I scan the room for anyone else I know, actually hoping to find that Hunter has arrived so I can steal him away from his wife and my nephew who's always stuck to his fathers side like glue for just a moment to speak to him.

ॐ

Seeing him walk in about twenty minutes later, I grab his arm and ask, "Hey Hunt, do you think we could talk about something?"

"Yeah Quent, just give me a minute to find Savannah and I'll meet you outside." He crosses the room, seeing Savannah talking to some local women. After whispering in her ear, she nods and picks River up to hold him against her hip.

Hunter comes back over to me and he follows me outside to sit on the bench seat by the pub doors.

Reassuringly when we sit down he touches my arm, asking, "So what's up little brother?"

"It was fucking hard Hunt, watching her get married you know."

"I know it was hard Quent, but I'm sure your happy ending is right around the corner," he says, a soothing tone in his voice.

"Thanks Hunter, but I'm not so sure about that."

"Why Quentin? What makes you think that?" he asks, his tone concerned.

"I don't know…I just feel broken."

"Broken? I don't get you."

"Yeah, broken and I need to tell you something about my past."

He nods, rubbing his hand comfortingly up and down my arm.

"You can tell me anything Quent."

"I know, but it's bad Hunter," I say, dipping my head in shame.

"Quentin, you're my brother. I love you no matter what."

"I know…and well it's kinda actually about why Sam and I broke up too."

"Ok, so what really happened then?" he asks, nodding.

The knot in my stomach feels like it's being pulled by an invisible rope, and my heart is pounding hard but I have to tell him.

I have to tell someone.

"I…um…I drove her away…because I wanted too much from her."

"What do you mean Quent?"

"She was too innocent for me," I declare, feeling like a weight has lifted off my shoulders.

"I'm sorry I'm not following Quent."

"With sex, Hunter," I blurt out, feeling a blush rise up my cheeks.

Shock crosses his face, and I pull my arm back, cursing myself for even thinking that sharing this with him is a good idea, but I have to. When he doesn't reply I force myself to continue.

"It started when I was at the Police Academy. I kinda just fucked anyone willing and got into some darker things."

"Like what Quentin?" he asks, a hint of what sounds like anger in his voice.

"Like wanting to control women to pleasure them as well as make them feel pain."

Again the shock crosses his face, at hearing the words I can't believe I've just said to my older brother.

"Whoah Quentin! Tell me why you'd even want to get into that stuff?"

And there it is, the million dollar question and the answer to that question has plagued me since I'd left Ridgehope for the police academy years ago.

"Because I couldn't have Addison."

"But why that stuff Quent?"

"I don't know. It was like a way of punishing myself...like I felt not good enough for her and you were."

"Quentin, honestly I'm sorry but you and I both know that neither of us can really be with Addison, regardless of the fact that she's found Zane and I've found Savannah."

"I know Hunter and I'm so glad she's happy, and you are to but I don't want to down that dark path again and I feel like I am."

"Oh Quent," he says soothingly, before continuing with a question, "Is that the only reason you broke up with Sam?"

"No, I really liked her, but her being so innocent I don't know I just couldn't fall in love with her."

"I get it Quentin. You can't help who you fall in love with."

I laugh, wondering when my brother got so wise.

"Yeah, I just want what you have with Savannah, that kind of love."

"I know Quent, but do you still love Addison though?"

"No, I don't actually," I admit, feeling the weight of acknowledging it lifted from me, "Being with Sam kinda helped me get over Addison, even though I'm not in love with Sam."

"Yeah, I'm sure your someone is out there Quentin."

"Maybe, but I'm not counting on it."

"Oh, Quent, maybe you need to get out of Ridgehope for a while again."

I shake my head frantically. "Fuck no brother! I'm not leaving you, Savannah and River! You guys are my everything!"

"I know Quentin. You're the most amazing uncle but I just want to see you happy."

"I know that Hunter, but I'd rather stay forever single than leave."

"Oh Quent, I don't know. I don't want you to be lonely."

"I'm not Hunter, I have you guys and my mates. Hugh and Mark don't let a man drink alone," I say reassuringly, not completely convinced of my words.

I can't help but notice that he gulped hard when I'd mentioned my mates as though he's hiding something he wants to say.

Shrugging he speaks, "Yeah but well you deserve to be happy Quentin. That's all I'm saying."

"I know Hunter and being here with you and your little family makes me happy."

"Really Quentin? Even if you can't have all you desire?"

Laughing, and running a hand through my hair, I say, "Yes desire and happiness are two very different things Hunter."

Again he speaks with words that seem wise beyond his years, "Are you going to be able to deal without giving into those desires though Quentin?"

"I'm not saying it's going to be easy Hunter, but yes I'm going to try to suppress those desires again."

He doesn't reply, urging me to continue, as though he knows I have more to say.

"Sam brought them back, but she also took them away again."

"Yeah I guess I see what you're saying. I'm never going to completely understand that side of you, but if it makes you happy then I'm all for it Quent."

I sigh deeply, laughing. "Thats enough of this sap. I need a hard drink!"

He slaps a hand against my back when we stand up. "Sounds like a great idea."

Heading back inside the pub, the whole place is abuzz with chatter and music.

Hunter walks up to the bar and orders two whiskeys straight up.

Looking straight at me, he takes his glass from the bar top and clinks his glass against mine in a toast, "To happiness brother."

We both down the whiskey, slamming the glasses down on the bar top. Hunter then wraps an arm around my waist, pulling me closer to his side in a brotherly hug, and whispers in my ear, "Love you little brother."

Those words mean the world as the fact that he still loves me after what I'd just told him, makes my heart happy and confirms that leaving Ridgehope is something I'll never be able to do again.

Doctor Attraction

It's home. And I'll never believe the saying that, *'home is where the heart is'* because even though I don't have love from a woman in my heart I have so much more.

Ridgehope, my Mum, my brother and his family are my heart and my home.